MW00937016

A KISS FOR EMILY

a novel by

J. P. GALUSKA

Book One of the Emily Stokes Series

Enjoy!

Jennifer J Galuska

A KISS FOR EMILY

Copyright © 2011 by Jennifer Galuska

All rights reserved. No part of this book may be reproduced or transmitted in any form or by any means without written permission of the author.

Cover art by Jennifer Finerty

All characters and events in this book are fictitious. Any resemblance to actual person, living or dead, is strictly coincidental.

For my children, who inspire me to write wonderful works of art.

ACKNOWLEDGEMENTS

With God, all things are possible.

Thanks to my sister Julie, who told me it was great right from the first draft. Thanks to Scott L., who then bought me my first books on writing.

Thanks to my niece, Janelle, for turning me onto Muse.

Thank you Muse, for helping me feel, more.

My deep gratitude goes out to my writers group – Ann Noser, Mike Kalmbach, and Christa Worrell. Good luck with your own stories.

I love you Ashley, Cortiney and Lindsey.

Thanks to Joan Sween, friend and founder of the Minnesota Writer's Alliance, Connie L., and the members of the Rochester MN Writers Group of 2009.

A big shout-out to my YA test-readers: Kelly Ziemer, Brianna Allen, Cindy Turner, Ashley McGowean, and Alexa Sundeen.

Thank you to the rest of my supporting family and friends. You mean the world to me.

ORDER OF SEQUENCE

Prologue

PROLOGUE

I ALREADY KNEW I was going to miss his kiss more than I'd miss my friends, and we hadn't even kissed yet.

CHAPTER ONE

THE END

STARING OUT MY BEDROOM WINDOW with my forehead pressed against the windowpane, the hot air from my breath fogged the glass in a tiny circle with each jagged exhale.

This had become the worst day of my life.

Late in the evening, the temperature of the window against my skin felt more like autumn than spring. Outside, the sky had lost its color. An unanswered question continued to threaten the core of my stability I'd come to trust: *How could he do this to me?*

Within the giant "how" tumbled two more thoughts, each specific to "now what?" I had pretty much narrowed my choices down to two options: drown in my pit of misery, or rise above myself and embrace the move. Either way I'd have to say good-bye to everything I'd ever loved.

Bits and pieces of previous conversations tumbled inside my brain. Dad, Mom, my sister Kat, and I all agreed that a new house would be good for us. A bigger house, better suited to our needs--toy storage for Kat, a place for me to practice my guitar, and whatever it was that parents thought necessary. We agreed as a family.

Somehow, I'd been deceived.

For the past twenty-odd years, Dad has been the owner of a gun shop located on the edge of Topeka. Once rural, the area was now prime for development. On more than one occasion, I had overheard his worries concerning possible new homeowners objecting to his outdoor shooting range. Once, I even saw him wink at Mom when he told her that he was all right with her wearing a tight skirt to the judge's chambers in order to keep his zoning license and permits.

I hated him, but not because of his business or crude sense of humor. I hated him because he didn't even have the decency to apologize for ruining my life.

Just a few hours ago, Dad came speeding home from work happier than usual, calling for Mom, even before getting the white diesel truck into park. Kat and I were outside playing basketball.

"Hey, kids!" Dad shouted. His boyish grin still outshined the gray at his temples. I inwardly laughed as I watched him skip into the garage where Mom was, preparing flower pots.

"Izzy! Izzy!" I heard him call. "I bought a house!"

The basketball bounced off my head. At the very moment I opened my mouth to laugh because I had not been hurt, my ears began to burn at the horrific words my mother spoke: "We can make the commute, but this means new schools for the children..."

Like a shock wave from a huge explosion, the news hit me full force, almost knocking me to the ground; my perfect world had just ended prematurely. Kat looked up at me, her words echoed in my head, "Are you okay?"

No, I was not okay. My father, the hero that I trusted without waver, had just stabbed me in the back.

Mom grumbled something and headed in the house, wiping her dirty hands on her apron as she walked. Dad trailed off after her. Filled with disbelief, I felt compelled to follow. I had to see the man who had just demolished my life.

They made it as far as the entry way; he was standing there, excitement radiating from his smile. "It's so beau-ti-ful out there," Dad said without hearing what Mom was implying. "We'll have eleven acres."

She didn't take the bait. "Emily is a junior this year."

"Kathryn will love it. She'll have room to run around and play. It's just what every seven-year-old needs."

Mom didn't return the smile. "You had no right to do this, John! Your midlife crisis should be about buying a little red sports car, not a—"

"I don't like sports cars," Dad retorted, rather meekly.

Mom stomped off. The next thing I heard was a slamming door. Probably the bedroom door; the one place a woman could go to hide, no matter her age. I slammed my own next.

Still in my bedroom, frozen in a catatonic stupor, I sensed a presence behind me. Turning awkwardly, I kept my head pressed against the glass. Pain radiated from my mother's eyes despite her otherwise neutral expression. By now she had changed out of her work clothes and into a pair of lounging pajamas, her straight deep auburn hair still pulled back in a clasp.

"Although you may feel like it, Emily, it's not the end of the world." Mom took my hand and led me away from the window. "And you have Bunny. I know she'll help."

Bunny was like a Band-Aid for my heart. The white stuffed rabbit dangled beside me as I held it by its ears. Yes, I was too old for a stuffed animal, but I didn't care. It didn't seem right to cast her away. After all, I'd had her for as long as I could remember, and she was a wonderful friend, never complaining about her missing black button eye or her fluffy cotton-tail worn smooth. Plopping down on the edge of my bed, Bunny sprawled out next to me.

"You just don't get it, Mom."

Her eyes asked her question.

"Alex asked me to be his partner for the English project today."

"You and Alex have been friends for a long time…"

Yes, that much was true. Pictures of the two of us were scattered about my room. "But it was different today." Pain swelled in my heart. "I could just feel it."

"You're hoping he'll ask you to prom?" she asked.

"It's not just about prom. It's bigger than that." I knew I was getting ahead of myself, but I'd been dreaming about this fairytale with a happy ending for a while now. I'd been dreaming about… a kiss.

"I wish I could say I understand, but when I switched high schools, well, that was a long time ago."

"Did you ever get over it?" I looked at Mom, hoping to hear something good.

She hesitated and finally exhaled loudly through her nose. "Derek Houser was the boy I left behind. I don't think anyone ever completely gets over their first love. Still, if you focus on the good in your life, it will help you get through the rough stuff. Besides, the new house is just a few miles past Silver Lake. Maybe it won't be so bad." Leaning over, she pressed her lips against the top of my head. "I love you, and I'm always here for you." Then she added a smile. "Now get some sleep and I'll see you in the morning."

Mom turned and left me alone in silence. The forced smile on my lips began to quiver as my brave façade started to crumble. I needed a new hero.

Mom had a hero. It was Job, a persevering man described in the Old Testament. I considered adopting him as my hero. Then the second passed. Persevering was something I could not fathom at this particular moment. Hope of a quick and painless death was more like it. Imagining a meteorite falling from outer space and making a direct hit while I slept in my bed, felt oddly comforting at this particular moment.

As I sat in the stillness, my life took on a surreal quality as the realization that my very room, my school, my friends, my *fairytale,* were all about to evaporate in the aftermath of an atomic explosion. Everything would be gone. The thirty miles to the new house might as well be three hundred. My father had dropped a bomb. And somehow I'd become an unarmed soldier summoned with draft papers to a war I didn't know existed.

I looked at my stuffed white rabbit. Her expression told me she understood. I swooped Bunny up in my arms and held her tight. Nuzzling into the soft patch of fur between her long ears, I rubbed my chin across her fuzzy white hair, becoming lost in thought.

Kat startled me when she came in to say goodnight. "You should be in bed," I said.

"I was reading a book with Dad," she replied. "Are you going to bed soon?"

"Soon."

Her small face brightened. "Can I sleep with you?"

"Not tonight."

Her lower lip plumped.

"Some other time. Now leave me alone." Watching Kat mope back out into the hall made me feel bad, but there was no way could I deal with life if she were in my room, and that's assuming I could deal with it at all.

Emotionally drained, my body tipped over and my head bounced on the pillow. "It's not the end of the world. I can do this."

Then I waited for the statement to take hold.

Who was I trying to kid? *This move is going to kill me.* Tears that were strangely cold rolled off my cheeks and soaked my pillow. *Traitor.*

CHAPTER TWO

ALEX

THE WEEKEND PASSED BY in a slow-motion fog. If someone were to ask me what happened, I wouldn't be able to give any details except that my father had crossed over into enemy territory and blew up my life. I wasn't certain about anything anymore, except that I was suffering from shell shock, Post Traumatic Stress Disorder, or some other form of psychological war trauma.

Now Monday morning, I'd soon be facing my friends for the first time since hearing the "good news." I had no idea how to tell them about it and I looked upon this task with the same feeling as walking in front of a firing squad. Standing in front of the mirror, I tried out a few ice breakers:

"Hey everyone, I'm moving in a month and I'll probably never see you again." Too histrionic.

"I have terrible news…." Too emo.

"Guess what, I'm moving!" Too animated.

"My dad has single-handedly ruined my life!" Too dramatic.

Crap.

Just as I was about to cave into self-pity, a new idea began to take shape. Maybe I'd just pretend I wasn't going to move. I loved denial! It made life so much easier to cope with.

Continuing with my pre-outing prep and blow-drying my hair, thoughts of the school play popped into my head, cutting short my new-found enthusiasm. Opening night for the school play would be here in no time. Rather than being excited, the idea made me feel a little ill. And overwhelmed. Somehow, I'd have to find the energy to keep up the long rehearsal hours *and* pretend my life wasn't about to end.

A new brigade of hot tears rolled down my face, reinforcing the idea that nothing in life was certain. The hollow pit lingering in my stomach swelled against my heart, interfering with the love I felt for the stage. *Why did Dad have to ruin my life?*

After dabbing my tears with a tissue in an attempt to save my mascara, I leaned in close to the mirror to check for damage and caught a glimpse of my internal mood-rings which revealed a brownish-hazel color. Depressed: go figure. I doubted my eyes would ever be blue again. Returning to my hair, I brushed it until it shone, but I still didn't feel pretty. I never felt pretty, even though I was often told I was. Leaning to the side, the long strands fell into open space, exposing the dark brown low-lights Mom added to the under-layer a few weeks back. Mom's comment to keep track of the good things rang through my head. Shiny hair was a start.

With my morning routine complete, I headed for the kitchen to grab an apple out of the fruit bowl and considered sneaking off to school without all the normal morning conversation. That was my other favorite coping skill, avoidance.

"Stop right there, young lady," Mom called from the dining table where the rest of the family was gathered.

I let go of the doorknob.

Mom was big on the family eating together. "Gangs!" she would state. "If you don't have family, you have gangs." She got up from her chair and repeatedly pointed to her cheek as she approached me. "Sorry, Mom." I pecked a kiss on her cheek. Mom was known to the public as Elizabeth Stokes, an avid volunteer at the Boys' and Girls' Club. She was always in the news. She was less known for her love of Edgar Allen Poe, fascination with criminal psychology, or her paid work as a probation officer in Shawnee County.

"I get one!" Kat bellowed as she tore around the corner. Her semi-curly brown hair was wild, still not combed.

Arms out, I leaned down, trying to prepare myself for the assault.

With a track and field style long jump, Kat launched herself into the air and hooked her arms around my neck, nearly causing permanent damage.

"You must be practicing," I groaned, staggering backwards.

"How could you tell?"

"I'm psychic. So, I also know you're going to have a great day at school." Prying her arms off my neck, she dropped to the floor. "See ya later, Kitty."

Grabbing my backpack, I ignored Dad, who was sitting at the table looking my way.

Walking out to my car, I knew I had to pour the charm on Alex if I was going to get him to ask me to the dance. My stomach tightened as I tried not to think about how thirty miles was long enough to kill friendships, force me into a new school district, and wreak havoc in my life, but short enough for parents to commute to their same jobs every day. Placing all my faith in the English project, I begged God to work a miracle. After cranking the ignition switch, I added a final *"please"* and began the short drive to school.

Until a few months ago, I didn't want a boyfriend. All because of Zachary Melcomb. He had been the boy who'd completely destroyed my childhood fantasies of the romantic first kiss, and any dating that could lead to another kiss. His kiss made me not want to kiss another boy for five years. It wasn't just nasty, it was naaasty! I still remember his fat slimy tongue jetting into my mouth like some trained walrus searching for a treat, the feeling of extra spit sloshing in my mouth—his tongue whirling wildly beside my tonsils until I gagged! My body still responds with a repulsive shudder just thinking about it.

But as of late, when I look at Alex Hibbs, I secretly desire a romantic kiss. Not just any old kiss, but one that makes you weak in the knees and defines true love. The all-important, all-encompassing kiss: that's what I dreamed of. That's what I wanted.

Not like there was any pressure or anything.

I knew if I could make it to English, I'd make it through today. Alex always made me feel better. His hysterical sense of humor made me laugh. And how I loved to imagine running my fingers through his thick, black hair that was always kept at the perfect length of needing a haircut yesterday. He definitely made it a little easier to get up this morning, but a whole lot harder to face the move.

But I had my plan! A *great* plan that involved wooing.

My insides seemed to grow warm just thinking about it. Indeed, I was beginning to believe I could survive.

As I pulled into the Topeka West parking lot, I noticed the girls already huddled together. Bailey, Clair, and Rayyan each already had steady boyfriends, and of course, they were going to prom. Making a quick search further down the parking aisles, I felt my cheeks tighten as I spied Alex's black Jeep. At least I had three good things going for me today. Getting out of my car, I could hear the girls' conversation. Dress shopping for prom. Tonight.

"Where do you want to go?" Rayyan scanned our faces.

"I think we should look at Sylvester's, the fancy little boutique at Fairlawn Plaza." Clair's eyes lit up like fireworks.

"Isn't that really expensive?" Rayyan began the procession to the entrance.

"I've always had really good luck at J.C. Penney," Bailey offered.

"Really?" Clair looked skeptical.

"My mom would like it if I could keep the cost down," Rayyan admitted. Everyone nodded in agreement, even me.

Rayyan noticed. "Did Alex ask you?" All eyes locked on me.

"No…" I heaved a sigh. Somehow my diabolical plan suddenly seemed stupid.

"I'm not surprised. He's so…" Bailey made a face that included sticking out her tongue.

"Stop picking on Alex. He's a nice guy! Besides, you can't hold him responsible for all the crap that has happened in his family," I responded hotly.

"I guess every dysfunctional family has its normal member." Sarcasm oozed from Bailey's words.

"I think you and Alex would make a nice couple," Clair said. "You should come with me to Sylvester's after school since it's so close. You want to impress him, don't you?"

"Ah…"

"But you *think* Alex will ask," Rayyan asked, no doubt wanting details.

"Yes!" The word ended in a hiss. "I think Alex will ask me." He *had* to ask.

"Why don't you just ask him?" Bailey scoffed.

I stopped walking and faced them all. "Because that doesn't count. If *I* ask, we're still just friends. But if *he* asks, I'll get a kiss at the end of the night." I turned and stomped off for the door without them. "I want a kiss!" I yelled back.

With my good mood squelched yet again, I knew it would take every last ounce of energy I had to get through this day. As I drew near the school building, even the simple brick design annoyed me and I wondered when architectural flair went out of style? *Why couldn't Dad have picked a new house next to Topeka High? At least they got to enter through a majestic entryway every day.*

Find the good, Mom's words rang in my head.

"Okay, Mom," I murmured to myself. *They get a spectacular building, but T-West has* "the best band in the land," *and I was part of it.*

"See you later, Emily," one of my friends called from behind.

"At lunch," I mumbled, still irritated.

As I hurried down the hall, the day's priorities and events tumbled into order. I liked starting the day with band; our teacher was great. He actually seemed excited whenever I asked permission to add yet another woodwind to my repertoire. I suppose my gratitude should belong to my ex-hero father who never tired of buying me instruments, including my real passion, the guitar.

Life wrecker.

I never looked forward to second hour, trigonometry. Insider information claimed that all higher mathematics were created by the Devil himself, but then I knew not to believe everything I heard. Other rumors had my third hour teacher dating the math teacher, which may explain why she always showed a movie on days following really hard math tests. Unfortunately, she had a movie scheduled for today.

Up until this past Friday, Spanish had been my favorite class. It had been a goal of mine to convince Mrs. Linz to approach the school board and suggest the course be turned into a cultural-language class that focused on the impact Spain and Mexico have had on our nation's history with a mandatory trip to Spain!

But, starting today, the newest reason why I liked third hour was because it came directly before the only truly important class of the day: English. With Alex Hibbs! And today, *that's* what mattered most.

Entering the door to my first class, I checked the clock on the wall and then my pocket to make sure I had a piece of gum so my breath would be fresh when fourth hour came.

7:40 am. Have gum.

C-sharp-not-B-flat-8:11 am…8:22 am…Bell-has-rung-time-for-next-class-8:35 am…Pain-of-death-math-test-8:51 am…8:55 am…9:01 am…9:03 am…9:04 am…9:20 am…Thank-God-that-is-over-9:37 am…This-movie-is-boring-10:06 am…10:15 am…10:17 am…

Finally! 10:35 am. Time for English!

Even though I sat by Alex every day, today I had butterflies. He was already sitting in his chair when I walked into the room. I popped the gum into my mouth.

Please, let the plan work.

"Hi," I said, a bit overzealously as I took my seat next to him.

"Hey, how's it going?" It sounded more like a statement than a question. He was messing with his cell phone, but shook his head, briefly exposing his steel blue eyes that were usually hidden beneath his thick black hair.

"We get to start on our project today." I leaned in towards him, trying to appear irresistible.

"Yeah, this should be good," he replied without looking up.

Hello! Girl trying to flirt.

Mrs. Stoffer began distributing the project outline before the bell rang. "If you are not already sitting by your partner, please do so now."

He put his phone in his pocket and looked at me.

I smiled what I hoped to be a sexy smile. Butterflies fluttered through my stomach a second time.

"Is your cell broken?" he asked.

What? The butterflies turned into lead. *I can't believe I didn't even look at my cell phone over the weekend...he looks mad.* "I'm sorry. Family stuff came up. You know how it goes," I said.

"I suppose," Alex replied, not appearing completely convinced.

"The final project for the year will be a documentary based upon the characters you and your partner create. It can be presented in either written or video form, as described in the outline," Mrs. Stoffer continued.

"What would you like to do?" Alex whispered close to my ear resulting in an involuntary shiver and an image of him and me locked in a steamy first kiss.

My thoughts felt exposed as Mrs. Stoffer slapped the outline down on my desk, making both Alex and me jerk back against our chairs.

I couldn't very well tell him what I was honestly thinking, so using my best flirtatious luscious-lip-lick, I said, "Wouldn't it be great to make a movie?" instead.

He smiled. "I knew I hung around you for a reason. You're a lot of fun."

Well, that made four things going for me: shiny hair, being a member of the best band in the entire state of Kansas, sitting next to Alex, and him thinking I was fun.

"So, what should the movie be about?" he asked.

I glanced over the paper Mrs. Stoffer gave us. "It says we need a minimum of two characters in our story."

"Well, we have a male and a female." His hand motioned between us.

"How about pre-dating jitters?" I regretted my words as soon as they were out.

Alex's face went flat.

"Or not." I winced.

"But a boy-girl meeting seems to be a logical direction," he said.

As we created the characters for our plot, I found myself thinking about other things—like his hair, his secretive blue eyes, going to a movie together, holding hands… him leaning over and kissing me.

"Why are you being so resistant!" *What just came out of my mouth?*

Stunned, Alex stared. "Excuse me?"

I gawked back. *Oh crap!*

"Something about resistance?" His eyebrow curved as he tapped his pencil on the desk.

I had to think of something fast. "Ahh…The Renaissance. You know, they could meet…never mind. Dumb idea."

"Blondes," Alex sneered, smacking his elbows on the desk to create a doubled-fisted platform for his chin.

Thankful I didn't blow my plan before I had the chance to implement it, I stuck to the assignment from here on out. Our story evolved into the plot of a self-made documentary made by a serial killer. Alex would star as the psycho killer and I would be one of his tortured victims. It was deliciously bad. We laughed so hard at our tasteless project I was surprised the teacher didn't kick us out.

Then all too soon, the bell rang, eliciting the entire class to their feet like a group of Pavlov's dogs.

Alex's expression turned serious. "We should get together and work on this after school." His tone of voice turned somber, quite different from our hysterical laughter. Then he reached for my hand and turned it palm side up, drawing in a smiley face with his finger.

"Oh." Not expecting the question or the hand holding, my knees became a bit wobbly. I could tell that this was different from the other times he asked me to hang out. "I have plans tonight, but, I could change them. You could stay for dinner." The butterflies went crazy in my stomach.

"That's okay. Keep your plans, but I work tomorrow so how about Wednesday?"

"Play practice. Thursday?" I was sure my heart was thumping so hard he'd be able to hear it.

His lips curved to a grin. "That will work." Then he patted his stomach. "Is dinner still in the offer? I love your mom's cooking."

"Sure is," I said, hoping he was more eager to see me than to eat my mom's food.

"We'll just keep working on the story plot in class until then." Scooping his books up off the desk he said, "I don't want to be late for my next class. See you later, Em."

Alex left me standing on cloud nine with dreams of a happily-ever-after fairytale. Watching him walk away, I was curious what it must be like for a guy who was interested in a girl. Did they ever get butterflies or weak in the knees? Or was it limited to the boner inside their pants? And if so, did he ever get one for me?

Shame on me! At any rate, the plan seemed to be working and it was going to be outrageously fun. I had to get to the cafeteria to fill in my buds—he held my hand!

CHAPTER THREE

THE DRESS

"HOW DID YOUR DAY GO, EM?"
Mom asked as she handed me a china bowl of steaming mashed potatoes. Mom was big into family dinnertime, too.

"Lovely," I cooed, taking the beautiful bowl from my mother's hands and twirled toward the dining table, feeling my long hair flow with me. Magically, over the course of the school day, my shell-shocked daze had been transformed into a ballet dance performed to the melody heard only in my head.

"Lovely, huh? Do please tell, what makes a school day 'lovely?'"

Returning to the kitchen, I distinctly recalled drawing hearts on notebook paper that surrounded the initials E.S. + A.H. during the last two class periods. "I'm doing a fun project in English, that's all."

"That's all?" Mom stopped whisking the gravy and looked up. "Strange, I've never heard you describe English in such a way before."

"I was right, Mom. He *likes* me."

"Alex?"

The words blurted out, "He held my hand today in class."

"In class?" Dad repeated, walking into the kitchen, just in time to interrupt. "That Alex kid? And you let him?"

I resisted the urge to stick my tongue out at him.

"You sure know how to ruin a moment." Mom scowled at Dad, then looked at me. "Having a date for prom is looking a little more promising." She went to check the calendar hanging on the side of the fridge. "Let's see, he has about three weeks to ask?"

"I hope he asks sooner than later. I don't want to be stuck with an ugly dress."

"Don't worry! Now if your hands are washed, please sit down. Someone call Kathryn first."

"I think it's important to finish the last few weeks of the school year with all the enthusiasm as we normally would," Mom proclaimed as she passed another china bowl filled with fresh green beans laced with sliced almonds.

She was no doubt referring to Kat's track and field season and my regularly over-booked schedule of band concerts, art club, year book committee meetings, and the upcoming school rendition of *Prelude to a Kiss*.

And don't forget about prom (with Alex Hibbs).

"What's the play about?" Kat asked, and then applied another layer of milk-mustache.

"It's about an old man who kisses a bride-to-be and they swap souls in the process."

"Creepy." Kat crinkled her nose.

"And disturbing. But it's still been a lot of fun."

"I can't wait to hear the band concert." Dad smiled and reached out to touch my arm.

I pulled it away, pretending to have something in my eye. My ex-hero father went back to eating his mashed potatoes dripping with excessive gravy. He made me nauseous.

"After I kick butt at McCarter this year, I'm gonna kick some more at the new school next year!" Kat blurted.

Obviously she was okay with country living. Dad found a new smile. "That's my girl," he cheered.

I sat and wondered if it was more of a self-serving cheer than for her athletic ability. And what about Kat? She seemed not to care at all about moving. How could she not be sad? Wouldn't she miss her friends, too? Perhaps she was just too young and couldn't fully understand the impending loss. Stirring the chocolate powder into my milk, I thought to ponder this later. I really didn't want to spoil my good mood.

"What's on for tonight?" Mom asked as we cleared the table of dirty dinner plates and empty serving dishes.

"We're going to West Ridge Mall to look for dresses." I didn't have to tell her that the individuals included in "we" were Rayyan, Bailey, Clair, and of course, me. "I'm not going to get a dress just yet," I pouted, "but I do want to be prepared."

Mom kindly withheld the judgment I saw in her eyes, and tried to cover it up with a smile of endearment.

I grabbed my purse and reached in for the car keys. I loved my car. That was another positive thing in my life. It was a blue VW Love Bug with green flames painted on the front. Dad even sprang for a customized license plate that read ONFIRE. I got it for my seventeenth birthday present, a reward for being an accident-free driver. That was about the only perk of having a November birthday—I got my license earlier than most other kids in my grade.

Just as I was ready to slip the gearshift in reverse to back out of my spot along side the house, Kat came bounding out through the door yelling and waving her arms.

"Wait!" she screamed, running to the driver's side window. Poking her head inside, she asked, "Can I come?"

I took a deep breath and held it. I looked at her cute little face and her cute little eyes and her cute pouting lower lip quivering in exaggeration. Little sisters were so annoying. "Get in, Kitty." I said, pointing to the back seat with my thumb.

"Yesss." She smiled, clenching her fist and pulling it in toward her belly. "I gotta tell Mom. Don't leave." She darted back inside the house, with her hair still appearing uncombed.

She returned moments later accompanied by Mom clutching her gardening supplies. I blew Mom a kiss which she quickly snatched out of the sky and planted on her lips.

Shopping for the perfect dress with my three best friends became quite the adventure. With our arms loaded down with a heap of dresses, the fitting room became a fashion runway. We tried on long and sleek, short and frilly, bold and pleated, beaded and scratchy. My favorite worst dress was the very short, super ruffle-y dress Bailey tried on.

"I look like the frickin' tooth fairy," Bailey piped.
"Somebody get me a magic wand."

"You have to get it," Clair exclaimed. "I'll pay you
fifty dollars if you wear it."

"I have sparkly wings you could borrow," Kat
added.

Although the dress was way too short, I had to
admit Bailey looked...like the tooth fairy. And no one
wants to look like an elf at a school dance.

I couldn't remember the last time I laughed so hard
or had this much fun. Even Kat had a blast pretending
to be a famous know-it-all fashion critique as she
announced each dress as we walked down the
imaginary runway. I'd have to thank her later.

As the mall announced it was closing in ten
minutes, time became relevant. Bailey and Rayyan each
purchased a dress from J.C. Penney. Clair decided to go
back to Sylvester's Boutique to compare. We laughed
some more on our way through the parking lot as we
relived the trial and error process of trying on nearly
every dress in every single store. Mom would kill me if
she knew what a mess we left behind in the dressing
rooms.

Rayyan tossed her purse into the passenger's front
seat of Bailey's car. They lived close to each other so
often shared a ride. A heated wisp of envy dashed
through me as I watched them carefully pack their bags
containing brand new shoes and jewelry that perfectly
matched their brand new evening dresses.

"I'll see you all tomorrow." Clair reached out to
begin the exchange of hugs. Kat looked up and did her
pouting lip thing. My friends hugged her, too.

"Let's get home, Kitty." I grabbed her hand and walked towards my fiery painted Bug. Clair turned and went the other way. Then the sickening pains of moving jarred me again. I was going to miss the convenience of the city. We were just minutes away from everything, living on a cul-de-sac just off Fairlawn. Both our schools were just south of our house, off Fairlawn. The shopping malls were just off Fairlawn. Everything that mattered was just off Fairlawn.

Although it seemed like forever, it had only been six days since Dad had informed us we'd be moving. While it was my intent to embrace the move, I was failing miserably and my scheme to cope with life was seriously malfunctioning. The part of my plan that included "denial" kept faltering and I never knew when another round of random tears would break through. Not even play practice stopped the tears today. Then there was the other part of my diabolical plan that involved Alex, which was not working as I had hoped, either. In fact, it didn't seem to be working at all. Desperation was setting in.

I was sitting at the kitchen table eating chocolate chip cookies and feeling the need to succumb to childish ploys that involved my friends asking Alex seemingly innocent questions about topics like prom, when Mom came home from work, disrupting my thoughts. She was holding a very long bag over her arm.

My mouth dropped open in surprise. Knowing exactly what it was, I grabbed it out of her arms asking, "What is it?"

"Kat told me about it," Mom began. "She was all worried about it being the dress you admired the most and the only one in existence."

"Where is Kitty anyway?" The nickname began as a taunt but now it just seemed to fit.

"Dad took some time off and the two are practicing the softball throw."

Hearing his name, I realized I was still mad at him. *Home wrecker.* But that didn't matter now. I refocused on the very long plastic bag and held it up just as if I could see the dress that was hidden underneath.

"You're the best!"

"I love you."

"I love you, too, Mom. Thanks." I bounded off to my room for the unveiling.

To prolong the anticipation, I removed the plastic covering a little slower than necessary. As I untied the bottom of the bag, soft white silk began to spill out like a graceful waterfall. The intricate beaded flowers decorated the front of the dress, starting at knee length and bloomed lavishly up the bodice. It was not gaudy in the least. It was just as delicate and beautiful as I remembered. Thin spaghetti straps held the masterpiece on the hanger. I had to try it on again to make sure it still looked the same.

The day's clothes were in a pile on the floor. The room felt warm as I stood there in my undies. After pulling down the zipper, I lowered the dress to step in. The cool silk warmed up quickly as it glided across my skin. I couldn't quite reach the top end of the zipper to fully close the back of the dress but that didn't matter all that much right now. I stepped in front of the mirror to rate my reflection. This dress…this amazing dress! For the first time ever, I thought of myself as beautiful. I dared myself to keep believing in the fairytale.

CHAPTER FOUR

LIFE SUCKS

IT WAS GETTING HARDER and harder for Alex to crawl out of bed. He hadn't slept well in months. It always seemed that he finally got to sleep just when the alarm was about to go off. He grabbed his jeans from off the floor and a clean shirt out of the closet. After pulling a comb through his wet hair, he headed out the door.

He hated to walk past the garage. It was the reason he couldn't sleep.

CHAPTER FIVE

FEARS

I AWOKE TO A BITTERSWEET MORNING. I smiled because Alex would be coming over tonight to work on the video, yet, as the move drew nearer, I wondered why I continued to kid myself. Even if Alex did ask me to prom, I doubted that a relationship would survive the miles. Looking over at the amazing dress that hung from my closet door frame, I felt fear, but not about prom. Prom was just the cover-up. I was afraid that I'd never find another Alex, I'd never get my kiss, and I'd never live my fairytale.

Shifting back into my comfort zone of denial, I waited for the hot water to run from the showerhead. I gave myself a pep talk to not waste time dwelling on the future.

"I must be strong," I spoke the words aloud, hoping for greater effect. Or, at least some effect.

Finally stepping into the shower, the spray washed over my face, making my tears indistinguishable from the rest of the water. I had no right to say it, but I really hated life. I wanted to stay in the shower until every last bit of sorrow washed down the drain.

I emerged just as miserable as I had entered. Like every other morning, after dressing, I put on a little make-up. I liked the way it accented my eyes. But then instead of my usual clear lip-gloss, I opted for bright pink lipstick. Like a clown, my smile needed to be painted on.

It was Thursday, which meant a late start. Mom would already be at work. I made my way to the kitchen and found a note next to a bowl of deep red strawberries waiting on the counter, both from Mom, telling me that she loved me, to eat my breakfast, and have a great day. As I popped a berry in my mouth, I became aware of Dad and Kat sitting at the table.

"Good morning, Em," Dad called out at me. I didn't realize it until this second, but we hadn't spoken since the foreboding news. I looked down at the floor, then back up at him. I nodded my head.

"Good morning, Grumpy-pants," Kathryn, the annoying, spouted off. At least it broke the tension.

"You'd better run!" I shouted and chased after the screaming, wild brown hair that still didn't look like it had been combed.

The school parking lot was already filling up with the other one thousand or so students that attended T-West. Some kids like to park close to the doors. I liked to park near the exit to avoid the always-congested dismissal rush. Bailey, along with Rayyan, parked next to me.

"Hey, when do tickets go on sale for the play? It's next weekend, right?" Rayyan asked.

"Yeah," I said.

"Don't be so excited." Bailey shifted her books to the other arm.

"I think they go on sale Monday. Where's Clair?" I asked as I reached behind the back seat of my car to grab my woodwind instruments from their hiding spot.

A moan escaped as the lack of practicing skimmed my thoughts.

"She texted me that she'd be late," Rayyan responded, grabbing her backpack from the floor of her car. "Something about a hair appointment."

"What? Missing school for hair?" I rolled my eyes.

"She's all freaked about a hairstyle to match her dress from Sylvester's," Rayyan continued.

"Prom is 'only two weeks away,'" Bailey piped in, making fun of Clair.

A lot of people thought Clair was stuck on herself because she spent so much time on her looks. Once I got to know her, it was obvious she was just insecure. Still, it didn't help her case for her mom to let her miss school for a hair appointment.

Making our way toward the entrance, I finally saw Alex's big black Jeep. An elusive smile spread across my face.

"You know," Bailey said, after noticing my eyes on Alex's Jeep, "that must have been really awful, to walk into the garage and see your Dad with his brains blown all over the wall."

I tried to ignore her.

Rayyan elbowed her in the ribs.

"I wonder if it was as bloody as the rumors claim?" Bailey didn't catch the obvious hint to shut up. "I heard it took two bullets."

"Maybe you should go *wonder* somewhere else," I said.

"I don't mean to be critical, but it happened over a year ago. A normal person would be over it by now. Quite honestly, Emily, I don't know what you see in him, anyway. He gives me the creeps. His eyes are so pale, they're almost white."

"Man, I can't believe you are so insensitive."

"I think he's cute," Rayyan said.

Oblivious to the surrounding mood, Bailey began nodding in self approval. "Maybe he has a fear of attachment or something because of it. Maybe that's why he wouldn't ask you to prom."

"Who died and made you Dr. Phil? I don't care what you think. I like Alex, so just keep your opinions to yourself!"

"Like I said before, I don't mean to be rude." Bailey shrugged her shoulders.

"Then stop bashing him. I still believe he's going to ask me."

Bailey's expression changed from disgust to mild glee. "I think you should find someone else."

Rayyan groaned. "Don't start this again."

"Who? Zachary Melcomb?" I asked through clenched teeth.

"Don't be such a baby. There are more boys out there than Zachary and Alex."

"Not the way I see it."

"Oh yeah, I forgot about the fireman who rescued you when you were little. Maybe he'll come back and marry you."

My heart jumped to my throat. I couldn't believe she would use that against me. "I still cherish that memory!"

"Like I said, don't be such a baby."

Some days I really hated Bailey. Mostly because she was right and not afraid to say it. Unfortunately for me, Bailey's words infected the rest of my school day.

Like a simple sliver that started out painless, it became an oozing sore. Doubts about Alex asking me to prom were becoming hard to ignore.

Walking back to my car, I recapped my entire day with one single word: crap. Especially after Mrs. Stoffer decided to show a documentary, leaving me no chance to flirt with Alex. Throwing my books and instruments in the passenger seat, I looked back over to where Alex's Jeep had been this morning.

"Oh criminy!" His car was already gone. "He's going to beat me home." I looked around to see if anyone noticed I was talking out loud to myself. *Safe.* Suddenly, life didn't seem so bad.

Luck saw to it that I arrived home first to clean up the pigsty decorating the living room. Alex was going to be here at any moment to work on the movie and this place was a disaster! I grabbed the tablature sheets for my guitar that were spread out all over the floor and stacked them in a sloppy pile on the coffee table. Then I found seven dirty socks Kat had scatter-bombed around the couch. The eighth one must be lost somewhere in the cushions. Mom made it clear that her job title did not include "maid." Kat made it obvious she was okay with that. I threw the seven down the laundry chute and came back for a final inspection. It would have to pass.

Realizing Kat was not in the middle of my business, I surmised that she and Dad must have been practicing for track 'n' field days again.

Just as I was about to plop on the couch, I heard a car pull up in the driveway. I saw Mom's car. The front door opened and in walked Alex.

"Alex, what are you doing here?" He was carrying a bag of groceries.

He gave me a puzzled look. "I thought we were working on the movie today."

Realizing my stupid question, I rephrased. "I mean, I didn't hear you pull up."

"Thank you for your help, Alex." Mom smiled.

"You're welcome, Mrs. Stokes." He put the bag on the kitchen counter and added, "You are looking exceptionally nice this afternoon."

Mom liked his flattery; she knew he wasn't really interested in her so she enjoyed it. "I hope you like shrimp fettuccini," she replied as she unloaded the bag.

Alex and I headed for the living room and laid out our storyboard on the coffee table. I sat on the floor across from him so I could look directly at him. It made for easier flirting. We decided to change the character from a serial killer to a random guy committing a single murder for the sole purpose of filming it. We had most of the work completed and just had to come up with a plausible ending.

"How about after he makes the movie, he is so overwhelmed by his actions, he decides to take his own life?" The thought of his father popped into my head and I grimaced. "Or not. I'm sorry."

Alex exhaled loudly. "No foul, it's cool. It could work. We could have him hang himself."

Relieved I didn't ruin our fun, my enthusiasm grew. "Yeah, like you can hear him talking as he puts the camera down on a table or something, and the lens is pointed off to the side so you only see part of him, he could be throwing a rope up over a beam...."

I didn't pay much attention to the tantalizing smell coming from the kitchen; of Kat complaining it was not her night to set the table with dishes, or anything else that occurred in the house over the next hour and a half. Lost in the moment and each other, it felt strange talking about murder and death while seductive thoughts lingered just below the surface.

"Time to eat!" Kat yelled at ear level directly behind us.

Alex got up off the couch first and extended his hand to me. Accepting his help, I tried not to smile too big when he kept it, all the way to the table. At last the plan was working, and I could visualize the fairytale ending in the romantic kiss I dreamed about.

"What a delicious looking meal." Alex inhaled deeply while his eyes scanned the table.

I was proud of Mom. She was an excellent cook and found pleasure in presenting the meal so it looked as good as it would taste. I think it actually made it taste even better. God forbid Alex would ever expect this from me. I was not into cooking, of any kind.

"Well, let's get this thing started," Dad said. "I've got to get to the bowling alley."

"Do people still play that?" Alex gawked in disbelief.

"Yes they do," Dad answered back, undaunted by the youth.

"I always thought that to be pretty lame," Alex jeered.

"Shut up." I took offense as a wave of memories poured into my mind. I used to have a lot of fun going glow-in-the-dark bowling with Dad, and it abruptly reminded me why my father was my hero. He was patient, kind, loving. But hugely, he gave me the greatest gift of all—his time.

"Easy there, Blondie," Alex said. "It's just bowling."

I wasn't sure why, but I felt like I'd been completely dissed. Yeah, actually I did. Because I was.

I tried to let it go.

"Just bowling." His words echoed in my head.

Who did Alex think he was, insulting us like that? After all, I defended Alex from Bailey all the time. As the conversation turned elsewhere, I couldn't move past the bowling thing, and I questioned the real source of my bitterness. After dinner, I walked away from the table with a blackened fairytale.

Alex took to the couch and I sat on the floor opposite him. "I have a pounding headache," I said, swirling a design against the nap of the carpet.

"You don't look very happy. Maybe we should stop here and pick it back up tomorrow?" Alex suggested.

"I think that would be good." My voice sounded harsh, even to me.

Alex tugged at his chin. "Is everything okay with you?"

OMG. You are being a dork, my fairytale is more like a nightmare, I'm about to move to an entirely different city, and you are wondering if everything is all right?

"Yeah, I'm fine. Maybe just a little tired." I tried to sound more pleasant.

"Well, I guess I'll see you later then." He stood up, straightened his shorts and proceeded to stretch his arms high above head, allowing his stomach to peek out from under the bottom of his shirt.

My eyes liked what they saw, but my heart was still mad. Why couldn't he just ask?

Alex walked over to the front door. I hovered a few feet back.

"Talk to you tomorrow," he said, closing the door behind him.

Wishing I could divert my preoccupation about Alex with a cucumber facial, I was patting my face dry when mom poked her head in through the open door. She stepped in and waited for me to say something.

I threw my towel on the counter. "It's just not fair!" I blurted out. "I know you're going to tell me that life doesn't have to change with the move, but it's going to. I won't see my friends anymore and—"

"Emily, dear."

"Sure, maybe for a while, but that will be all. A while!" I heard myself nearly yelling but I didn't care. "Just like when Jill Jenkins moved away. How long did it take—three weeks? She was my best friend, Mom."

A sense of betrayal hit me hard in the stomach, making me wince. I'd never allowed myself to acknowledge that whole painful scene before. Now here I was, faced with complete exile.

"And all the stupid hoopla over prom!" Within an instant, my mother vanished beneath the wall of water welling up in the rims of my eyes. Just as quickly, the salty tears flooded their confines and poured out like a burst dam.

Mom approached me with her palms stretched out. My tears flowed too fast and she disappeared again. I blinked to reveal a distressed smile embedded in empathy. She reached for my hands and gently worked her fingertips into my fists.

"You are right, my dear little one." She held my hands and searched my eyes. "It is not fair. But there is an entire world outside of Topeka waiting to be discovered."

I longed to be small enough to be cradled in her arms. Mom seemed to sense this and led me to the overstuffed rocking chair that used to belong to my grandpa. She sat first and I snuggled up on her lap. Just like when I was little, she pushed back against the floor with her feet and set the chair in motion. Mom began to sing.

"Hush little baby don't say a word, Mama's gonna buy you a mocking bird," her sweet voice was just louder than a whisper. "And if that mocking bird don't sing, Mama's gonna buy you a diamond ring. And if that diamond ring don't shine—"

Although she had sung this song to me countless times before, I choked out a laugh at my epiphany of the entire song. "It's no wonder why women find comfort in shopping."

A sad smile crossed her face. "We are pathetic creatures at times." She caressed my leg even though it was probably cutting off her circulation.

"When did you meet Dad?"

"I met your father shortly after moving to Kansas back in 1989, during the BTK serial killings." Joy replaced the sadness as she spoke.

My eyes grew wide. "The bind, torture, and kill dude?"

"Yes. Even though the murders had been taking place in the lower half of the state, it was a dormant time for him. I was young, and paranoid that the BTK murderer might relocate in my area to start another killing spree."

"How can you tell this story with a smile on your face?"

"Lord knows I dislike guns, but I went to buy one, just for that false sense of security. And, well, there was this very charming man who helped me..."

"Was it Dad?"

A distant glow warmed her eyes. "I never bought a gun; I got your father instead."

"Mom! Picking up strange men." Her story made me smile too.

She cringed and laughed at the same time. "It's not like I made a habit out of it."

"I know. Just teasing. But you never knew each other in school?"

"Never." Mom's smile came to a close. Then, as loving and supporting as a mother holding her newborn infant, she gave me another hug. "Remember Em, life is an adventure."

Friday passed with little consequence. Alex and I finished our storyboard, but without the flirting. *Stupid jerk.* I still had an entire week before prom, but the constant ache in my stomach seemed to be telling me that I waited in vain.

And, it was getting harder to face my friends. I knew once I confessed the move, my whole scheme of denial would fall apart, and I just didn't have the energy to come up with something new. Why did life have to be so hard?

When Saturday morning arrived, the house was quiet. A note on the counter explained that my parents were already busy with plans of their own, and reminded me that Kat would still be at her friend's house after last night's sleepover. Yay for me.

I enjoyed being alone. It left me free to create my music. So upon my bed, I closed my eyes and began to play. Instantly, rhythmic sounds flowed from my guitar. It seemed I had just started when the phone rang. Caller ID revealed it was Alex Hibbs.

"Hello."

"What time do you want to get together?" he asked in a cheerful voice. "We still need to work on our project."

A part of me wanted to see him, a part of me wanted to shake some sense into him, and yet another part of me wanted to yell, "never!" and hang up the phone. His reluctance, coupled with my own issues over moving, was definitely making me crazy. I could hardly stand being seventeen and already plagued with emotional baggage.

"Oh, how about some time this morning? Where?" I asked.

"Your house." His excitement came over the line. "I'll be there in an hour." Then he hung up.

"Why do women like men?" I complained out loud to myself. *"They're all morons."*

I hurried up my relaxing morning.

The doorbell rang. Before I could pull the door open, Alex let himself in, thrusting a bouquet of mixed flowers in my face. "Since I am killing you today, I thought this would be a nice gesture."

This is why women like men, they…are…morons!

"Thanks, I guess." I took the flowers from him and he followed me into the living room. "I'll put them in water."

Although I liked the flowers, I liked the way he looked even better. He was dressed in a pair of tan shorts and a wrinkled, untucked, dark blue button-down shirt. He had the sleeves rolled up to his elbows. The unkept-style looked good on him, like a model posing in some fashion magazine. I wondered if he ever noticed what I was wearing.

He flopped on the couch to wait: feet on the coffee table and legs crossed at the ankles. Sometimes he acted more like a brother than the cute guy I'd like to make out with.

"Where is everyone?" he called out nonchalantly.

"Gone," I called back. Realizing we were alone, I froze in my tracks. I was alone with Alex Hibbs! I was definitely back into the "love" mode. Hormones raced through my body and I felt my checks flush and goosebumps rise on my arms. We'd been alone in my house a hundred times before…. But this was different.

This was the time my mother warned me about. Fear crept in my consciousness, but of what? Myself?

"Em?" His voice only heightened my arousal.

"Ahh, just a minute." I became paranoid like he could see my x-rated thoughts.

"Hurry it up, we don't have all day."

Disappointment set in abruptly ending the fantasy. "Why?"

"Emily, it's just an expression."

"Oh, okay." Smile back on.

Rather than taking the time to arrange the flowers one by one, I simply crammed the clipped ends into the first vase I found. Returning to the living room with the vase in hand, I set it on the coffee table, and plopped myself next to Alex.

He's so...yummy.

The urge to spring a big kiss on him was intense. What if I was a bad kisser? Like Zachary Melcomb. While I contemplated the idea, Alex opened the folder he brought and glanced over the storyboard.

"Okay, Blondie," his voice became deep and sinister, "are you prepared to meet your doom?" He turned his head from the papers and gave a devilish smile. Then he leaned closer and widened his grin.

Hot flash. Melting body. Must use self-control.

In a burst of energy unrelated to the lust I was experiencing, he slammed the folder shut.

Yikes!

Hopping to his feet, he offered out his hand. "Come on then, daylight is burning. I've got the camcorder in the car."

What's the rush? You haven't even kissed me yet!

He wiggled his hand impatiently.

Rats! I wanted lips and he offered me a hand.

"Do you want anything to drink before we go? Lemonade?" I asked.

"Stop stalling. This is going to be too much fun."

With the nagging sensation like I had unfinished business to take care of, I begrudgingly took his hand and we headed toward the front door.

"Wait!" I yelled, bringing Alex to a stop with an exaggerated jerk. I looked down at myself, running a hand across my clothing. In a tone too serious, I asked, "Do I look alright to die?"

Rolling his eyes, he swung his arm around my shoulders, pulling me into his body. "Emily, it's going to be a downright shame to have to kill such a beautiful young lady."

Did he just say beautiful?

I never imagined dying would be so much fun. We drove to several locations while making our fake documentary. We forgot about a script so we made up lines as we went. He met her in the park. He killed her in the woods. We used ketchup bottles for squirting blood. He hung himself in a tree. His body twitched while he hung there. It was great!

It was about suppertime when Alex pulled his Jeep in front of my house. He put the gearshift in park but left the engine running. An awkward silence filled the air. I was not getting the romantic good-bye kiss I was expecting.

"Um, that was a lot of fun," Alex finally said.

"Yeah, it was." The words came out hampered, laced with embarrassment by my foolish wish and confusion by this afternoon's closeness. "Thanks for driving." *Why did I say that?*

"Any time." His words were polite, but aloof.

I tugged on the door handle. The latch clicked.

"Em—" his voice broke off.

He should be asking me out, or to prom, but something felt very wrong.

"What, Alex?" I turned and looked at him, trying to play it cool. He had his hair brushed away from his eyes and I noticed how intense they were. There was pain.

He hesitated more. "Have a good night. I'll see you in class on Monday."

Monday? It's only Saturday. "Thanks, you too." *Crap! He didn't ask, but there is still hope! The fairytale isn't dead yet!* "Is there anything else you want to talk about?"

"I gotta go, Emily."

That was it. A sledgehammer delivered squarely to my chest. Tight lipped, I gave him the only smile I had in me before sliding out of the leather seat. The distance from the Jeep to our house looked like a mile as I desperately began hoping, dreaming, and bargaining with God, *if only Alex would ask...*

But before I took my third step up the front walk, the black Jeep sped off and the hum of the oversized tires became silent. He didn't even wait for me to get to the door! My head dropped—and I watched my own tears splatter against the pavement, painfully aware that he would not be asking me to prom. My dreams of a beautiful fairytale were shattered.

By the time I entered the house, I was sobbing. Dad arrived first, to hold my shaking body.

Mom came running from the kitchen. "What's wrong?" she gasped, visually inspecting me for signs of physical abuse. Kathryn stood cautiously behind mother.

Sobs continued so heavy I could not speak.

"Are you hurt?" Dad asked as he stepped back to check for himself.

All I could do was shake my head no.

"Is she going to be okay?" Kat asked. She eyed me with the same curiosity as watching the aftermath of an auto accident.

Dad took his hands and placed them on my checks. He looked me squarely in the eyes, searching.

"Yes, Kat, Emily will be okay," Mom reassured her. With a little prodding, Mom led Kat off in the direction of the kitchen, arm in arm.

Dad and I were left in privacy. With the utmost care, my hero released my face and returned his strong, loving arms around me until my tears subsided.

CHAPTER SIX

CHAINS

ALEX'S MUSCLES ACHED from the relentless tension that plagued him. Dramatic memories lingered, ready to overtake and infest his normal functioning should he ever drop his guard. The sight was gruesome. Feelings of abandonment stung deep.

Then there was her. He loved her; there was never any doubt about that. Alex tried to erase the pain he saw in Emily's eyes today. He should have asked. He knew that's what she wanted. Hate raged upon himself. But then he hated himself long before he hurt her.

For a fleeting moment, as he pulled into his driveway, Alex considered stomping on the gas and crashing into the garage. They'd have no other choice but to tear it down.

Maybe *then* he could be free.

CHAPTER SEVEN

SEVERANCE

"GOOD MORNING, EMILY." Mom sat down on the edge of my bed. "It's time for church."

"I don't want to go." I didn't even bother to open my eyes.

"It will make you feel better."

"So would fifty pounds of chocolate."

"True, but then what?" she asked.

I waited for her to leave.

"Your performance last night was the best one of all. Too bad there weren't more people in the audience."

"It's always larger opening night. I just want to take a really long shower, is that all right?"

Silence.

"Maybe you could go to prom with a group of girls." It was not a question.

I stared at her in disbelief. "It's just a stupid dance, anyway. It doesn't matter."

"Stop the drama. Let's put the whole thing into perspective. Alex has been ignoring you for a week now. It's obvious he has his own issues to deal with and actually, I'm glad you're not being dragged through the middle of it. "

"Is that supposed to make me feel better?"

"In two short weeks, we'll be moving, and you'll have brand new opportunities. In fact, let's celebrate and start packing tonight." She remained perched on the edge of my bed, looking at me like she hoped I would say something that would make her feel better. Finally, she got up and left.

Mom's words twisted my stomach. Ignoring the feeling that my entire body might somehow spontaneously collapse in dehydrated rubble, I threw my covers aside and slipped into my fuzzy slippers. Next, I turned off my cell phone so I wouldn't have to ignore the texts I was or was not receiving. It had been an entire week since I'd seen Alex. The coward even skipped English every day this week.

After my shower, which accomplished very little, I picked up my guitar and started to play. My music described my feelings in a way that Freud could not. Not that it mattered; it's all a bunch of crap anyway.

Later in the evening, Mother gathered us in the living room for a brief meeting. "Professional movers will be hired for the furniture and other large items. You get to pack up your own personal items."

"If we had a pet, like a hamster, would we pack that in a box too?" Kat asked.

She was such a dork.

"No, you would not," Dad replied dryly.

"Can we get a pet when we get out to the country? There'd be enough room for a dog to run out there."

Dad didn't like pets. He always said no.

Kat began to whine.

"I'll let you and your father discuss that at another time," Mom said, glaring at Dad who was making a face.

"Before you begin packing what you want to take to the new house," Mom continued, "go through your items that you no longer want and we'll send them over to Goodwill."

"Boxes are located in the garage for your convenience," Dad added with airline steward gestures.

Discarding unwanted items were directions Mom didn't have to repeat twice. As I headed out to retrieve a box from the stash, a twinge of sorrow zipped though my heart. Still, the directions remained uncomplicated. Even before entering my room, I knew exactly what I was going to put in the box. I placed the container in the middle of the floor and opened the four flaps.

I took a moment and savored each second as I carefully noted the four walls surrounding me. They were painted the faintest lavender and had bold, deep purple curtains to match. Framed photos of my childhood memories surrounded me, cluttering every wall. My favorites were the pictures of various characters I portrayed in numerous theatrical productions throughout the years. Next came the vast array of athletic attempts and me dressed in the according attire: me wearing a plain, pink leotard and black ballet slippers, a frilly dress with tap shoes, a Tae Kwon Do uniform, me with cleats and a soccer ball, kneepads and a volleyball, me on a balance beam, and lastly, me on horseback. The photos seemed to fill the void created by a lack of trophies or metals.

A heavy sigh escaped from my lungs as I reminisced all the times I used to lie in bed at night imagining what it would be like to say goodbye to my room. Sometimes I'd be going off to college, or other times leaving to start the rest of my life with a loving husband.

It wasn't supposed to happen like this.

I walked over to my closet, opened the doors and pressed its contents to the far left. My heart began to beat faster as I saw the amazing white satin dress with the delicate floral beading. Reaching inside, I slowly retrieved the evening dress from its hiding spot and held it at a distance to admire its beauty. I loved this dress. I clutched it in both my hands and buried my face in the soft, silky fabric. I inhaled deeply, expecting to smell romance itself.

Abruptly, the nostalgia was severed. I turned around and dropped the dress into the Goodwill box.

I was finished.

***

An unusual thing happened the day I discarded the dress: my feelings seemed to go along with it. I stopped feeling angry. I no longer felt depressed. I especially didn't feel joy. I didn't feel anything at all, except that I agreed with Bailey; I had been wasting my time with Alex.

The last two weeks of school went off without a hitch. Prom came and went. I spent that evening with my family watching a rented movie about ninja guinea pigs. It wasn't long after the dance that I calmly told my friends I was moving and just like I thought, they promised to stay in contact. *We'll see.*

On the evening of our move, our overnight bags were already in the vehicles previously gassed up and ready for the westbound lane on Highway 24. After checking the house a third time for forgotten items, I placed Bunny in the passenger seat of my car.

While reaching for my car keys nestled safely in my pocket, I heard the low hum of oversized tires approaching fast. The familiar black Jeep came to an abrupt halt at the curb in front of our soon to be ex-house.

The first thing I noticed was the damage to his perfect, treasured vehicle. The left headlight was smashed out and several pieces were missing from the grill. The hood and front fenders were dented and several scrapes marred the onyx-black paint. Mom, Dad and Kat disappeared as Alex jumped down from behind the wheel.

"I was worried I'd miss you!" Alex blurted as he ran up to me, trembling and out of breath. His hair was tucked in beneath a backwards ball cap, allowing me to see his eyes that moved about wildly.

I'm sure my facial expression was not very welcoming as I struggled to make sense out of what was taking place. I found it to be very strange.

"I was an idiot!" He admitted, searching my eyes for perhaps some kind of understanding or forgiveness. His hands settled upon my shoulders. "I was scared, and confused….but I'm here, now." He was out of words and seemed to be terrified by the silence. "Please, Em!"

I bit at my lower lip nervously, but my overall expression remained poised.

He reached into his pocket and pulled out a delicate silver chain. A small silver heart, about the size of a quarter, dangled at the bottom. "This is for you." He took my hand. "Promise me you'll think about it," Alex pleaded as he lowered the necklace into my palm.

"I want you to call me—I want you to be the one to tell me it's not too late." Perhaps he thought he was starting to ramble. He changed his pitch. "I should have asked you to prom the day I had you in my Jeep, Emily. I'm sorry. Please forgive me."

Once again, I found myself lacking feeling and words. He leaned over and kissed my cheek, tenderly. His gesture awakened my senses. But it wasn't enough.

"I won't say good-bye, and I'm foolish enough to wait by the phone. Don't make me wait too long." He smiled timidly before walking back to his Jeep.

The scene could have ended in a million different ways. He could have come running back to me. I could have gone running to him with my arms outstretched. I could have called out his name, teasing him with hope, only to crush him with, "good-bye." But it wasn't theatrical at all. He just got into his big black Jeep and left.

"Are you okay?" Mom asked as she walked up behind me.

"No."

"I can't believe he had the nerve to come here and show his face," Dad growled as he returned to the yard.

"John!" Mom cautioned. "Diplomacy. Tact."

"You want me to take him out? We can use one of the guns from the shop." An evil grin curled up the corners of his lips.

"Dad!" I gasped and whacked him in the arm.

"Ow," he feigned.

Kats eyes nearly bugged out. "Would you really do that?"

"Are you trying to make the situation better, or do you really think you're funny?" Mom asked.

"Both," Dad chuckled. His eyes twinkled as he looked my way.

"Would he really 'take him out?'" Kat looked up at Mom.

Three "NO!s" surrounded her in stereo.

"Excuse a girl for asking." Kat stuck out her tongue.

A moment of peaceful silence overtook the scene before we automatically lined up in a single row and walked arm in arm toward the caravan of cars ready for departure. Alex provided the distraction I desperately needed for the drive. Although I was not ready to leave, I was ready to go.

"Kitty, do you want to ride with me? We'll make it an adventure.

CHAPTER EIGHT

A NEW BEGINNING

THE ONLY ADVENTURE KITTY and I had getting to the new house was a flat tire.

When we finally drove down the dusty gravel driveway, I thought my father had gone completely insane as I gazed upon a brown cedar house that looked as small up close as it did from a distance.

"We left the city to move into a one-room house?" Any optimism I had dissipated into thin air while the familiar queasiness returned to my stomach.

Kitty scrambled to the front seat for a better view. "It'll be great! Just like the olden days!"

Leave it to Kitty, she always saw the good.

I glared at Dad as I pulled in beside the house. "Where's the outhouse?"

Dad bent down to face me through the window. "Don't get your undies in a bunch, Em. I promised you room to grow."

After opening the front door, the house proved to be nothing less than spectacular. It was then I realized the rest of the structure was strategically hidden behind a wall of trees and other greenery.

"Hello?" Kat called out. Her voice echoed throughout the barren rooms and off of the wooden floors. Dropping her overnight bag in the middle of the entryway, the door bounced back open as she dashed off to explore.

Walking around, there seemed to be a room for everybody and everything. Electric light reflected off the many windows that decorated room after room. Upstairs, an open loft divided a master bedroom and two more bedrooms, each side having its own bathroom. In the center of the loft, a music stand stood at attention, and I realized this area was for me. My dad was right, it was the perfect house. Only, it was in the wrong location. It was in the middle of *farm country*, for heaven's sake! Despite the translucent excellence, I could not appreciate the tranquil beauty of country life. I did not ask for it and I did not want it.

Over the course of a week, we managed to unpack most of the boxes with little family bickering. Arranging the furniture was another story. With each failed attempt, our grumbling grew louder and louder. Especially while moving the five-hundred pound couch Dad made us lug from the living room, to the family room, then to the sun room, and finally up to the loft. The stupid thing still didn't look quite right. On our way back down, Kitty lost her grip and dropped her corner.

"Grab Kathryn!" Mom yelled as the couch tumbled down the stairs.

It actually flipped over. Its hide-a-bed mattress ejected like a jack-in-the-box and acted as a launching device. The couch took air, then burst into pieces at the bottom of the stairs.

Dad blew his top.

Then he apologized. "Yes, I do love you more than the furniture."

"You didn't act like it," Kat sputtered, wiping tears and snot on her shirt.

Dad grinned. "Would ice cream help?"

"Maybe," she said, looking up at him with curious eyes.

"Great! Let's go find an ice cream parlor."

"Yippee!" Kat squealed.

"Then a furniture store!" Dad cheered.

"Awh…" Her smile vanished. "I should have known I'd get suckered into more work."

Mom and I exchanged looks. He was so predictable. She was so gullible.

It turned out that Silver Lake didn't have an ice cream parlor, so we ended up with a container of Cookies and Cream and box of plastic spoons from Wehners grocery store.

"Do you really think it's pronounced 'wieners?'" Kat pounded her fist on the seat, emphasizing her uncontrolled laughter. "I think they should have name tags in the *shape* of a wiener."

"Oh man," Dad laughed under his breath.

"Don't say another word," Mom scolded.

I wasn't sure, but I think Dad visualized the wrong kind of wiener.

Aside from shopping at a store named Wehners, moving over summer vacation sucked. Instead of keeping busy with homework, I found myself restless. The new property wasn't all that far from Topeka, less than twenty miles in fact, but the distance had already proved to be far enough to discourage spur of the moment outings. Rayyan even thought she was being kind by not making me waste the gas driving into town to join them for a movie. Whatever.

And I had no desire to call Alex, even after considering his apology, or whatever that was, the night I left. I didn't miss Alex, and I was finished with childish fairytales. I wasn't trying to be mean. I was simply protecting my heart.

So with little to look forward to, I took refuge in my favorite part of the house. Actually, it was outside, on the large deck that surrounded the back. I liked to sit out there and strum my guitar. I played the melody I heard in my head; it was my own work in progress. My sorrow fighting to find my inner happiness, or better yet, peace.

At times I'd look out upon the forest for inspiration, but my view somehow became restricted by the giant brown tree trunk cell bars that surrounded this place of exile. Other times, I heard a toad or frog calling out its mid-day doldrums from a nearby creek, and it gave me a strange comfort knowing I was not the only lonely creature here in this anti-paradise.

The one redeeming quality of the property was that the house lay just off the Pacific Union Railroad. We literally had to cross the tracks to get to our house. The first time the train passed, Kat started screaming about an earthquake. She was such a dork. Personally, I fell in love with the powerful rumble that shook the house and the floor beneath my feet the very first time I experienced it. At night, I lay awake and waited for the silent rumble that always preludes the clickity-clack of the massive steel wheels charging forward.

I wasn't surprised the first time I dreamed about jumping aboard a passing boxcar, but I didn't expect the dream to occur so often. Freud would probably tell me that I was desperate for some sort of adventure.

CHAPTER NINE

HOMECOMING

IT HAD BEEN A LONG TIME since Sam had been back to the farm after the accident. He scanned the house with the sagging roof and noted the paint had long-since been worn off by wind and weather. He turned toward the open grassy field where the crops once grew. There was an unnatural rise in the earth's landscape that stood out from the predominately flat land. Although it too was covered with prairie grass, a barn had once stood there. It had been reduced to a pile of ash years back. He could still envision the flames and the screaming. He wondered why he'd returned.

A shift in the air current brought in the faint sound of a guitar song riding on the wings of the wind. He did not recognize the tune, but found it strangely compelling. Curiosity persuaded him to follow the melody.

He crossed the field and headed west into the woods. A nearby creek flowed northerly. It was here he used to capture crayfish when he was little. The music led him down stream. When he finally reached his unknown destination, he found himself close to a house he didn't recognize. It was a large home with a wraparound deck. He searched for the source of the music and found it. She was sitting on the deck, picking a guitar that rested comfortably in her lap. The sun reflected off her long blonde hair that moved gently with the breeze. She had long legs that were propped up against the banister of the deck. She wore a pair of blue denim shorts and a billowy white top. She was not the glamorous type, yet so beautiful it made him smile.

He was resting against a tree when someone called out her name, "Emily." It also brought attention to himself. Suddenly, he felt like a stalker, intruding on her privacy. He felt inclined to leave. The girl continued to play.

As he turned around to make his way back to the farm, he began to hum along with the melody. When he reached the open prairie, he settled upon a very large rock. Propping himself up with his long arms stretched out behind him, he closed his eyes and soaked up the sun's rays. Like a moth drawn to the candle, he was uncomfortable with the way the music called to him.

CHAPTER TEN

VARMINTS, STRANGERS AND OTHER DANGERS

BY OUR SECOND SATURDAY, Mom felt it time to get acquainted with a local church. Dad flipped open his laptop to do some on-line church shopping. We had either Baptist or Methodist to choose from. Because Dad said that he liked to enjoy his beer without guilt, he drove us to the Methodist church that following Sunday morning. Once there, the minister seemed friendly enough, and I saw a few kids my own age, but laryngitis must have been going around.

Soon after getting home, Mom busied herself with staking off an area that would eventually become a colorful garden of flowers. Dad and Kat headed out for fishing in the near-by creek, hoping to catch anything.

I retreated back into my bedroom, which by now, was turning claustrophobic…and life threatening. I felt as if the stark white walls were literally sucking the life right out of me, absorbing my energy with each passing second. I was sure if I stayed much longer, my family would enter my room to find a dehydrated corpse of skin and bones.

Hearing the sound of Kat's voice coming in through the deck door, talking to Dad about their fishing excursion, interrupted my wallowing in self-pity and visions of being dead. She sounded so happy and excited. It made me even more depressed. And angry. I reminded myself that I had originally decided to be optimistic and embrace the move.

"Just snap out of it," I scolded myself, sitting upright on my bed. I grabbed bunny and shook her. "You're not being very helpful, either." I tried to imagine something I could do. "Ahh....Hmmm..."

Sigh. I should have caught a ride into town with Mom and helped her pick out flowers. Looking about my room, wishing I was back in Topeka, I noticed a green book jacket on the shelf. *The Giving Tree.* I tossed bunny aside and took the book down.

Like always, by the end of the book, I was crying for the tree.

And maybe for me. I could be that boy. Maybe I was. A self-absorbed teenager. Everyone else was managing to enjoy all this land, why couldn't I? Hanging up my church clothes, I eyed the white, billowy babydoll top and snatched it off the hanger. Wearing it made me feel sweet, and kind. Then I grabbed a pair of plaid shorts out the dresser drawer and slipped them on next.

As I made my way downstairs, I could hear excitement coming from the kitchen. "What's going on?" I asked, seeing fish in a frying pan.

Kat turned around, holding up another fish. "Hi, Emmy. We're making lunch!"

"It's still alive!" I gasped in mild horror.

"It won't be, after we're finished with it," Dad snarled in his best "Igor" voice, waving the knife in his hand.

"Would you like to join us?" Kat asked.

"Thanks, but I'll pass." I grabbed a piece of fruit out of the bowl, took a bite, and headed to the couch to finish eating. Glancing around the area, the stark, white walls seemed to reach out with a suffocating effect.

Run, Forrest, run, before the life is sucked out of you, I thought to myself.

With half a pear in hand, I grabbed my tennis shoes on the way out the door, and headed towards some kind of adventure. Hopefully.

"Now what?" I wondered aloud, standing in front of Mom's plot of ground for her floral garden. That's when I heard my friend, the amphibian, croaking. Maybe it lived near the stream. A stir in my stomach told me that it might be fun to investigate; maybe I'd be lucky enough to find the little thing.

I wasn't sure how far the creek was from the house, but common sense led me to believe it wouldn't be too far off. I looked to see if Dad and Kat had already forged a path, but couldn't find their trail. Not that it mattered; I really wasn't worried about getting lost.

And then reality set in. The trees quickly progressed into a forest; the spring canopy was already thick, making the sun useless as a compass. It took me a while to realize I had no idea where I was. It took less time to notice one thing about trees: they all looked alike.

Even fallen trees began to look like one another. Everywhere I looked, green leaves and brown bark followed more green leaves and brown bark. An uneasy feeling settled in, but I was too afraid to stop walking, even though I was unsure what direction I was headed.

The sound of my racing heartbeat pounded so loudly in my ears that I could no longer hear the moving water. Hot, sticky air made it all the more hard to breathe. I felt disabled, and vulnerable. Visions of my family organizing a search party clouded my head. My chest tightened. Just as panic was telling me to scream as loud as I could, I caught a glimpse of something…shimmering…the sun reflecting off the water! Like someone excited to greet an old friend, I ran to the water's edge. Tearing off my shoes, I put my feet into the stream. I had made it.

Now with panic behind me, I laughed at my own wild imagination.

Feeling safe, I poked around the rocks at the shoreline, hoping to find the frog. Since he wasn't croaking, I had no idea where to look, but much to my surprise, I found a tiny crayfish instead. They were such interesting creatures.

Scanning the water to my right, then left, I decided to follow the creek upstream to the north. But first, I collected a bunch of small rocks and piled them together to make a marker for when I returned. I had enough of being lost.

Nature was easy to fall in love with. Wild bluebells, yellow violets, and white Dutchman's Britches dotted color along the bank's edges while dragonflies skimmed the water. Splashing through the liquid sidewalk, I marveled at the stark contrast to Fairlawn. It became easy not to miss the litter that decorated the city's walkways. Too engrossed in the beauty, I wasn't looking where I was going and—

The rocks felt very slippery. Up went my feet, out from under me.

I opened my eyes and saw nothing but bright blue. The trees were nowhere in sight. Rushing water sounded loudly in my ears.

"Oh crap!" I winced, as I felt the back of my head pound to the rhythm of my heartbeat. Tilting my head to the side, I came face to face with rocks. I was lying in the dirt.

"Smooth move, Grace," I said only to myself. As I sat up, I reached for the source of pain and rubbed the lump under my hair. Short of a miracle, I had landed mostly on the edge of the bank, rather then the water.

Rising to my feet, I brushed the dirt off my clothes and visually inspected myself for injuries. In the absence of gushing blood, I retrieved my shoes I'd tossed while falling, and decided to keep to the grass for the duration of my adventure. Although I had a headache, it was slight enough to ignore.

Once again, I was easily drawn into this new enchanting world: the crystal clear water, the birds singing high above my head, and so many kinds of trees I'd never seen before. Everywhere I looked, the bright foliage waved its green leaves in the gentle breeze, as if to say, "Hi, welcome to the neighborhood."

With each step, feelings of inner peace replaced my residual pain of loneliness. I couldn't remember ever feeling such contentment in my life before; the urge to go home and paint my room green welled up inside me. As I continued with this thought, I came upon a small crossing made from various rocks stretching to the other side.

Accepting the invitation, I hopped across the rocks and discovered a natural archway in the trees that also looked very inviting. A sense of mystery filled my imagination and I began to tiptoe. I found myself holding my breath as I crept further into the archway.

Hiding behind the last tree, I peered into an open field. My heart raced.

I gazed upon a scene that held all the charm from another era. The picturesque white two-story farmhouse standing proudly in the middle of an open field reminded me of old photographs I'd seen in school textbooks. A worn dirt path lead to a nearby red barn, complete with a wooden wagon parked in front.

The simple beauty drew me in for a closer look. Forgetting the probability that someone lived there, I made a bee-line toward the structures, and then noticed an old-time truck next to the house. I was almost there when I noticed someone standing behind the truck with his back towards me.

"Oh!" I exclaimed in embarrassment, stopping abruptly.

The figure turned around to face me, casually, unstartled.

"Hello," came a friendly greeting.

I stood frozen in my embarrassment, unable to speak.

"The name's Sam," he offered, in a deep but gentle voice. His face was round. His chin, cheeks, and brow were all in perfect proportion, but paid homage to his deep brown eyes.

I guessed he was a few years older than me. And tall, very tall. Thick biceps emerged from the plain white shirt that stretched tightly across his wide chest. He had manly hands that looked too clean for a farm boy. A well-fitting pair of jeans loudly hinted that muscular legs matched his upper strength. An old pair of brown leather work boots scuffed across the grass in my direction.

I wondered how long I had been staring when it dawned on me to speak. As much as I tried, I couldn't wipe the smile off my face and I became hopelessly tongue-tied over the most handsome boy I'd ever seen in my life.

"Hello," I finally stammered, still smiling too wide. "I wasn't expecting to find anyone here, um, I'm sorry."

"Think nothing of it." He stopped walking a comfortable distance from me.

"My name is Emily," I spoke a little too slowly, finally introducing myself. "I live over that way." I turned around and pointed behind me. "So, you live here?"

"'Yes, ma'am, I do." His head nodded, seeming quite proud.

I looked beyond him towards the truck. "Does it run?" My inhibitions began disappearing faster than an Olympic sprint.

"You like it?"

"I love it! That's the coolest truck I've ever seen."

"Why, thank you," he said. "Unfortunately no, I can't get it to run."

Sam started back toward the vehicle, then stopped, apparently waiting for me to join him.

Naturally, I did.

"It's a 1933 Ford half ton." Pointing to the wooden bed rails, he added, "Short bed." His eyes twinkled and his grin looked genuine. I found myself smiling just because he was smiling.

"If you ever get it running, can I have a ride?" I couldn't believe it when the question came out of my mouth, or how comfortable I felt talking to a complete stranger. An incredibly handsome stranger. In the back of my head, I could hear my mother's voice warning me not to talk to strangers, but here I was, doing it anyway. And, what was Mother's second safety rule? Dismissing her words of warning as irrelevant, fear was the last thing on my mind as I immediately became enamored with this country boy.

"It'd be my pleasure to give you a ride," Sam replied. "Only it hasn't run for a long time." He stretched out the vowel in long.

"I suppose vintage engine parts are hard to come by, huh?"

"Vintage? Well, yes ma'am. That they are."

I shot him a puzzled glare over the word ma'am.

"'Ma'am' is just being polite, but if you don't like ma'am, how about Miss?"

"How about just Emily."

"Just Emily it is," he said. "So tell me, Just Emily, are you new to these parts?" He laughed at his own humor.

It made me wince. "Yes, we just moved in about a week ago."

"First time in the country?" He leaned against the truck, crossed his arms, and rested them on the wooden bed railing.

I copied his movement. "Yes."

"Has anyone warned you of varmints?" He seemed serious.

"Varmints? Like what?" *Was there a real danger?*

"Well, you know, the usual type: rattlesnakes, coyotes." His grin returned. "And bobcats."

I could tell he was amused by my expression that grew more alarmed with each animal listed. "Sam!

You're teasing me!" I liked the way his name rolled off my tongue.

He chuckled out loud, shaking his head, "No, ma'am, I am not. In fact, they love this area. All this green grass draws a lot of rabbits and other little critters. It's a perfect food chain."

I wondered if something ate the frog and that's why it had stopped croaking. "Well then, I'm appointing you to keep me safe—from varmints."

Seriousness replaced his smile. "I'd be obliged," he said, gazing deeply in my eyes before turning his attention to the dirt he was scuffing with his boot. Finally, he stood up straight and took a deep breath of fresh air. His chest went from massive to mammoth, and I noted he must be a good six inches taller than me.

"So, you probably moved here with your family?" he asked before turning and walking into the open field. I followed his lead.

"Yes, my parents and an annoying little sister."

"Sisters aren't so bad."

"I guess not really."

As we strolled across the grassy field, I spoke about my love for drama. He truly seemed fascinated about the silly details of my school-age adventures on stage. His curiosity made me feel important and I liked it.

"What was the last play you were in?" Sam asked.

"*Prelude to a Kiss*."

"I'll be!"

"You know this play?"

His voice softened. "Do you reckon there's any truth to souls switching bodies?"

"I don't know about that," I said, shrugging my shoulders, "but my grandpa claimed to have had an out

of body experience while having surgery. He said that
he was floating in the corner of the operating
room...able to watch everything that was happening.
Doctors say that he nearly died on the table." I watched
Sam's face for a reaction, and then continued. "Grandpa
said that it was fascinating, yet upsetting. I was really
little when this happened, but I remember he didn't
want my mother to say anything to anybody else
because he worried that people would have him
committed."

"I believe it." Sam responded with interest.

"So you think it's possible?" My question seemed
to carry a tone of unnatural creepiness.

"Yes, Miss Emily, I s'pose it could be possible.
Getting back to soul swapping, take your grandfather's
case. If a wandering soul would have been traveling
through the operating room at that particular time, I
reckon that other soul could have taken over your
grandpa's body."

"You really believe that?"

"Yes, yes I do. But I don't think it could really
happen as the play portrays. Completely trading souls
with just a kiss is a bit hard to fathom," he said.

"Any circumstance that includes taking over
another person's body is hard to fathom."

"Why? It's even in the dictionary."

"What is?"

"Body snatching."

"Seriously? That's gross." A prickly tingle shot
down my spine.

"The official term is transmigration," Sam rattled
off. "The act of passing the soul to another body at the
time of death."

"Isn't that reincarnation?"

"Not at all. The original body has a different soul, just like the play you were in."

"You are kidding."

"No, Miss Emily, I am not. Look it up if you don't believe me." Sam looked down at me and smiled, showing off his pearly white teeth.

Wow, he is good looking. "You really can't believe everything you read, you know."

Sam laughed. "I take you for the type that needs to see things with her own eyes."

As I looked back up at him, I couldn't believe what I was actually thinking: love at first sight. *Was it truly possible?* My *eyes* certainly did not object to this reasoning. Of course Dad always said that he knew he'd marry Mom from the first moment she walked into his shop. And he did.

"What else do you like to do?" Sam asked, leaning forward anticipating my answer.

"I like sports."

Sam nodded as he gave me a look over.

"But just for fun. I leave the competitiveness to the real jocks. I really love history. Actually old buildings and stuff like that. Like Topeka High. Have you ever seen it?"

"Heck, everyone from these parts remembers when the first million dollar school was built," Sam replied. "That was big news."

"1931," we both said in unison.

"Although I can't say I *remember* it being built," I laughed, expecting him to laugh, too. He didn't. "What about music? I bet you're into Toby Keith."

"I looove music, but I tend to favor jazz."

"Really?" I couldn't quite calculate how a farm-type boy ended up liking jazz, not that I had anything against jazz in the first place. "I've played a few jazz pieces for school band concerts."

"What instruments do you play? Let me guess...the flute?"

"Not even close. I play the oboe and the bassoon, with hopes of my new band teacher letting me try the contra bassoon this year. That's assuming Silver Lake even has a band program...you know, with all the budget cuts and all. But guitar is my most favorite."

"Well I'll be. All that talent, and you haven't been discovered yet. My folks were into music, don't you know. I always wished I had inherited some of their musical talents."

"Were they famous?"

"In a way, I reckon. But enough of me. I s'pose you play your guitar often?"

"Yeah, it fills up my day. I'm kind of bored out here."

Sam stopped short. "Bored? In the country? You just said the wrong words, little lady." His grin turned sly and his eyes lit up like stars. "I wasn't going to sow the land this year, but you just volunteered yourself as an unpaid hired hand."

"What?" My eyes widened at the comment my ears heard but my mind had difficulty comprehending. "Oh....no. No, no, I can't." I backed away, scanning the grassy field that suddenly appeared much larger.

Once again he found humor in my reactions. "Relax, it can be a little garden, for personal use. A man's got to eat, you know," he said, rubbing his hand over his stomach.

"That might be fun." I envisioned a little garden of radishes, beans and lettuce.

"You can take some home, too," he offered, still smiling.

I smiled back. Looking at him, I think I would have agreed to eat beets. I loathed beets.

Time became irrelevant as we continued wandering through the field. I told Sam about my dad's great escape from city life, and how unfair it felt to me. I shared my jealousy of my little sister because she really could be free out here and up until today, I'd been struggling.

"Life is what you make it, Miss Emily." Sam's words were kind, not judgmental.

"Actually, my new thing is adventure."

He looked confused.

"It's a long story," I said, shifting my eyes so he wouldn't think I was staring at him. Which I was, of course, because he was so darned good-looking.

"Maybe someday you can tell me about it, but in case you haven't noticed, it's getting late."

I followed Sam's gaze to the west and saw the beginnings of a spectacular sunset with beautiful hues of deep pink and orange fanning wide into the sky. "I didn't realize how late it was. I gotta get back before they start missing me."

Sam arched an eyebrow. "You mean no one knows where you are?"

CHAPTER ELEVEN

ENDORPHINS

MOM'S FIRST RULE, *Don't talk to strangers* was quickly followed by her second rule, *Leave a note.* But what would I write? "Went for walk"? Like that would help. I would have to be attached to a GPS out here.

"I reckon you ought to be more careful, Miss Emily. You never know where you might meet up with danger." His voice was smooth and cool.

My heart lurched. Was he referring to wild animals, or an event like my slip on the rocks? Or was he the bad guy my mother warned me about? Would my first real attempt at adventure end with me getting axed by some stranger in the woods?

"Stop it," I snapped, hoping to appear unafraid just in case he had evil intentions. "I took Tae Kwon Do."

Sam smirked and shook his head. "So you're just gonna karate-chop a snake?"

An awkward moment of silence passed. I felt like an idiot for thinking terrible things about him. "Yes," I said as confidently as I could, like I was a woman in charge of things.

"Just remember, you have about five minutes to get the venom sucked out before you die."

I looked at him, mouth open.

"Kidding. Plus they advise against the sucking part nowadays."

My face flushed. Even my ears turned warm. "Since you are the expert, I guess that makes me all the more glad to have you as my defender against evil and perils. Now if you would be so kind as to assist me with another problem."

We were still standing in a field... a body of water was up ahead. A line of trees stood behind me. And to the left... I chewed my lip.

"Do you even know how to get home?" he asked; muted laughter rolled off his lips.

I squeezed my eyes shut, not wanting to speak the word that would humiliate me completely. A very tiny "No," slipped from my lips.

"City girls!" He turned abruptly and headed off toward the tree line. "I can tell that you're going to be a full-time job."

"I thought it was that way!" I shouted in a missed triumphant moment, running to catch up with his long strides. After about five more of his steps, and seven of mine, it occurred to me, "Hey! How do you know where I live?"

He stopped sharp and paused before answering, "You pointed behind you when you first showed up, remember? I happen to know there is a house or two on the other side of the creek." He seemed a bit defensive, his muscles tense. Maybe I'd offended him with the Tae Kwon Do comment and he'd had enough of random accusations.

"Well, actually, our house is the only one in the area." I looked up at him, smiling to let him know I meant no offense by my question. "How about you? Do you have neighbors on this side?"

"Not for a few miles. Jedd is my closest neighbor and actually he's on *your* side of the creek as well. He lives under an old stump."

"Who's Jedd?" I asked as we ducked into the trees.

"A badger."

A long leafy branch nearly smacked me in the face as I concentrated more on what a badger looked like than where I was going.

"An' you better watch out, 'cause he's a mean one." Sam's voice became deeper still. "You're lucky he didn't come out and chew your foot off at the ankle when you crossed the water."

"He lives by the crossing?" I imagined myself viciously attacked by yet another animal.

"Yes, ma'am. He's supposed to scare people away."

"Oh, stop it, you and your...dangerous varmints. How gullible do you think I am?"

"I'll admit he's not as scary as the Grim Reaper," Sam said, leading the way across the creek. "But he does exist. And honestly, badgers can be mighty ornery if they feel threatened."

Badgers. Hearing about all these animals out here filled me with awe. I felt like I lived in my own personal zoo.

"Hush now, while I try and fetch him out." He knelt down beside a hole in a rotting tree stump, barely visible in the tall grass, just about a yard from the stone bridge. I crouched beside him.

"Seriously?" I whispered. I could hardly believe that I was going to see a real live wild animal.

Sam made some sort of an animal calling noise to lure the animal out. "Jedd.... Jedd, come out and meet Miss Emily."

I leaned in for a closer look, peering into the dark opening. I half expected Sam to be playing some sort of unfunny trick on me. Then two black shiny eyes appeared from the darkness. I gasped in delight as the larger than anticipated animal emerged from its den.

"Oh! Look at it." I glanced from Sam to the badger, in mild disbelief.

He remained calm, careful not to spook it. "Come here, sleepy head." Sam held his hand out in a welcoming gesture. The badger sniffed it.
"Hello, Jedd." Sam scratched his head. "I'd like you to meet my new friend."

After a stretch and a yawn, the badger looked my way, like he understood. He lifted his head and sniffed the air. I didn't offer my hand, afraid of being bitten. Then, without prompting, the animal turned around and went back into his den.

Sam beamed in delight at how well the introduction went.

"That was so cool," I marveled as we both stood up.

"Yeah," he agreed. He took a wide, comfortable stance, crossing his thick arms across his mighty chest and looked directly at me. "The creatures you find in the country can be quite amazing."

I blushed. My heart began to beat a little faster as I looked away from the most handsome, brawny, beautiful boy I'd ever laid eyes on. The word *boy* seemed too young for the large figure standing in front of me. Still, I didn't want to use the word *man* because that sounded too old. How about guy? A really, really hot guy. Whatever he was, he made me weak in the knees. Even without a kiss.

"Do you know which direction to go from here?" Sam's question interrupted my silent ogling.

Pretending not to be caught in my fixation, I responded with great articulation, "Um, I need to go this way?" I pointed to the left, fairly confident.

He arched his eyebrow in approval. "Do you have any idea how far?" He glanced up at the sun, which was casting deeper shadows of pink across the sky.

"I stacked a pile of rocks at the water's edge to give myself a marker," I proudly informed him.

"Good thinking. But if we make it quick, I'd like to tag along, just in case."

"That's probably for the best. You have obviously picked up on my poor navigational skills. Even my dad pokes fun at me, stating that I could get lost in my own back yard."

"It's lucky that Lewis and Clark didn't have to depend on you to lead them through the wilderness," Sam teased.

My jaw dropped. "I can't believe you just said that." Yet I was compelled to tell more. "But that's so true. I hate to admit it, but I got mixed up trying to find the creek."

The sound of Sam bursting into laughter burned my cheeks.

"I'm not really surprised," he said, pulling himself together. "To tell you the truth, this creek has many twists and turns. Unless you're familiar with it…"

Just when I was about to go into a female pouting routine, his grin ended abruptly.

"You know something?" he asked.

"Could you be more specific?"I asked back.

"You are a special young lady, Miss Emily, and I am sincere when I say that."

I looked up to study his face. His words sounded so genuine. "Thanks."

His eyes twinkled just a little bit more. "You're welcome."

Together, we chatted our way down the riverbank when my attention was drawn toward the abundant wildflowers. There were far more colors and varieties than I remembered.

"This is a pawpaw flower." Sam handed me an unusual small red flower that looked more like a bud than a full bloom. "In the fall, the bush will produce fruit that can be made into some pretty delicious jelly."

I held the flower in my fingertips, spinning it from right to left as I inhaled deeply. "It doesn't have much of a scent, but it sure is lovely." I slipped the flower into my blouse pocket and returned my attention to the dense splashes of color. "I still can't get over all the flowers!"

"They must be blooming just for you."

"This is incredible!"

A wide grin spread over Sam's face. "That's the magic of spring time in the country."

His enthusiasm grew as he told me about other native berries that could be turned into jelly. I was fascinated, listening to a walking encyclopedia.

"How do you know all this stuff? I always thought farmers knew about corn, and that was about it."

He looked at me sideways. "And you were offended by *my* comment? At least *I* was joking."

"That's not what I meant at all. I keep sticking my foot in my mouth, don't I?"

"It must come with the color," he said, pointing to my head.

"Excuse me?"

"I love to learn," Sam stated, still laughing, tapping his finger near his temple. "I know all sorts of facts."

The more I thought about him, the more I didn't know what to make of him. Aside from his preference of jazz, and his overwhelming knowledge, I still knew very little.

I was trying to come up with a noninvasive question to ask him when he began to fidget.

"What's wrong?" I asked.

"I'm figurin' we passed your house."

I looked about the shoreline. "We haven't come to my pile of rocks, yet."

"That's right, Sacagawea, but you mentioned that you lived by the railroad tracks. I'm telling you they're closest to the water from back there." He pointed behind us with his thumb.

I wasn't sure if Sam saw me stick my tongue out at him before he turned around, but from the way he hacked out a laugh, I thought it possible. Trailing behind him, I couldn't remember telling him where I lived, but I didn't remember *not* telling him, either.

Within a few yards, Sam moved in closer to the edge of the forest, bobbing up and down, looking in between the trees. Finally, he stopped, straightened up and smiled. I knew he had found my house. Sappy as it may be, my heart beat in admiration. He had saved the damsel in distress, otherwise lost in the woods only to be eaten by coyotes, bobcats, or who knows what other kind of hungry varmint.

Sam grinned a cheesy grin, almost like he knew what I was thinking. I kind of hoped he did, and would say something like, *I've been waiting for you my whole life*. But he didn't. Instead, "Look there, Miss Emily," came out. And he pointed into the dense woods.

Retrieving my head from the clouds, I took a stance next to him.

"Straight ahead, you'll see some poplar trees."

I cleared my throat and tried to follow his path of sight. "You're too tall. Crouch down."

Resting his hands on his knees, Sam matched my height. He turned to face me and unexpectedly, his lips were even with mine. Instantly, whatever point he was trying to make became immaterial. Suddenly I was filled with a new fantasy about being lost in the woods. Together. Just him and me. Now *that* would be an adventure.

"How's this?" he asked.

Another shiver flushed my skin. "Nice?"

Looking back into the forest, Sam pointed. "Look for the three trees that seem to be tied together in the middle of the trunks. Notice how they curve in and then back out."

Affirming my feeling of love at first sight, I forced my attention toward the trees. "The ones with the white bark?"

"Yep, the aspens. Your house is in a straight line from here." Sam pointed with a stocky finger. "I reckon you can keep a direct path if you use the trees as a reference."

I looked up at him, in gratitude. "Thank you, Sam." I felt my cheeks flush red, realizing I would have been completely lost had it not been for him.

"It'd be a mighty shame to find you mauled by a bear or something," he laughed under his breath.

"Bears, too?" My eyes widened.

He chuckled louder. "It would be mighty unlikely, but one can never be too careful..."

"Sam, you stop all this nonsense. We are in Kansas, not in the Land of Oz," I shot back, a bit miffed, but secretly enjoying his sense of humor. "When can I see you again?"

My forwardness seemed to surprise him. Then he stuffed his hands in his back pockets. "Tomorrow, I hope. There's work to be done in the garden. I reckon the seeds can't plant themselves."

Returning the smile, I waved a childish goodbye and headed towards the trio of trees.

I was nearly there when his voice echoed through the woods, "Stay on the yellow brick road, Dorothy."

I spun around quickly, but he was already out of sight. Running back to the water's edge, I looked up the creek. He was gone.

Disappointed, I turned back around for home, when some markings in a tree trunk caught my eye.

"This way to Sam's" was carved in the trunk, with an arrow pointing upstream.

I was in love.

CHAPTER TWELVE

NOW YOU SEE IT, NOW YOU DON'T

MOM WAS BUSY IN THE KITCHEN when I walked in from the deck door.

"Mmm! Something smells good." I hugged her before peering into the simmering pot of homemade stew. "I'm glad I didn't miss dinner." Setting the lid back down, I turned a graceful pirouette over to the fridge and pulled out the jug of milk.

"I was getting worried. God only knows where we'd begin to look for you if anything ever went wrong."

"I'm sorry," I offered meagerly. Twisting off the cover, I held the plastic container to my lips and chugged four gulps. "Ahhh!" Wiping the white residue off my upper lip I asked, "Can I help you with anything?" I felt on top of the world and eager to share my happiness.

Mom paused from arranging the sliced tomatoes on a plate and gave me the look that expressed, "So you had a good day?"

"This place might not be so bad after all. Call me for dinner, I'm going upstairs."

"Dinner," she said, matter of factually, adding, "You can tell us all about your day over supper. Now, call Dad and Kat. We've been waiting."

"DAD AND KITTY, TIME FOR DINNER!" Since I was standing in the middle of the kitchen, I wanted to be extra loud.

"Thank you, dear." Mom handed me the plate of tomatoes and then opened the oven door. The aroma of hot biscuits filled the room.

Kat came racing from the sunroom and sat down at the table, "Last one sitting down smells like skunk poop."

"That's enough of that at the table, young lady," Dad warned as he rounded the corner from the opposite direction.

With dinner served, a lively conversation erupted at the table. I patiently nodded at all the right moments as I listened to Kat, who needed a bigger container for the insects she was collecting, and questioned the ethical practice if she were to freeze them alive in ice cubs, just to see what happened. Next, Dad was pleased with how comfortable his new hammock felt and had the best nap in his life. Mom took her turn next.

"I saw a fawn and its mother today," she said.

"Sweet! Kat squealed with glee.

"It was not!" Mom shrieked.

"Oh?" Dad asked, wearily. Mom never said anything even remotely negative about any animal.

"There they were, strolling through our yard." Her expression clearly indicating this normally in control woman could go off at any second.

"And?" he asked bravely.

"They ate most of my new flower garden!"

Mom loved her flowers.

"Bastards!" Dad pounded the table with his fist. "Do you want me to get the guns?"

For once, I kinda hoped that Mom would take the easy option. I could just see her forcing us into building some giant crates, like when we trapped and released the five rabbits that ate Mom's tulips at our old house.

"John, you are no help at all."

Dad put on his best *I care* face. "Don't worry, Izzy. I'll buy you some new flowers." It was obvious he hadn't purchased flowers before. She swooned at his generous offer.

Even without a resolution to the deer problem, I couldn't wait any longer to tell everyone about Sam. Just thinking about him made me go giddy.

"I went for a walk today!"

Smiles surrounding the table faded into vacant expressions.

"Good for you, Honey," Dad offered. "And you found your way home, too."

"I had a perfect day," I insisted, ignoring his sarcasm, "well, except for when I fell and hit my head." *Uh-oh. Now I did it.*

"What?" Mom's brow rose in worry, "You hit your head? Where? Let me see." Mom got up from the table to inspect my head. "This is exactly what I was referring to. You could have been laying there for days and no one would have known where to find you."

"No, Mom, I'm okay. Really." I tried to shoo her hand away.

"Oh, you have a big lump on the back of your head." She continued to sift through my hair.

"Mom!" I growled, annoyed, mostly because my story was ruined.

"When did this happen? We need to put some ice on it. John, we shouldn't let her sleep alone tonight with such a big goose egg on her skull." Mom continued fretfully. "I think I see a small cut."

Dad rolled his eyes as he headed for the freezer to retrieve the bag of peas marked "Do Not Eat." Mom always overreacted when it came to head trauma.

"Did you lose consciousness?" she asked, almost sounding frantic as she continued her interrogation.

"I don't think so."

As Dad walked past me, I saw him wince at my choice of words, which included the word "think." It would give Mom an opening for more obsessing. Kat, who was also used to Mom's overreactions, kept busy eating, avoiding eye contact. She couldn't hide her smirks from me though. I kicked her underneath the table.

"Ouch!" Kat said.

"Did that hurt?" Mom asked me, still examining my head.

"No, Mother, that wasn't even me."

Kat giggled again. Returning with the frozen peas, Dad handed them to Mom who took them and gently laid them on my head.

"I'll clear the table," Dad offered, probably as an excuse to escape, taking several items with him to the sink.

"Mom! Really, I'm fine," I stated as firmly as possible. "I'll tie the peas on my head for a while if that will make you happy, but I don't think it's necessary. It stopped hurting almost right away." I turned sideways in my chair to look at her.

Mom smiled at me with such love in her eyes. "All right, my Emily. But first we need to wash the cut." She bowed her head and kissed me on my forehead.

"I'll get the ACE bandage to wrap up Emmy's head." Kat jumped up off the chair, excited to play medic.

Hiding out in my bedroom with the bag of defrosted peas tossed on the floor, I absentmindedly flipped through a magazine. Luckily, Mom didn't press the injury issue and take me to the ER to have an MRI. That would have prevented me from reliving my afternoon with Sam, over and over again. And the sign Sam left for me in the tree.
At least I hoped it was for me.
What if the message was old—meant for a past girlfriend? What if he has a girlfriend now?
Mom poked her head around the corner of my door, interrupting my new worry. "How are you feeling?"
"Fine."
"Let me check your pupils." She was on the verge of restarting her obsession.
"Mother!" I glared.
"Okay, okay. I just worry," she confessed.
"Too much." I tossed the magazine over the bag of peas in hopes she hadn't spotted them yet. "But I love you, anyway." I got up off my chair to hug her and to let her stare at my pupils. She hugged me again. I dared to ask a seemingly random question, "Can I paint my bedroom green?"
"Green? Where did that come from?"
"Today, walking in the woods. Green is just so, calming. And cheery." *And Samish.*
Without so much as a blink of an eye, she gave her consent. "Let's go look at paint samples this week."

"Yeah!" I squeaked, a bit over excited, clapping my hands together in tiny movements.

"I'm off to bed. Don't stay up too late."

"'Night, Mom."

She turned and left but not before getting her official goodnight kiss. Flopping back on my lounger chair, I realized I was a bit sleepy myself. Sliding my tongue across my teeth, I felt little fuzzy sweaters covering most of them. After a good brushing, and other bedtime rituals, I headed back to my bedroom. On the way, I noticed a dim glow coming from Kat's room.

"Are you still up?"

"Yeah, I'm not tired." She was watching a video on a small TV that sat upon her dresser.

"Guess what?" I taunted.

"You hit your head and now you can't remember who you are."

"Whatever," I sneered. "I met someone today." I whispered, almost like it was a secret.

Kat sat up in bed, "Who?"

"His name is Sam. Come here, I want to show you something. He gave me a flower." I grabbed her small hand and pulled her out from under her quilted bedspread. Grabbing my shirt from the back of my desk chair, I reached into the pocket to retrieve the delicate red bud from its place of safety. Only there were no soft petals. Instead, I felt…grit. I pulled the pocket open wide and peered into its depths. It was filled with dark, dry dirt.

"That's strange."

"What is?"

"I must have lost it," I said disappointedly, shaking the dirt out into the wastebasket.

"It's just a stupid flower."

"And you're too little to understand."

She crossed her arms. "All right, tell me more."

"He is the cutest guy I've ever seen in my life. No one at T-West even begins to hold a candle next to him."

"Even Alex?"

"Especially Alex. I'm going to see Sam again, tomorrow. We're going to plant a vegetable garden together."

Kat's face cringed. "You?"

"I know, it sounds weird, but he is just so—cool."

"Did ya kiss him?" Kitty's eyes gleamed, waiting for details.

I imagined him and me in a romantic first kiss. "No."

Her eyes dimmed.

"But I'd like to."

Kat's nose crinkled.

CHAPTER THIRTEEN

A ROAD LESS TRAVELED

DRUGS PROBABLY WON'T kill a person the first time they try them. But sometimes, there are worse things than dying. The road to hell always begins as planned... excitement, comfort, numbness—whatever it is the person is after. If not, Satan would never get anyone to play along.

Alex was after anesthetic qualities. He could no longer stand the pain that resided in his otherwise barren heart that was first betrayed by his wreck of a family, his father's suicide, and now dismissed by the girl he'd loved since seventh grade. He used to spend many nights imagining himself as the Prince Charming type, rescuing the girl from herself. The only problem was that she never needed rescuing. She was everything he was not.

It was him that needed the rescuing.

He closed his eyes, hoping to end the torment, as he relived his desperate, unorganized display of affection, at which he failed miserably. After five years of wishing, *hoping*—she was gone. Emily was gone, forever. He knew she wouldn't call.

All of his energy had left him. He hadn't showered since the night she left Topeka. He hadn't found the desire to eat. He hadn't done anything in the past miserable week, except today. He went to the side of town where no one should be, to buy the stuff that no one should buy. Other than that, he remained confined to his bed, with the shades closed tight and the lights turned off. He felt less in the dark. He craved less pain, if there ever could be. His pain was excruciating, even in the dark.

CHAPTER FOURTEEN

LOST CHANCES

AFTER TUCKING KITTY BACK INTO HER bed, I went outside to play my guitar. I was no longer tired and my head was full with thoughts. Warm night air still lingered in the breeze, and the partial moon shined brightly, unveiling varying shades of gray. An owl's hoot rose out from the darkened woods while a pair of frogs took turns at filling the otherwise quiet night sky. The frogs were safe for now, but I wondered how long before their croaking would lure in one of the varmints Sam talked about.

I strummed my guitar.

God, I hope he doesn't have a girlfriend.

I knew I shouldn't let my emotions get the best of me, but it was difficult to deny these feelings. I'd never felt this way before in my life. If it wasn't love, what else could it be?

There were so many things I didn't know about Sam. What exactly do farmers do all day long? Or maybe, he planned on giving up farming and that's why he wasn't going to plant crops this year? And what about his family? Where were they?

Butterflies tickled my stomach in anticipation of seeing him again tomorrow. I could hardly wait. Since he was a farm boy, I assumed he woke up at sunrise. Was that too early?

Probably. And what about Kat? I didn't want her tagging along. Being annoying. I wanted it to be just me and Sam.

The call of the wild let itself be heard off in the distance: howling. Whether it be a fox or a coyote, I had no idea. Nevertheless, Sam was telling the truth. There were creatures out there. Some of them no doubt ferocious. Not that I thought he would lie, but this just seemed to add to his credibility. He was amazing.

Something brought my attention back to myself and I was surprised to realize I had stopped playing my guitar. A smile spread across my lips. It was a good place to end the day.

Without turning on a light, I cranked the windows open in my bedroom and continued to listen to the sounds of nature. No honking horns. No screaming sirens. Just nature. The passing of a train began to vibrate the floor beneath me. Maybe Sam and I could jump aboard the train together.

I opened my eyes to the bright sunlight shining directly into my room. Spring not only extended the evening daylight hours, but also brought an earlier morning. I looked at my clock, seven am.

After rolling out of bed, I shuffled to the top of the stairs and overheard my parents talking. They hadn't left for work yet. Mom stated my name and Kat's name in the same sentence. I decided I'd better see what it was about and trotted downstairs.

"Good morning, Sunshine." Dad seemed chipper.

I smiled a tired smile, trying to appear enthusiastic.

"Oh, Emily, dear. I'm so glad you're awake. How are you feeling?" she asked, walking over to me with raised hands, ready to inspect my head.

"Still fine, Mom." I looked over at Dad who was twirling his finger beside his temple in a "she's crazy" gesture. "Thanks for asking."

"Emily, dear," Mom began again. She needed a favor, I could tell. "Will you take Kat into town today for day camp?"

I knew it. I was about to protest when I realized this could work for me. I would be free to spend the day with Sam. "Sure, I'd love to."

Mom and Dad shot a look of surprise at each other. "Who are you, and what have you done with our daughter?" Dad asked.

"Ha, ha. What time does she need to be there?" I sounded too excited for the task. *I must remain calm,* I reminded myself, but I thought I was going to bust, just thinking about it.

"I was just leaving you a note that explains the details. It starts at nine am.," Mom said. "You don't need to worry about picking her up. We'll bring her home with us after work."

"Perfect!" I agreed, and it really was.

With high expectations, I got myself ready, and then went to wake up Kitty. Surprisingly, she was already awake. I found her sitting at the table, sipping chocolate milk from a neon green straw.

"You get to go to camp today!" I celebrated her fun, as well as my own freedom from babysitting.

She released the straw from her lips. "Yeah." She solemnly returned to taking another long sip.

"Come on, sleepy head." I tousled the top of her hair. "It's going to be a great day!" Again, I was thinking about my own day more than hers.

"Did you ever go to camp?" Kat asked, probably after much consideration for a seven year old, the straw still resting on her lower lip.

I looked Kitty over. She was not acting like the wild monkey she usually imitated. I pulled a chair from the table to sit down next to her.

"Sure I did, Kitty."

"What was it like?"

I realized Kat was afraid. "It was *lots* of fun!" I said, putting my arm around her. "I still look back at camp as one of the most fun times of summer. Ever. We'd sing songs, make crafts, go swimming…."

She looked up at me with her dark brown eyes, full of trust, and smiled. At that instant, I felt a deeper level of love for my sister.

"You're going to have a great day!" I said, giving her an extra hard hug. Then I did what any other big sister would do: I tipped her chair far over on its side until she fell off onto the floor.

"Ow! Knock it off." She got up, rubbing her rear end. Then her expression turned from fake pain to attack. "You're going to be sorry for that." She took the stance of a boxer, ready for a fight.

"Not if I get you first!" Like a wannabe ninja, I grabbed and pinned her down on the floor. Sitting on her middle, I tickled her armpits until she cried for mercy.

Somehow, the ten minutes it should take for a youngster to get dressed turned into twenty-five.

Growing more frustrated by the second, I ordered her to wait in the car so she couldn't find any more ways to waste time while I threw a sack lunch together. If I hurried, I could still get her there on time.

Sliding into the driver's seat, I came face to face with the locket Alex gave me on the night I left Topeka. I hadn't known what to do with it at the time, so I hung it around the rearview mirror. It'd been there, forgotten, ever since. Seeing it this morning, I didn't experience the feelings that Alex was probably hoping for. Instead, it reminded me of the day he broke my heart. I should have thrown it out the window on the drive out here.

"That's Alex's locket," Kat stated, like I needed reminding.

"Umm." More painful memories reran through my mind. I unhooked the necklace from the mirror and tossed it in the glove box.

"Don't you think it's pretty?"

"Yes."

"Why don't you wear it?" she asked, obviously not understanding what it represented.

"Mmmm." I didn't want to start a graphic name-calling session. "I don't know."

"Can I have it?"

"I don't think so."

Reaching for the volume, I pretended to like the song playing on the radio and turned it up. While Kat sang along to the radio for the duration of the drive, I replayed the dreadful night Alex dumped me off at my house. Apparently he didn't notice that my heart got caught in the door of his big black Jeep and was dragged through the streets of town, bouncing unmercifully on the pavement until there was nothing left but shreds.

Alex had been my Prince Charming, a knight in shining armor. Now, he was simply the moldy cherry on a melted hot fudge sundae.

Check-in for camp went without a hitch. Within minutes, I was headed back for the house as fast as I could. It seemed strange rushing towards the destination that only last week I viewed as my demise. Well, it wasn't the house I rushed to. It was Sam.

Before heading to the farm, I brushed my hair one more time just to make sure there weren't any tangles, then shoved a hair tie in my pocket for later when it became too hot outside. When I finally looked in the mirror, the reflection staring back at me didn't seem to be dressed appropriately for farming. Denim shorts, layered cream and blue camis, with blue on the top, to show less dirt.

It would have to do.

Just as I was closing the door behind me, the phone rang. It continued ringing for too long…the answering machine part must be off. Making a dash, I answered with a heavy hello to a dial tone.

"Man, I hate that," I hissed.

The Caller ID came up "Alex Hibbs."

Just as well, I thought, setting the phone back in its charger. There could never be a second chance for him now...now that I found Sam.

CHAPTER FIFTEEN

SAM

AS GIDDY AS A GIRL CAN GET, I set off out across the lawn in search of the trio of poplar trees. By the time I passed them, my breathing had already turned rapid, but not from exhaustion. I felt energized, and my skin prickled despite the hot temperature.

Reaching the tree that read, "This way to Sam's," I examined it more carefully, trying to determine if the carving might be old. Although the exposed wood looked dry, there was a single bark curl still attached to one of the letters. I concluded this meant the letters were fresh. At least that's what I hoped for.

Ready to continue on, I slipped my shoes off to wade in the clear, shallow waters. The cold water felt good flowing past my feet and helped to keep me cool. Even though it was still relatively early, the air already felt hot. The last thing I wanted was to show up at Sam's all sweaty first thing in the morning. Like that would be attractive.

Making my way up stream, I expected a repeat of fabulous colors along the water bank. Instead, only a few flowers were in bloom compared to when Sam had walked me home. I scanned the terrain for the red pawpaw flower Sam had given me. No sign of them either.

Did I only dream about them last night? No, because I distinctly remember being impressed with all his knowledge.

Feeling the hot sun against my own skin, I reasoned the flowers must have a short life, due to the intense heat.

Finally reaching the rock crossing, I smiled, thinking of Jedd. Peering into the small hole underneath the tree, I called out the badger's name, "Jedd—"

I tried to imitate the animal sounds Sam had made, but my sound sounded like me kissing the air.

"You'll never call him out like that," a deep, gentle voice said behind me.

Embarrassed, I spun around to see Sam standing on the other side of the creek. A huge smile erupted across my face.

"Are you stalking me?" I joked.

"You shouldn't ask that question with a smile. It might lead people to the wrong conclusion," Sam retorted. "Actually, you are very loud. I heard you a mile away." He hopped from one rock to the next, coming closer. Butterflies tickled my stomach just seeing him. He knelt down next to the den and summoned Jedd.

Once again, I peered into the black hole. Two little shiny eyes emerged from the darkness, but hesitated within the confines of its den. The eyes blinked twice before disappearing.

We both laughed.

"I reckon he's had his fill of you," Sam chuckled, standing back up with his back against the sun. The sun shone so bright, it appeared to shine right through him, causing me to squint. "We should get to work before the sun gets any higher. Are you ready?" Sam asked, apparently eager to put me to work.

"As ready as I'll ever be," I replied, wondering what I was getting myself into.

As we crossed the prairie field, I was surprised to see that he had already tilled a small area of land into long rows, revealing dark, rich soil. A workbench displayed a large assortment of seeds. Lying beside the bench were rope, spades, thin wooden dowels, and other items I guessed necessary for planting vegetables.

"What do you usually plant?" I asked as I examined the packages of seeds lying on the bench.

"My parents were wheat farmers, but this land hasn't been sown for quite some time now." Sam said as he took a stance next to me.

His answer made me think that his parents were no longer living here. "So are you alone?"

"Yes, ma'am," he replied.

"Where are your parents now?" Sensing the question made him uncomfortable. I offered a weak apology, "I'm sorry, I didn't mean to pry."

"No, that's okay. They're dead."

"Both of them?" I wished I could take back my question.

Sam wedged his tongue in between his front teeth and upper lip like he was retrieving a stuck piece of food. He seemed to be thinking. "It's been a long time," he finally said. "But I still miss them."

I thought of many questions, but asked none.

With a deep sigh, Sam's expression recovered and he took a step closer to the bench. "How do you like the variety?" His thick hand brushed over the tops of the seed packages.

"I like it very much." I looked up at Sam and he seemed pleased by my response. Unfortunately, I couldn't keep the smile going.

"What's wrong?" Sam asked.

How could I tell him that I was already worried? I looked at all the packages, then at the size of the newly formed garden. The novelty of gardening was already wearing out. "This is going to be a lot of work," I groaned.

Sam covered his face with his hands as he tipped his head back towards the cloudless sky. "City girls!" He raked his hands through his thick hair. "I'm up at the crack of dawn breaking dirt while you're fast asleep, probably snoring—"

"I don't snore!"

"Probably snoring…" His eyes twinkled at me. "Just so you wouldn't get here and complain."

I went to give him a whack on the arm, but must have misjudged our distance. My hand whizzed past the point of intended impact. He looked a bit shocked.

Hoping he didn't think I was some violent lunatic and regretted inviting me here today, I decided to not acknowledge his reaction. Picking up the package containing peas, I waved them in the air. "Shall we start with these?"

Planting seeds proved to be easier than I anticipated. Plus it really helped working with someone like Sam.

In between nesting the seeds in dirt, I imagined what it would be like to kiss him. I tried to pretend I hadn't seen the locket that Alex gave me because it reminded me too vividly of how painful love could be.

But Sam seemed different.

"If you're lucky," he said, striking up a conversation, "you might find an arrowhead. I remember finding a few when I was a little kid."

"Here, in the dirt?" I knew that the Potawatomi Indian Reservation was located north of here, but hadn't given much thought to the fact that Native Americans actually once occupied the land. This land, right here, where I was sitting. "I think it's cool how many Kansas counties, towns and cities are named after Native American tribes." I think I said that just to make myself feel better for forgetting about them in the first palace.

Sam nodded in agreement. "Except that most names aren't tribes."

"Oh?"

"Take the city of Olathe for example. That word best describes *you* in the native Shawnee language."

"Me?"

Without answering my question, Sam returned to work. So did I.

As I watched Sam work, I wondered what happened to his parents. It definitely had to be a tragedy. How else would such a young person not have living parents? It was obvious, however, that Sam didn't want to discuss the matter. Maybe that's why he worked so hard, as a diversion. I continued to watch his large muscular frame, hunched over, with his knees firmly planted in the dirt; my heart felt a twinge of pain as I imagined the emptiness he must be experiencing.

Suddenly, the spray and scatter of incoming dirt
redirected my thoughts to a happier time, the present.

"You've become awfully quiet over there, Miss
Emily."

I hadn't realized that I had stopped working, only to
be caught ogling at the incredible work of art on the
other side of the garden.

"This is labor-intensive work! I don't know how
you do it." I took the last sip of water from my bottle.

"Are you whining again, city girl?"

"Not at all. I'm trying to tell you that I'm
developing a keen appreciation for farmers."

Sam arched his back and smiled. "You do fine work
yourself."

By now, the sun hung high in the sky and it was
miserably hot. The dirt on his shirt had turned into mud
and the white cotton material stuck to his damp skin. I
wondered if I looked as hot as he did. Pun intended.

What was wrong with me—are all single girls this
boy crazy? What about Sam? Did I even stand a chance
of being attractive to him? How old was he, anyway?
What would I tell my parents? Would they ever begin to
approve? What if they forbade me to see him?

Wiping the sweat from his forehead with his arm,
Sam strolled over towards me.

"I think I heard a coyote last night," I said.

"I bet you don't hear that in the city."

"It sounded so close! Will they ever come into the
yard?"

"That's what I was trying to tell you yesterday.
They are close!"

I tensed with fear. I'd never seen a coyote before,
but always imagined them to be fairly lethal.

"Don't worry yourself too much, little lady." Sam looked down at me. His deep brown eyes made me want to throw my arms around him. "You've already appointed me to keep you safe and I intend to honor that agreement." Like a mighty warrior, Sam thumped his fist against his wide chest. "Besides, those varmints are more interested in eating rabbits than you."

"It *is* difficult being a city girl in the midst of the country, you know." I gave him my best pout.

"Well, this ol' country boy thinks this here city girl just might make it if she's careful."

"Really?"

Ignoring my rhetorical question, Sam asked, "Are you thirsty?"

"Parched!" I said, holding up my empty water bottle. The feel of sweat rolled down my back and I hoped to God I put on enough deodorant.

"Follow me," he said, leading me past the house and around the corner. Much to my surprise, an eighteen-foot windmill sat behind the classic Ford truck. I faltered a bit, not recollecting the windmill being there yesterday. We had walked all around the house and field, and I couldn't recall seeing a windmill being *anywhere.*

"Take this ladle." Sam handed me an old tin cup welded to a long handle. Dismissing my incongruent memories, I watched Sam clench the metal pump lever and pull back. Instantly, the blades of the windmill twirled in the wind. The pump gurgled and with a belching *whoosh*, ice-cold water gushed out from the spout, splashing up freezing mud all over me.

Slapping his knee, Sam laughed so hard I thought he was going to fall over. Fuming, I grabbed a metal bucket that hung near the spigot.

"You dare to laugh at me?" I asked, filling the bucket with more freezing cold water. Taking aim at the still laughing tall target, I launched the water with deadly precision.

"What the?" I uttered in disbelief. I couldn't believe it. The water missed him.

He just smirked all the more and filled his own tin bucket.

"Don't you dare." I shook a pointed finger at him.

Holding the full bucket, Sam cocked back his arms. Like something out of a Tom and Jerry cartoon, Sam let the water fly.

"Nooo!" I shrieked as I struggled to keep from slipping in the mud, dropping my pail in the process.

"Missed me," I taunted, scrambling to my feet to take cover on the other side of the house. When it didn't seem like he was going to follow me, I waited another few seconds, just to be sure, and finally peered around the corner. Seeing no one, I stepped out to face the open end of a garden hose. Three seconds later, I was drenched.

"Gotcha," he said.

As quick as it began, the water war was over and I suffered heavy casualties. I stood there, trying to be brave, as the water from my wet hair and clothes ran down my legs. The well water was painfully cold and despite the hot air, I began to shiver. As the remaining drips fell to the ground, I wasn't sure which, but I either looked like a drowned rat, or a contestant in a wet t-shirt contest. By the way his laughter exploded, I figured it was the first.

"Sss…S… Ssaaamm, I nneed to knnow your llllast nananame so I cccan yell at yyyou pppropperlllly!"

Somehow, my chattering only increased my outrageous state and he responded with greater intensity.

Letting out a girly growl, I charged straight at him. Expecting a hard impact against his tall frame, I prepared myself.

Landing in a pile of dried straw was the last thing I expected. Rolling over onto my backside, I held up two fists of the yellow stuff. "Where did this come from?"

"Ah, I picked it up late yesterday," Sam explained without missing a beat. "I'm making plans for a few chickens and I'll need it for nests."

I dropped the straw and pressed my fingers into my forehead and temples. I was starting to think I was losing my mind. All day long, things were not as I expected. Flowers went missing while windmills and straw stacks popped out of thin air. I couldn't even seem to focus accurately because I missed whacking Sam twice. Totally confused, I let my head drop to rest my on my knees. "I think the heat is getting to me. Maybe I need to take a break."

A much quieter Sam disengaged the windmill, but not before filling the water pail. He came back over and took my hand.

Suddenly, I tasted something weird. I needed to spit. I began fishing for foreign objects.

"What's wrong? Did you manage to eat the straw as well?" he asked, picking it out of my hair.

"It doesn't taste like straw. I'm not sure what I got into." I licked my lips, trying to wipe off the smoky residue that had settled on my tongue. It reminded me of men's cologne, but I had no intention of telling him that.

"Sit down here." Sam gestured to a very large rock. I climbed up on the boulder and pulled my knees tightly against my chest. "Take a drink of water." He held out the bucket.

Despite being wet on the outside, my throat was dry. Maybe I'd become dehydrated or something. I appreciated the offer and took the cup eagerly. As I took the sip, he climbed up next to me.

"Did that help?"

I nodded. Besides peculiar, I didn't really mind the taste, it was rather sweet.

Between the sun and the heat radiating off the rock's surface, I was warming up nicely. A bit more relaxed, I closed my eyes and tipped my chin to the blue skies.

"Are you mad?" Sam's gentle voice inquired.

"No, unless you are referring to crazy. That, on the other hand, might be true." I said, with my eyes still closed.

"Why would you say that?" The presence of anger marked Sam's voice.

Opening my eyes, I rubbed the lump on the back of my skull. "I hit my head yesterday. Last night, I wasn't worried at all, but as today continues, I wonder if I should be."

"Tell me. What's happening?"

I tried to explain the unusual ways I'd been perceiving things; however, the further I went with my story, the more it reinforced my theory of crazy.

When I was finished, Sam looked up from the ant he was pestering. "I haven't heard anything *that* unusual."

"That's because it's not happening to you. It's really scary for me. It makes me think I hallucinated the flowers."

Sam grew quiet. "Maybe you had a dream last night and added in extra flowers." His eyes hid more than his words said.

"Sam—"

He put his finger against my lips. The unusual taste returned. Maybe, it *was* his cologne. Or some other kind of hallucination! Nevertheless, it was obvious the conversation was over.

"My last name is Easley. It originates from the word iron."

He removed his finger from my lips and I found the remnants of a smile. The taste disappeared with his finger.

"The name fits you well. You most definitely are a strong man." My words lacked enthusiasm.

"The Yankee spelling is Ei. As folks moved south, they changed the spelling to Ea. Probably as a Confederate thing."

"You do like interesting facts. But you don't seem very rebel-ish to me."

"I've had my share of scuffles in the dirt," he smirked. "I must get it from my great grandma Hatti—consorting with the forbidden." Then his grin turned mischievous. "I am definitely an E, A, Easley."

Curiosity filled my imagination. I had only witnessed a kind and gentle Sam. Yet judging by his size, I'm sure he could pummel the other guy if he ever found himself in a precarious situation.

"You don't approve?" Sam interrupted my daydream.

"Oh, it's not like that at all," I said, embarrassed to be caught daydreaming again.

"At any rate, I told you my last name so you could yell at me, if you still wanted."

I tried to smile.

"Still not feeling well? Do you want to go home?"

I want a hug and to be told everything will be all right. "It's probably a good idea. Between smashing my head, moving here, and—" I nearly mentioned Alex, but why mention him? "I think I need to lie down for a while."

"Your head is fine, Emily," Sam said sternly. "You are not nuts. Trust me."

"How would you know? You weren't there when I slipped. Maybe I gave myself brain damage."

Sam searched the sky and heaved a heavy sigh.

That only made me angrier. "Whatever is going on is not normal."

"Miss Emily," he said as he rubbed his chin with his hand, "some of the best advice I ever received was 'don't over-analyze life.' Sometimes you just have to accept things at face value."

"I am. Right now, my eyes are telling me I need my head examined!"

"That's not what I meant."

"I'm sorry if you think I'm being overly dramatic. I shouldn't have said anything." Hopping down from the boulder, I apologized again for behaving like a girl, and pushed back the sting of tears.

The last thing I wanted to do was cry in front of Sam. Without saying another word, I left him, sitting there.

Walking home in silence, I purposely avoided looking at flowers, birds, or even trees lining the water pathway. I was too afraid to look at anything. Too afraid of what I may or may not see.

The journey home seemed much too long, probably because I was exhausted from all the gardening. Fatigue weighed heavy in my legs and the idea of a nap sounded pretty good. That was my plan. I'd go home and lay down for a while.

"Mom, I found her," a little voice whispered just outside my bedroom door, raising my level of awareness.

"Here you are." Mom's soft hand brushed across my forehead and temple.

I laid there for a moment, not moving. My brain was like a computer just being turned on, and needed time to reboot. Then, in an instant, my day flooded my memory.

"Mom!" I bolted upright. "Something weird is happening to me."

Obviously she heard the concern in my tone, but tried to remain calm, "What do you mean, Emily?"

"I don't know if it's from hitting my head, or the stress of moving, or stupid Alex, or what it is, but I think I'm going crazy!"

Mom lifted my chin. "Tell me why you think this."

I told her about meeting Sam, the way I missed him with the bucket full of water, and the mysteriously appearing objects at his farm. "And the flowers. Where could they go?"

"I don't think you are going crazy," she said reassuringly, "unless it's boy crazy." She tapped the tip of my nose. "But I will call the doctor and have an appointment scheduled."

She smiled and informed me that dinner would be ready soon. I returned the smile, but it was insincere. I didn't believe her, and I'm not sure she believed herself. Add in Sam's reaction, who didn't put on a convincing act either, and all we needed was a fourth to start a game of liar's poker.

"Emmy's got a new boyfriend." Kat taunted, looking at Dad, who was already sitting at the table twirling his fork in the spaghetti.

Dad made a fake surprised expression, "Oh?"

Kat's face brightened up, and I sank in my chair. "He's a farm boy across the creek."

Dad tilted his head to the side as Kitty continued. I shot her a look to stop. "He lives there by himself!" Apparently, she was having too much fun.

At that, Dad looked at Mom, who suddenly took interest in the ingredients on the salad dressing label.

"Elizabeth…" Dad began, although he looked directly at me, "Do you know about this?" I could feel the blood drain from my face.

"Dad!" I lurched forward in my own defense. "It's not like that! Sam is a nice guy!"

"A *guy*, who is old enough to have his own farm!" Dad countered.

"Yes, but barely. It's like he's an orphan, his parents are dead." I said, getting mad and feeling the need to defend Sam, as well as myself, which turned my attention to Kat, who started this whole conversation. "You brat!"

That's when Mom finally engaged. "All right. Let's not jump to conclusions." Mom gave Dad a warning look. "From the way Emmy described him to me, he seems to be a nice young man."

Dad silently echoed the word "man."

Kat wasn't finished yet. "She thinks she's going nuts, too!" I looked at Kat in disbelief. What was she trying to accomplish?

Dad's face turned sour. "Would someone please tell me what is going on around here?"

Putting her fork down on her plate, Mom let out a heavy sigh. "No one is going crazy. Emily is concerned because she experienced some hand-eye coordination problems earlier today. Since she hit her head yesterday, she's worried the two might be related.

"I'm the one who over reacts to head injuries, and I am sorry if I have infected any of you with my own paranoia. I will call Dr. Lui in the morning and see what she recommends." Grabbing her fork, Mom stabbed another section of spaghetti and began twisting.

No one had anything else to say over dinner, only exchanging words in polite requests. The table was cleared in a similar fashion. Once everything was put away, we scattered in our own directions. Mom and Kat went to work on the bird journal while Dad retired to the family room to read the newspaper. I grabbed my wooden companion and together, we headed out for the deck. It was a perfect evening to play my guitar.

The sun hovered deep on the horizon and the telltale clouds indicated late night rain was likely. At least I hoped so. I yearned for the chance to lie in bed and listen to the rain pitter-patter down upon the rooftop.

After placing a chair alongside the wooden railing, I sat down and propped my feet up. An invisible place called serenity began to appear as I played the melody flowing out of my memory. Once again, my loyal friend helped me work though my sorrows and grief. I could feel the stress being taken from my body and released high above the treetops note by note. A small gust of wind blew my hair around my face, tickling my nose. Within the wind, I smelled the new and familiar scent that reminded me of Sam. The smoky taste touched my tongue for a brief moment. Tiny goosebumps rose upon my flesh. Standing abruptly, I searched the yard and woods for him. Without thought, I called out, "Sam?"

I scanned the wooded scenery in vain. Disappointed, I sat down and placed the guitar back in my lap. Like a loitering fascination, I had no choice but to smile as my thoughts continued of Sam. With my eyes closed, I slowly strummed my guitar, carelessly and without much thought. The notes were soft and delicate, becoming a love song.

CHAPTER SIXTEEN

CHOICES

SAM WANDERED THE OPEN FIELD, regretting the recent decisions he had made. *What a fool!* He shook his head in disgust at himself. Who was he trying to kid? Himself, obviously. He never should have allowed it to go this far.

Their worlds didn't mix. He could try to blend in, but questioned how much longer he really expected to keep the illusion going. Close to talking himself into ending the escapade, the winds turned and blew in from the south. Within the breeze, a melody called to him, much like a forgotten promise.

CHAPTER SEVENTEEN

THE GOLDENROD

"DID YOU PACK ME A LUNCH?" Kat asked as she bounced down the steps in an adorable summer outfit. It was too nice for camp, but I decided not to say anything just because she looked so darn cute.

"Mom did last night," I said, handing her the insulated bag.

"What are you going to do today?" she asked, probably to blackmail me later.

"I'm not sure yet."

"Are you going to see Sam?"

"I don't know. I'll have to wait and see how my brain is functioning."

"You're catching Mom's paranoia." Kat stood with her hands on her hips, analyzing me. "Do you really think you're crazy? Maybe we should call a cab."

"Thanks," I muttered, grabbing my purse off the counter.

Kat shook her lunch like a present. "You're the one that brought it up."

"Let's get you to camp." I gave her a gentle push.

The walk to the car refreshed the conversation.

"Kat?" I asked in lingering tones.

"What?"

"You look nice today."

She beamed with pride. "Thanks!"

"How did you do in your track and field this year?"

Ecstatic that I asked, Kat provided me with an animated play-by-play recap of the entire day. She won a total of four blue ribbons, two red, and one pink ribbon for fourth place in the relay because one of the girls tripped. Her recount of the story lasted all the way to the sign-in desk.

"Have fun." I gave her a one-armed hug, preparing to leave.

"I will. Camp is a blast!" she said, jumping up like she going to dunk a basketball. Two arms squeezed around my neck instead. "Have fun with you-know-who."

As I made my way back to the car, I knew I wouldn't stay away from Sam. Despite common sense yelling things like, "Don't be rash" and "Slow down!" I pushed them aside for barely justifiable reasons like, I enjoyed being with him, and I liked the way he made me feel. Plus, thinking about *not* seeing him made my stomach hurt.

But today, I intended to get answers. He had used the "enough-about-me" more than once. It would be my turn to ask the questions.

Waving to Kitty one more time before she ducked out of sight, I realized we were both lucky, each having an adventure to look forward to. A happy little giggle escaped my lips; never in my wildest dreams did I think my adventure would revolve around farming.

After all, I was a city girl.

As I began my journey up the creek bed, I kept my eyes busy with the water and out of the tall grass where the wildflowers might be. Even though I relied on denial for so many unpleasant things in life, it was hard ignoring my fears of being crazy. I still didn't know what, but something was very wrong. So, in an attempt to distract my mind, I decided to listen for song birds.

But the only thing that caught my attention was the stillness in the forest air.

"Where are all the little creatures?" I looked around in the treetops. I listened for rustling leaves.

Nothing.

Not a single peep.

My stomach tightened.

Is everything vanishing?

Then a wave of reality spoke to me, but that wasn't good news, either. Recalling from grade school, I learned that animals would leave an area if they sensed danger. Since they didn't seem to mind me before, it could only be one thing, *Varmints! Oh crap! I'm going to get eaten by a frickin' wolverine.*

"Keep calm," I told myself. "No panicking." I started to run. *Bobcats, coyotes, and bears, oh my!*

I was out of shape. My chest burned. *I'm going to die.*

Bobcats, coyotes, and bears, oh my!

I scanned the banks for a foaming-mouthed, large-fanged, snarling animal.

Just keep running, just keep running, just keep running, running, running.

Certain that a rabid animal was going to charge at me any second, I regretted knowing that the forest was a dangerous place full of flesh-eating creatures. I would much rather have been killed in a surprise ambush instead of waiting for the strike to come. Glancing repeatedly from side to side, each step became heavier than the last, and I couldn't stop the maddening rhyme inside my brain, *bobcats, coyotes, and bears, oh my!*

Jedd's place was just up ahead. If I was attacked now, Sam would hear me scream and come running. At the same time, I didn't want to go into Sam's yard running like some lunatic. I'd have to take my chances. Slowing down, my legs began to feel like rubber. I had to stop.

"I'm such a coward!" I gasped, slumping over in an exhausted mess. I braced my hands on my knees to keep from falling over. Still panting, I stared down into the grass to view a grasshopper inches from my foot.

Gray-brown fur leaped from under the brush, directly at me.

A breathless scream escaped my lips as I prepared for pain. Hopefully shock would set in quickly.

Nothing happened.

I opened one eye and saw motionless fur. I opened the other eye and saw a rabbit nibbling on a piece of grass.

"For Pete's sake!" I huffed, scaring the small furry animal into the woods.

Collecting my nerves, my thoughts returned to Sam and my heart began to race again, but this time, not from fear. Making my way through the clearing, I caught sight of the house and barn, but he was nowhere in sight.

Approaching the house cautiously, disappointment set in as I worried he might not be home. "Sam?"

Out from around the side of the house, Sam walked into view, dressed in another white cotton shirt and a pair of well-fitting jeans, smiling his fabulous smile. "It's nice to see you today."

A quick sigh of relief escaped my lips before curling back into a huge smile. "Thank you. It's good to see you too."

"I wasn't sure if you'd stop by today. Are you feeling better?"

"Yes," I said, stuffing my worries into a place called repression. "Besides," I said, feeling impish, "I had to check on my radishes."

Sam quickly put both his hands over his heart, staggering backwards, as if he'd been shot. "You've come for the vegetables and not me?"

"Don't quit your day job; you'll never make it as an actor." I laughed as he dropped to his knees.

"What?" His theatrical presentation ended abruptly. "I'll have you know that acting runs in my family."

"Really?" *That answers one of my questions about why he knows so much about theatre.*

"Yes, my mother was a star," he boasted proudly.

"A star? Like in famous? "

Rising from his knees, Sam motioned to the garden. "Let's water while I tell you about my family." Oddly, he seemed eager to brag of his mother, unlike yesterday, when he barely spoke about her death.

Working quickly, he fitted a hose to the water tank, and then pulled back on the long lever that allowed the pump to begin its work. More gurgling noises preceded the crystal-clear water from the end of the hose. There was no water fight today.

As we approached the garden, I noticed that Sam had marked the rows of seeds by name after I had left. With its wooden stakes and handcrafted tags, the garden looked just as quaint as the rest of the farm.

"Dressed in his finest suit," Sam began, "Pa met my mother on a business trip in Chicago on New Year's Eve. He was in the Windy City negotiating last minute deals with area textile manufacturers for the next year's crops. He was into cotton, you see."

I nodded mostly to show I was paying attention, and noted how he loved to tell a good story.

"Well, on this particular morning, he noticed this particularly fine lady as she entered the Blackstone Theatre. He watched nearly every man's eyes follow her across the street before she entered into the theatre, but no one dared to greet her. She was much too upscale for the lot of them. Curious, Pa went up to the ticket booth to inquire about the lovely young lady. He was informed that she was Tilly Rushford, daughter to the wealthy factory owner on the south side of the city. She was back from New York with the theatre company for her career debut. This news did not intimidate my Pa in the least. He would simply order a larger bouquet of flowers than he originally thought. You see, Pa was not intimidated by risks; he thrived on them.

"While ordering the flowers, he learned that it just so happened to be the grand opening of the theatre. Naturally, he upgraded his order again. When it was all said and done, he arranged for sixty red long-stemmed roses to be delivered to her dressing room before curtain call. On the card, he signed, 'Love and jazz awaits you.'

"Now, it just so happened that Ma was disenchanted with theatre. She went to New York looking for adventure and found loneliness. She didn't know it, but she was waiting for someone to take her away, and Pa was the one man valiant enough to do it."

"How exciting! Did they elope? What about the cotton farm?" I interrupted.

"Not exactly. Pa already knew her daddy as Mr. Tom Rushford, whom he previously met negotiating cotton price. Pa knew well enough to maintain reputable business relationships with Mr. Rushford. Marrying the only daughter of an incredibly wealthy Chicago businessman was never the plan, but it could have really huge benefits." Sam rubbed his fingers together, indicating money.

"Now the cotton *plantation*, not a farm…" He looked at me, obviously thinking 'city girl' and continued, "my Pa inherited from my great-grandmother, Hatti."

"You mentioned something about her yesterday. Called her a rebel or something."

"She lived during the Civil War. She fell in love."

"With a Yankee?"

"During the last year of the war, a secret relationship developed between her and a *slave*."

Silence fell between us.

"A *colored man*, Emily."

I thought about all the *non-white* kids at school. It was hard for me to imagine this being a terrible thing.

"Well, at the time, it was *strictly* prohibited. In fact, it might have been *illegal*. Some die-hard Confederates might have lynched them both, just to prove a point."

"Hung? For being in love?"

"Yup. But Tom was a good man. Faithful. She went on to have a son, my grandfather, Charles. Of course Hatti hid her pregnancy from the public, and when the child was born, she passed him off as a distant relative in need of a home. His complexion was light enough and no one questioned her story. Charles eventually wed and they had a son, Garret, my father."

"But you don't look black," I thoughtlessly blurted out as he pointed to his curly hair, which wasn't black, either. I wondered if my dad got his curly hair from African Americans as well. Weird.

By now, the garden was thoroughly saturated and we were sitting in the grass by the pond further out past the barn.

"Hatti and Tom never wed, and kept their relationship hush-hush"

"Back up a minute. There's you, your Pa, Charles, and then Hatti? I don't mean to be rude, Sam, and it could be that my teacher was misinformed about the American History class he was teaching, but your family timeline is not making any sense."

The twinkle in Sam's eyes fizzled out. A serious look over took the rest of his features as he stared out past the pond and into the next field. "Time is only relevant to those who don't have enough, Miss Emily."

Apparently that blob of information was supposed to satisfy my question. All it did was raise more questions, but I decided to switch gears. "What did your parents do after they left Chicago?"

A smile returned to his face. "Ma loved to sing and Pa played the piano. There were six of them that toured together."

"So, your parents had their own band? How exciting!"

"Oooh, doggy! Don't you know it." Sam's eyes grew large with excitement. "Living right there on the Goldenrod, tooling up and down the Mississippi, performing all the way from St. Louis to New Orleans!

"What is the Goldenrod?"

"A showboat."

"What's a showboat?"

"Tell me, have you ever heard of the Mississippi Queen?"

"It's that big ship with the giant paddle on the back, right? My aunt and uncle got married on it."

"The Goldenrod is a lot like that."

"Gee, I wonder why I've never heard of that one then?"

"That's probably because the Goldenrod was built in 1910 and the Mississippi Queen was built in 1976. Strange that both are still around, but folks only care about the newest."

"I'd care," I said, trying to sound compassionate.

Rolling his eyes, Sam continued with his story. "When Ma realized she was with child, they moved to Kansas City, to be with her sister. Then after I was born, they took a claim on the land out here, away from big city life."

"Why didn't they live on the plantation?"

"Pa never cared for the humidity. So, being the entrepreneur he was, he decided to try his hand at wheat. He had the house and barn built, bought the equipment, and hired out the crop labor. I eventually had a little sister, Amelia. Life was good. Nearly perfect." After ending his sentence, he stretched out, crossed his long legs, and rested back on his hands, appearing satisfied with the ending of his tale.

"What? You're ending there?" I felt cheated, like someone had shut off the TV in the middle of the program.

Sam turned to look at me, a half smile on his face.

"What about your family? What happened next?"

"This is the happy ending I like. I'll save the tragedy for another day."

My chin dropped into a silent, "Oh."

He closed my lower jaw up with the tips of his fingers. An immediate, smoky sweet taste returned to my taste buds. Weird.

Not knowing how Sam came to be an orphan, and picking up on the word "tragedy," I got the impression it was beyond bad. A stick had found its way into my hand and I had been absentmindedly etching a design in the dirt. "It's nice to hear you can focus on the positive."

"But you can't?" he asked.

I flung the stick into the water. "Fairytales used to be my favorite kind of books. I think they set little girls up for disappointment."

Sam thought for a moment. "Maybe. So, what kind of books do you like now?"

"Adventure. I am definitely looking for adventure."

CHAPTER EIGHTEEN

RADISHES

Sᴀᴍ ᴘʀᴇꜱꜱᴇᴅ ʜɪꜱ ʟɪᴘꜱ ᴛᴏɢᴇᴛʜᴇʀ and nodded, perhaps in thought. "Hows about swimming? We could make it a *mini* adventure."

The sun gleamed high in the sky and my skin felt sticky. The idea sounded refreshing. "I'd love to. Where?"

He pointed straight ahead. "There."

"Sam! In the pond? Where would we change?"

He glassed over the landscape. "Behind those bushes."

"And what would I wear?" I could feel the heat in my cheeks.

He grinned. "I'm sure you could be resourceful."

My mind was racing a million miles an hour. Did I dare? Skinny-dipping? Definitely not. I could wear my bra and undies. Was he just trying to get me out of my clothes? Probably. No, probably not. He hadn't even tried to kiss me yet.

"Okay," I heard myself say before I had fully made up my mind, "but I get to go in first, while you face the other way."

The pond water felt refreshingly cool against my over-heated skin. It was spacious, sizably larger than a backyard swimming pool. "You said that this pond used to be a watering hole for the cattle. I'm not going to step in cow poop, am I?"

"Do I really have to answer that?" he called out behind me.

As I bobbed into deeper depths, I was quite relieved my bra was not a see-through style. Confident to turn back towards shore, I noticed Sam's boots and shirt already in a pile and he was now unbuttoning his jeans. I was thinking I should look away to give him privacy but couldn't force my eyes away. He didn't have the abrupt farmer's tan as I was expecting. Instead, his muscular body was evenly colored. I figured it must be a part of his black heritage that still ran in his blood.

I had to keep staring. Wow! *How'd he put it? Oooh, doggy?*

Without the slightest apprehension, Sam slipped off his pants. Daunted by his un-bashful nature, and surprised at my own voyeuristic behavior, I noticed his unusual style of boxers. Maybe silk—definitely not off the rack at Target, and very sexy.

I tried not to give away my smile as I watched him enter the pond. Visually molesting his muscular body, I think I was beginning to understand why my dad was worried about the age thing. *Whoa, doggy!*

"How's the water?" he asked.

"Nice," I said, a bit too hastily, referring more to his body than the water. Embarrassed that he might have made the connection, I shut my mouth, opened my arms wide and took a plunge backwards before I said anything else stupid.

"Ahhh, yes," Sam proclaimed, standing mid-thigh in the pond. If he did catch my intent, he didn't let on. "You won't find *this* in the city." Then I saw the tail end of a grin as he took to the water in a rough dive. I squeezed my eyes shut in anticipation for a splash that never came. He resurfaced a few feet away, and stood at waist level.

I felt myself melt as he looked at me with his dreamy brown eyes. I could definitely handle a kiss from him!

"But enough of me," Sam said abruptly, and with an edge. "Let's hear some more about you. I recollect that you play in the school band?" He took a step closer.

"Yes," I answered, thinking that his question seemed more like an interrogation than curiosity. I broke eye contact and pretended to be busy looking for my hand in the murky water.

"How many more years of high school do you have?" He took another step.

"One." I looked him square in the face and tried to appear confident.

"How old are you, Emily?" Still closer. His eyes become scrutinizing.

Suddenly my age sounded very young. "Almost eighteen," I lied. I wouldn't be eighteen for a good five months. I regretted my answer. "Why?"

Sam waded through the water until he was next to me. He crouched down so we could be face to face.

I was so nervous, I thought I was going to bust.

He searched my face, like he was still unsatisfied with my answers. A gentle smile finally appeared.

"Olathe," Sam said.

"What does that mean, anyway?"

"I told you. It describes you. Beautiful."

Beautiful? Yesss! He probably wouldn't say that if he had a girlfriend. Butterflies filled my stomach.

"And your eyes… like sapphires."

"Thank you. They turn blue when…well, thank you."

Sam continued his gaze, making me feel awkward. But not in a groping kind of way. He didn't seem like just another horny guy. Well, he was a guy: that probably made him horny, but there seemed to be more to him than that. No other guy ever took the time to compliment my eyes.

As I marveled over his sensitive side, he gently moved my hair away from my face. The strange sweet taste briefly tingled my taste buds. I was beginning to like it.

"How close to eighteen?"

Crap! He is worried about the age thing.

"November."

His expression didn't change.

"How old are you, Sam?"

He thought purposefully for a brief moment, and then grinned too wide as the simple question turned into an alluded confession. "Old enough to know better and young enough not to care."

Uh-oh, this can't be good. "Am I too young for you?" *Yikes, that sounded really terrible.*

"Emily—" His head dipped under the water and reappeared a short distance away. "I like you, and—"

Say what?

"—your age might be a problem, but that's not what concerns me the most."

Did he just say what I thought he said? A sudden wave of empowerment tickled my self-esteem: He liked me! What else mattered? Sam Easley liked me. Well, I certainly wasn't bothered by the age thing. I'd be eighteen soon enough. And he liked me! I stood up and walked slowly toward Sam, graceful and cat-like. This could be fun.

"Maybe it's the fact that my daddy owns a gun shop?" I asked.

Sam raised his eyebrows, taking a step back.

I stopped my prowl. Little giggles welled up from inside me. "However, he's usually very even-tempered. I don't *think* he'd shoot you."

Sam grit his teeth in a grin.

"At the very least, if he had you arrested, my mom knows all the judges in town—she'd get you out."

Sam's expression dulled. "Your words bring me such comfort."

"I know. I have a warped sense of humor. I think it's because I have one parent selling guns, and the other parent trying to get them off the streets. My life has been a dichotomy of good versus evil, and the lines of both are heavily blurred."

"This sounds like it could take years of therapy," he cracked.

"Wise guy." I slapped the water, spraying Sam over and over again.

"I take it back," he yelped, scurrying like a coon in hound country.

Although I would have liked to let my bra and panties dry before I put my clothes back on, I was not brazen enough to sit in lacy undergarments in front of Sam. I also thought it to be un-lady like, so from behind the bush, I wrung them out as best as I could. After I finished dressing, Sam stepped behind the same bush. He flung his wet boxers on a nearby rock and I blushed at the thought of him 'going commando.' There was such a difference between men and women. I liked it.

"Would you like to see a fox's den?" Sam asked while lacing up his second boot.

"Really?"

"Really. She's almost as beautiful as you are." Sam yanked the hem of his pants over his boot then walked over to me and put his arm around me, pulling me into his side.

Instantly, my tongue felt like it was on fire and a musky sweet scent filled my nostrils. The smell became so overwhelming I began to choke. An intense pressure pushed against my throat, cutting off my air supply.

At once, Sam released me. His eyes darted back and forth.

Immediately the pressure lifted and I was able to catch my breath. "I couldn't breathe," I managed to gasp, massaging my throat.

Sam's expression was torn. "What happened?"

"I don't know. All of a sudden…it was like I was on fire."

A flash of regret crossed Sam's face. "I'm sorry. I shouldn't have—" His hands shot up to his head and he combed his fingers through his hair.

"Why?"

He looked me over again. "A bee. Are you allergic to bees?"

"Luckily not. But I don't think I was stung."

His facial features relaxed as he exhaled a long breath. He tried to smile. "Then there's no cause for alarm. I'm glad you're feeling better now."

Something about his response made me uncomfortable.

"Let's keep on our way," Sam said, pointing his finger. "You will really like the foxes."

I crossed my arms and stayed put. "You're very smart, Sam. I know you know I wasn't stung by a bee."

He started walking. "It's this-a-way."

I ran up in front of him, blocking his way. "What's going on Sam?"

For the first time, he appeared angry. "Why do you think something is going on?"

I didn't know what to say. I certainly didn't have a valid reason for suspecting anything, yet it didn't feel right, just the same. It reminded me of when we were sitting on the rock: he had words that he refused to share with me.

He took a step forward, but I didn't follow. He made a move to grab my hand, but hesitated. Then his palm turned upward, making a gesture to proceed.

I thought back to our recent conversation in the pond and wondered just how many reasons he had *not* to be with me. After all, I still knew very little about him. A dark thought crept into my head: maybe *he's* psycho and he killed his parents as a young kid… and he's just recently been released from prison and being around minors is a parole violation!

Or maybe I watch too much CSI.

I tried to remember if I saw him wearing an ankle bracelet. *Stop It!*

"Maybe I had an allergic reaction to some pollen or something." I said after what seemed like eternity. "I'm sure there are plenty of allergens out here that are new to me."

Sam's creased forehead eased back into place. "That sounds like a highly probable explanation. I should have thought of that."

Hesitantly, I took the step to join him at his side, and we started walking. But I still worried. A silent war raged on in my mind, slinging wild accusations, desecrating Sam's reputation *and* asking the question if I should be in fear of my life. I had an urge to run. *Bobcats, coyotes, bears...and Sam.*

"What are you doing?" Sam asked.

"Thinking."

"I can see that, what about?"

"You."

Sam's shoulders hunched. "I'm sorry that I upset you."

"It's not that you upset me, it's that you are hiding something from me."

Sam let out a gasp of exasperation. "Fine. Ask me any question. I promise to answer it truthfully."

Somehow, the pressure flipped back onto me. And I felt ridiculous. What would I possibly ask? His promise to protect me vividly entered my thoughts. Followed by the law of human nature: no man is perfect. How bad could his flaws be? Certainly not as bad as me asking the question, *How did you murder your parents?*

I buckled under my own indecisive weight. "I'd like to see the foxes, if you'll still take me."

Sam grinned. "I'd take you to any place you wanted to see. All you have to do is say so."

So with stifled reservations, I followed Sam into the grass that was becoming thicker and taller, and farther away from anything remotely populated.

"So, where exactly is the den located?" I asked, feeling the knot growing inside my stomach. I couldn't say I was hoping to catch him unprepared to answer, but if he stammered, I'd already decided to make a run for it.

"To what degree do you understand latitude and longitude?" Sam replied.

That answer wasn't among any I'd anticipated. *Rats!* "Not like that. I meant approximately."

"Exactly and approximately are two very different descriptions."

"Sam Easley! You twist my words."

"Actually, I'm clarifying them."

"Oh, just never mind."

Sam laughed. "You are just so dang cute when you get all pouty. And in case you still want to know, the den is just over yonder." He seemed to point past a dip in the grass.

As my cheek color returned to normal, Sam began explaining to me how the ice age affected our area of Kansas uniquely. Somewhere between lush green plants and rich soil, I finished mentally chastising myself for ever thinking such ridiculous and horrible thoughts about Sam. He was wonderful.

I looked up at him in approval; he was still going on about fossils. I reached for his hand and held it. At first he stiffened, then relaxed. The mysterious taste that was becoming less mysterious as the day went by returned. *What kind of aftershave does he wear, anyway? And why can I taste it when we touch? That is soooo bizarre.*

"Have you ever hopped aboard a moving train?" I asked.

"What kind of question is that?"

"Oh, just a silly one," I said, thinking about the trains that rumble past my house.

Midway up an incline, about a football field's length farther than what I had expected *over yonder to* be, Sam pointed to some unusual looking plants called button snakeroot. He informed me that the Native Americans used it for healing purposes including toothaches and treating snakebites. Rattlesnakes came to mind.

"How many kinds of poisonous snakes are there in Kansas?"

"'Bout five."

"Five? Do any of them live around here?"

"Yep."

"In the grass?"

"And in the woods."

"Varmints." I scowled.

He smiled at my use of the word as I took notice to the grass, careful not to step on a snake.

"I wouldn't be troubled over a snake bite, Miss Emily, it's more likely you'll be attacked by a rabid animal," Sam warned.

"Like, as in foaming-mouth rabies?" My mid-morning paranoia came to mind and my stomach suddenly turned heavy. "I sure hope you can keep up with all this protecting I'm in need of, Sam Easley!" I went to poke him in the ribs.

"Stop!" Sam's entire body stiffened.

Our hands ripped apart. I stood there, blinking. Waiting. "What?" I asked, startled and wide-eyed.

"I'm... ticklish."

I looked at him, not believing a word he just uttered. The *something's weird* thing was going on again.

"*Very* ticklish."

A big, fat dilemma stared me in the face. Minutes ago, I told Sam I'd accept anything he told me as truth. Now I wasn't so sure that was in my best interests. But why would he lie about being ticklish? The knot in my gut told me to make up any possible excuse and leave. The palpitations in my heart insisted that I'd never find another guy like Sam. "Okay." The word slid slowly off my tongue as I decided *not* to hold his hand. "Are we almost there?"

"Yes ma'am, we are," he said, overly up-beat. He pointed to a very large boulder, presumably brought in by an ice age glacier. The den, he informed me, was thirty paces to the left.

We approached quietly, finally stopping a few yards from the boulder. Sam let out a whistle. His eyes danced as he smiled at me, then he took my hand and gave it a quick squeeze. I automatically licked my lips to brush the taste off my tongue. He whistled again.

Two ears stuck up from the tall grass. "Here, Lucy," he called, and whistled one more time.

I watched as the grass ruffled in a line towards us. A red fox, no taller than my knees, emerged from the trail and sniffed my shoes.

"Oh, Sam!" I exclaimed too loudly and startled the fox.

"Easy girl." Sam bent down to stoke her beautiful hair.

"Can I pet her?"

"You can try."

"Hello, pretty girl." I held out my hand for her to smell. She sniffed at it and seemed satisfied. I rubbed her head twice, and then continued down her back. She tucked her tail between her hind legs.

Obviously someone who can charm animals must have a good heart. Now I really felt foolish for thinking the terrible thoughts about Sam.

"This boggles my mind. How do you do this?" I heard myself asking.

"How do I do *what*?" Sam chuckled, squatting down to scratch the fox's belly.

"Get animals to trust you?"

"What can I say? I'm a likable guy."

I rolled my eyes, but had to agree.

Still squatting, Sam looked up at me with puppy dog eyes of his own. "You like me."

Blushing, but with all the coyness I could muster, "How do you know that?"

"You came to visit your radishes."

CHAPTER NINETEEN

SPECULATIONS

WE SPENT THE REST of the afternoon wandering like nomads through the field, forest, and creek, talking about stuff and discovering Mother Nature's natural food supply. First we found a late bunch of morel mushrooms.

"This is disgusting." I spit and scraped my tongue with my fingernail while Sam laughed.

"I forget that they are much better cooked in butter."

I gave Sam a curious look.

Then we found a patch of wild strawberries. He passed, stating that he was still full from a very large breakfast, but I stuffed one berry in after another. This gave Sam more time to talk about all the stuff he knew.

"Look at that." The sun was fading into another fantastic display of color.

"Wow! It's so easy to lose track of time when we're together. You should probably get going soon, huh?" His voiced sounded lower than usual.

I searched his face to see if I might have said something that offended him. His expression did not indicate so.

"Yeah, I guess dinner will be ready soon," I replied.

"If your Ma is anything like mine was, she'll want you at the table when it's still hot."

I nodded. "Would you like to join us?"

"Thanks, but no. It would be rude to show up unannounced. I have errands to run, anyway."

That bit of information made me feel a little better.

We followed the creek back to my house and were now standing in front of the tree that had the carved sign for me to follow. I could hear Kat trying to yell over the sound of the riding lawnmower.

"Sam—" my heart started racing. "Thanks." I began envisioning our goodbye kiss. After all, he said that he liked me, and he knew I liked him. Or at least his radishes.

"It's been a good day." Sam said. He shifted his weight to his other foot. "It's going to rain tomorrow, so I thought I'd let you know I'll be heading into town."

"Oh? I thought it was supposed to be nice all week."

"Trust a farmer for accurate forecasting. We know," he said, tapping his temple.

"I'm realizing that," I said with a nod. "Will you be busy all day?"

"It's hard to say."

I didn't do a good job covering up my disappointment.

"Not to fret. I'll see you again soon." His lips curved into a simple smile before folding his hands behind his back. Then he leaned forward.

Oh! My! Gosh! He was going to kiss me. Suddenly, I felt very unprepared and the butterflies came halfway up my throat. I swallowed hard. I closed my eyes.

I felt the slightest touch of his lips against mine. His kiss was gentle and— Whoa, baby! My whole body lit up. I must have made some kind of noise because the kiss ended quickly.

Looking very surprised he asked, "Did that hurt?"

I barely received a kiss at all and now he was asking me if I was in pain? I wanted to die…of embarrassment! No, I wasn't in pain. I think I had my first orgasm. "Um, I think I backed into a pricker bush."

Sam's face twisted in curiosity. "Can I kiss you again, away from the pricker bush?"

For Pete's sake! The kiss I'd been waiting for, dreaming about. Yes, I wanted another kiss but something very peculiar was going on. My heart was beating so hard it started to burn. *Heart attack? No, panic attack?* "I don't think I can."

"Oh." Sam gave me a look of confusion.

Still recovering, I hoped my inexperience with boys wasn't that obvious. I didn't know what to do next, so I smiled. "Um, are you sure you won't come in?"

He smiled. "Thank you again, but no."

Shuffling the leaves with my shoe, I tried to invent new ways to prolong our togetherness. Although totally unrealistic, I never wanted to be apart from him again. When I looked up he was gone.

How does he do that? There was something definitely baffling about Sam Easley.

By the time I reached the edge of our lawn, Kat was using a creative form of sign language to communicate it was time for dinner. Dad gave her the thumbs up signal and headed toward the shed to park the John Deere.

Kat noticed me entering the yard from the woods. "Where have you been?"

"With Sam. How was camp?" I noticed a silver necklace around her neck. "What's this?"

Kitty defensively held her hand across her neck.

"Hey, that's mine." I hadn't even noticed that the locket was missing from my car. "When did you take it?"

"You don't even like it," Kat said sourly.

"You should have at least asked." *You little thief.* I wondered what else she had of mine.

"Can I keep it?" A fake grin stretched from ear to ear.

"I'll think about it."

"Yea!" Kat jumped up and spun a three-sixty mid-air.

As we ate, Mom reported that if my hand-eye coordination continued to be a problem, Dr. Lui would like to see me, but otherwise, she suggested an appointment with an ophthalmologist. I let her know that it hadn't bothered me at all today, but when I was with Sam, I kept having the strangest taste in my mouth.

"Like what?" Mom inquired.

"Well, it's difficult to explain. It seems to happen whenever I get too close to him or he touches me." I felt Dad's eyes on me. I looked at him, annoyed. "Stop speculating things, Dad."

"Izzy, maybe we are sending the *wrong* child to camp this year." Dad always seemed to find great pleasure in exasperating me.

"Oh, John!" Mom's eyes hit the ceiling and then returned her attention on me. "Tell me more about the taste, Em."

"It was like a smell I could taste. If men's cologne would taste as good as it smelled, it's like that."

"Men's cologne?" Dad interrupted. "Who is this guy, and why haven't I been introduced yet?"

"Maybe you should stop licking his neck!" Kat blurted out.

"Shut up!" I didn't miss whacking her arm.

"Good Lord, I knew an older man was trouble!" Dad pushed his chair back from the table.

"John—"

Bedlam erupted. Voices escalated. A scene of mad confusion busy with pointed fingers blurred the dinner table. Somebody please, just load us up in the paddy wagon and take us *all* straight to the asylum.

CHAPTER TWENTY

ANOTHER DAY IN PARADISE

ALEX WAS ACCUSTOMED to the dark. Flattened cardboard boxes were nailed across the windows to prevent any light from entering his chamber of torment. He let the phone slip out of his hand and onto the floor. He wanted so badly to talk to her.

Of course he would never tell her of his recent acts—she wouldn't approve. Yet, he had no other choice. He had to have it. And he had to win her back. She would see it his way. He was sure of that.

Alex dropped the white rock in the end of the pipe, stroked the wheel on the lighter with his thumb, closed his eyes, and felt the rush; the voice of reason blurred further.

CHAPTER TWENTY-ONE

A GAME OF BACKGAMMON

SOMETIMES, waking up to rain can be interpreted as a natural way of cleansing whatever it is that needs cleaning. Other times, it signifies the start of a bad day. For John Stokes, rain equated to less than three customers so far this morning. He had already inventoried the entire store contents in an effort to resist the urge to use the computer to search his daughter's new love interest. A temptation he could stand no more.

Let's see what kind of a place he's got, John thought to himself as he typed in "Silver Lake, Kansas", and hit "enter." Clicking on "bird's eye view," John decided to start at his own property as a reference point.

After admiring the satellite image of his new house, he briefly fantasized about another sunny afternoon napping in his hammock. Once satisfied, he began his search. With a half-mile of his house, the only place he found was a small, dilapidated building to the northeast. Panning out another half-mile, he made another circular sweep. This time, he located a home to the southwest, but it appeared to be a residential home, rather than a farmhouse. Becoming annoyed, he panned out further still until his own home was a mere dot on the screen. The closest farmhouse was miles away. Puzzled, John sat quietly and thought back to the night Emily first spoke of the farm. Did she drive to his farm? John concentrated hard on the conversation. *No, she said she went for a walk!*

John stared at the screen. He searched the scenery for a clue. "Talk to me," he whispered beneath his breath.

He was deep in concentration when the door alarm buzzed.

"Yeigh!" John jumped completely off his stool, knocking a second stool over in the process. Holding his hand over his heart, he greeted his long-time friend. "Good God, Bob. You nearly gave me a heart attack."

"I thought you might be in need of an opponent for backgammon, seeing how it's raining today," Bob chuckled, holding up the brushed leather-bound case.

"That would be great." John loved any game that legally allowed cheating.

Bob peered around John, to see the computer screen. "Are you looking for more land already?"

"Oh, no," John snickered in embarrassment at being caught snooping into his daughter's business. "I heard there was a farmhouse located near my place and was trying to find it, that's all."

Bob happened to be a retired farmer. "The only farm near your place would be the old abandoned Easley farm that burned down back in '36. Years of the Great Dust Bowl." Bob's weathered hand scratched his chin. "I always wanted that chunk of land, but it's never gone up for sale. I even called Kansas Records to inquire about the land—turns out the property taxes are paid out of Louisiana."

Bob walked over to a counter near the cash register and set the leather case on top of the glass showcase.

"The story behind the land is real tragic, though." His face cringed as he continued to set up the game. "They were into moonshine, ya know, as a remnant from the Prohibition, and naturally, the still was kept out in the barn. Well, the story goes that the wife went out into the barn to fetch something and knocked the oil lantern over. She grabbed what she thought was a pail of water and threw it on the small fire to put it out. Only it wasn't water. It was whisky!" Bob bared his teeth as he grimaced at the thought of what occurred next.

John leaned back, guessing what was coming.

"The hay ignited, bursting like a bomb. Fire was everywhere. Rumor has it that the husband saw his wife running and screaming from the barn completely covered in flames. I s'pose since everything was so dry, the barn went up in flames in mere seconds. To make matters worse, the boy ran into the barn to save the horses, and the roof collapsed in on him almost immediately." Bob shook his head in sadness as he walked over to the computer, stooped over to pick up the stool still lying on its side, and returned to the counter.

"That's horrible!" John exclaimed, carrying his own stool to the counter. "I can't even imagine. Did the wife survive?"

"Nope, but there was a daughter." Both the men had their pieces set in position. John placed the dice in the cup and shook the first roll.

"Easley blamed himself for the whole accident, and became completely grief-stricken. Every time he looked at the ashes from the barn, he relived the tragedy—he couldn't take it no more so he packed his bags and took his daughter from the area. I never heard what happened to them after they left." Bob took a breath and continued. "But the place never went up for sale. Kind of a strange deal, if you ask me." Bob scooped up the dice, dropped them into the shaker cup and gave them a gentle toss.

"Louisiana, you say?" John watched his friend move his playing piece ahead. "And the last name was Easley?"

"Yup."

"And that's the only farmhouse around my place for miles?"

"You've got farm *land* all around you, but the Easley farm is the only one that has a house on it. Otherwise, it's your house and the Brogan's house for miles in any direction."

John made his way back over to the computer and pointed to the house. "So this is Brogan's place? Have you met them?"

"Sure. Nice people," Bob said, joining John beside the computer. "Their boys are already off to college, so you don't have to worry about them making the move on your girls. Er, unless they've come home for the summer."

"Don't get me started on that today, Bob."

"Fine, fine. This old thing is the remnants of the Easley place." He gestured to the old structure a short distance from a small pond. "Like I said before, it's been abandoned for years."

"For years, huh?" An uneasy feeling started to build in John. He regretted not listening closer to the details of the chaotic discussion about Emmy's knock on the head. "Excuse me, Bob, but I need to call my wife.

When I'm finished, would you like to go out for a drive?"

CHAPTER TWENTY-TWO

A GET-TOGETHER

MY RINGING ALARM CLOCK awoke me from a much needed deep slumber. Unfortunately, it wasn't deep enough to erase the memories of last night's screaming match at the dinner table.

With covers in hand, I hesitated, realizing there was an absence of blinding sunlight casting through my bedroom window. Taking a moment to relax, I closed my eyes and listened to the hypnotic sounds of rain falling down upon the rooftop in a rhythmic pitter-patter. Sam was right. The rain had come. Like the rumble of the nearby trains, I found the rain to be very soothing as well. Each of these two sounds, one delicate, the other so powerful, were both music to my soul, much like the dichotomy I found in Sam. He was strong, yet gentle. I regarded him as the true image of *gentleman.*

And he liked me!

As a smile spread across my face, the ache in my heart told me that I already missed him.

Dismissing my paranoid fear of a heart attack, I envisioned our future kisses. Crossing the floor of my room, cool damp air rushed in as I opened my window.

"So much for global warming," I grumbled and headed for the shower.

After slipping on a pair of jeans and a long-sleeved shirt, I headed for Kitty's room. As I walked down the hall, the open loft area came into view and I couldn't help but smile at the music stand still waiting to be used.

Sitting on the edge of my sister's bed, I gave her a gentle nudge and waited for the complaining to begin. Kat was not a happy riser; she was always too tired. The path from the bed, to the potty, to the breakfast table was always filled with moans and groans. Luckily, as we sat at the table, the grumpies in her pants seemed to magically disappear as she gulped down her chocolate milk with the aid of a fluorescent pink straw.

"It's rainy today," I said, mostly to break the silence.

"I can see that."

"Do you have a raincoat? I think it's supposed to rain all day."

"So I still have camp?" She looked hopeful.

"Rain or shine."

After dropping Kat off at camp, I decided to drive over to the hardware store to pick up some green paint samples since I'd be in Topeka already. I didn't think Mom would mind me going without her. Besides, I knew Sam was busy with other plans so I had no reason to hurry home. While driving, I wondered what it would be like to be a farmer's wife...doing farm stuff every day.

Contrary to the smelly farmer image I had, I got the impression from Sam that Garret and Tilly Easley were no ordinary farmers. He described them more like fancy citizens. I envisioned his mother putting on a pair of short white gloves, dressed in high heels and a hat that complemented a nicely fitting dress, preparing for a Sunday drive. Quite the image that fit right in line with the 1920s farm I was growing so fond of. It was such a stark contrast to the twenty-first century.

Missing him, I reached in my purse to get my phone to call Sam, then scowled at my own stupidity for never asking for his phone number.

Upon entering the paint department, I became a bit overwhelmed by the extent of green options to choose from. I guessed there to be over one hundred shades of green. Immediately, I ruled out anything "minty." I wanted my room to be calming, not make me hungry for chocolate. Teal greens were eliminated next.

Closing my eyes, I envisioned the layout of my room. I had two walls with windows, the hallway door in another, and a double bi-fold closet door in the forth wall. Could I really paint my whole room green or would it create the illusion of being lost in an overgrown rain forest? Maybe just one wall, and the large closet doors and wooden window jambs green. I was liking this new idea, and started incorporating a "happy spring" wallpaper border when the clerk walked up beside me.

"Are you finding everything you need?" His voice matched the lines on his face.

"I'm thinking about sponge-painting my room. Do you think Festival Green and Shamrock would compliment each other?"

He liked my choices. "There is also a newer technique you might like to try. The flat surface actually looks like brushed suede from the mixture of light and dark hues."

"Ooooh."

We chatted a bit more before I thanked the man for his suggestions. Excited to get home and tape the samples on my closet doors, I hurried to my car, still admiring the shades of green. Loud obnoxious honking from the street interrupted my peaceful state. At least, the noise bothered me until I saw who was responsible: none other than Rayyan and Bailey, both waving wildly out the car windows.

"Emily!" Rayyan shouted as she swerved sharply into the parking lot, sending Bailey flying against the car door and her arms flinging wildly.

Thank God for seatbelts.

Stuffing the samples into my purse, I ran up to the car window. "Hey! I miss you guys! How's your summer? Do you have time to head over to the coffee shop?"

"Girl time just isn't the same without you." Rayyan spoke too loudly. "That's a great idea."

"You call Clair, and we'll meet you there." Bailey added, already shifting the car in drive for Rayyan.

Although the weather called for something hot to drink, it had been a long time since I'd been to Java Hut so I ordered my favorite, the Vanilla Chiller, instead. After receiving our order, we took a table in the back.

"I got a job!" Rayyan was the first to brag about her summer news. "At the mall. It's mostly nights, so I still get to play all day. And no, discounts don't apply to friends, so don't even ask."

"What about you, Clair, anything new?" I asked.

"Yeah, that jerk Rob broke up with me, the day after school let out. Apparently he didn't want to waste any time finding a college babe now that he's done with high school."

I thought she seemed to be taking it extremely well when she admitted she was sick of him anyway and had been eyeing a guy who worked at Dillon's grocery.

"I'm always running to the store for Mom. She loves it." Clair giggled and took a sip of her caramel latte. "And you sure are tan," she said, pointing her straw at me.

The door opened and in walked a well-dressed couple. A breeze followed them in and it made me shiver. The man must have been wearing too much cologne because I could smell it from where I sat. I liked it though. It reminded me of Sam. I actually caught myself looking around the coffee shop just to make sure Sam wasn't here. Automatically, I licked my lips to brush the taste away.

"You're tan," Clair repeated her comment, recapturing my attention.

"Oh?" I looked at the shade of my arm. "Yes," I mumbled, embarrassed to admit my current hobby.

Dissatisfied with the lack of details, Bailey questioned, "So, what are you up to? Is country living as bad as you were dreading?"

Three pairs of eyes focused on me.

"Get this," I sidestepped the questions and pulled out my cell phone. "I haven't heard a word from Alex since—well, besides the night I moved out of town."

"You never told me he came over," Bailey scoffed.

"What did he say?" Clair's eyes were wide.

I wrinkled my nose and shrugged. "So yesterday morning, I get this text from Alex, which I just ignored. And then," I leaned in closer to the center of the table to whisper, "when I looked at my phone last night, I had

twenty-seven missed phone calls. All from him!" I
showed them my phone as proof.

"OCD," Rayyan said.

"Stalker!" Bailey sneered.

"Eww, creepy." Clair shivered. "Did you call him
back?"

"Oh, no. I put my heart through enough pain."

"Guess what I heard," Rayyan gossiped. "Danny
saw him over by the—you know where—buying you
know what." She cringed as she said it.

"Just say it, Rayyan." Bailey challenged. "The meth
house." She spoke louder than necessary. "No one is
going to arrest you for talking about it. In fact, no one
in this store would do *anything* even if you said you *did*
it. Watch." Bailey stood up, cleared her throat and
stated matter of factly, "Let's go to the corner and score
a bump."

Clair's expression turned to shock as she ducked
beneath the table. The look on her face was priceless.

I nearly fell off my chair laughing.

"It's not funny," Clair hissed, returning topside,
looking everywhere. "Somebody might see us."

"You're such a sissy," Bailey laughed, adding a
snort.

The pig sound took me over the edge. I couldn't
catch my breath. Tears streamed down my face and I
couldn't speak. The more I tried to control my laughter,
the funnier it all seemed.

"Snort!" went Rayyan.

"Not you too!" Clair groaned.

The mania quickly spread, and three of us were
snorting hysterically.

"Quiet over there," a man ordered from behind the counter.

"See?" Bailey observed, hushing her voice. "He's more worried about the noise level than our illicit drug use. Snort!"

Another round of laughter exploded from the table. Although I was laughing on the outside, a part of me was worried for Alex. This was not good.

"Seriously, how is Silver Lake?" Rayyan asked once the laughter died down.

"It's very small, but has a lot of unusual street names. I'd like to visit the city hall and read up on its past." Strangely, the taste of men's cologne settled upon my tongue again, but this time I thought of brain damage.

"You are so weird, Emily!" Clair remarked.

"You should talk, missing school for a hair appointment." Rayyan backed me up.

"I've actually stopped in the town twice now. Once to buy new furniture and then on Sunday for church," I confessed. "I've really just been hanging out at the new house—" A little tickle on my neck interrupted my sentence and I brushed it away.

"That's dreadful!" Clair said, probably imagining life without daily shopping.

"It was at first," I agreed, but not for the same reasons. "Country life has been growing on me." I looked at each of their faces and waited for a reaction. They remained silent. Nervously, I wiped the puddle of water collecting around the bottom of my plastic cup. We all took a sip of our drinks to fill the lull in the conversation.

"You are so full of crap." Bailey pointed her finger at my nose. "I know there's a guy involved."

I threw up my hands in surrender. "What?" I crowed pretending to be innocent. The girls wanted details and I knew there was no way getting around it. "Okay, okay," I caved in. Still, I was going to have fun with it.

With as little emotion as possible, I shrugged and casually mentioned, "I planted a vegetable garden." With cup in hand, I folded my arms across my chest, and leaned back against the chair. I took an extra long sip of my drink trying to hide my smirk.

Looks of intense disappointment stared back at me. "That's why I'm so tan." I attempted to sound as indifferent as I could.

Three damp napkins bounced off my chest.

There wasn't really an elegant way to describe Sam, so I went for the bold approach. "I met a farmer."

That was definitely the wrong approach. Three pairs of horror-struck eyes starred at me.

"A farmer?" Bailey gasped.

But the unavoidable smile spreading across my face just kept getting bigger. I closed my eyes to get a clearer mental picture of him in my mind's eye.

"We just met a few days ago, but I tell you, he is nothing I ever thought a farm boy would be," I said, basking in his memory. "Instead, he's turning out to be everything I could ever hope for. I'm completely in love with him."

The shop door opened again allowing two ladies to enter, carrying another round of musky cologne, but this time, the wind rushed past me from the other direction. Instinctively, I tuned to check the rear exit. It was closed.

"Wow!" Clair exclaimed, indifferent to the draft. "That's so romantic."

All three of my friends rested back in their chairs, pondering what could be so special about a farm boy.

Shrugging off the unusual airflow, I continued my stories about Sam.

"Of course he's gorgeous, but beyond that, he is so…amazing." Words continued to flow as I reminisced of our time spent together: the first time I saw him standing by the old Ford truck, the walks through the prairie grass, laughing as we planted the garden, swimming in the pond, talking to the animals.

"How long have you known him? It seems kinda fast," Bailey said. "Besides, I thought you gave up trying to date again."

"I know. I must seem so fickle, but I can't help myself. Plus, he is so smart! He seems to know everything. He's like this history expert, and makes the United States seem like this fabulous culture museum. And science, he would make an excellent science teacher." My cheeks were getting sore from grinning so wide. "And the best part about him, is that he never makes me feel stupid." Talking about Sam made me miss him terribly.

I looked across the table at my friends. Apparently, my words needed some time to soak in.

"He sounds too good to be true," Rayyan finally commented. "How old is he? He sounds older."

"Well, a little. I'm not sure how old, exactly," I confessed. "He avoided the question when I asked him." The girls eyed me with worried expressions.

"What did he say," Clair asked flatly.

"That he was old enough to know better, but young enough not to care."

"That's not good," Bailey stated.

"It's just an old saying," Rayyan added. "You're reading too much into it."

"He's admitting he shirks responsibility," Bailey scoffed.

"Can it, Bailey. I'm beginning to think you don't like anyone," Clair said. Then she looked at me. "How old do you think he is?"

"Oh—" I really didn't want to say a number out loud. It would make the gap too real. I chewed my fingernail for a second, stalling for more time. Then I noticed my knee bouncing nervously up and down. After a heavy sigh I looked them all in the eye. "Maybe even twenty." Their reactions were not as shocked as I was expecting. Maybe they were still recovering from the farmer thing.

"What do your parents think?" Rayyan asked.

"Of course Dad wigged out, mostly because he remembers what he was like when he was young. But my mom seems to be okay with it. I think she trusts me more than Dad trusts hormones."

"If not hormones, then some other artificial aphrodisiac," Bailey sneered. "He's too old."

Of the four of us, only Bailey had had sex before. And she doesn't even remember it. She went to a party and some jerk put something in her soda. She remembers almost nothing of the party, or the rape. An adult walked in while it was happening and pulled the guy off of her. Bailey said that her father was the one who supported her through the whole ordeal, never blaming her in any way for what happened.

Rayyan's eyes suddenly went wide. "You're a minor! He could go to jail for dating you!"

The disapproval was beginning. I didn't want to hear this. Eyeing the extra napkin laying on the table, I considered stuffing it in her mouth. "It's not like he's twenty-five. Besides, we haven't even really made out yet."

"And how long do you think he's going to be content with that?" Bailey asked accusingly. "Doing nothing?"

"Well, even *I* would not be happy doing *nothing.*" I answered sharply. "Besides, the police don't drive around seeking out illegal relationships. I'm going to be eighteen in a few months and he knows I'll be a senior in the fall. He has no qualms about it. Not all guys are horny pigs."

My closing statement was definitely not as elegant as my mom might state her closing remarks to a judge and jury, but I believed it to be just as effective.

"Well, when you're barefoot and pregnant, standing in the middle of this guy's kitchen cookin' up his homemade meal, don't blame us. Just be ready for 'I told you so.'" Bailey snapped.

Or not.

I should have just stopped my useless persuasion, but I couldn't. "It's not that way at all. He's past all the high school drama we are used to."

"So why would he be interested in you?" Bailey snapped.

Pretending not to hear her, I continued, "Sam is unlike any person I have ever met."

Understanding that I was not going to convince my friends of Sam's remarkable qualities, I decided to switch gears and try another approach. Before finishing the first word in my next sentence, the voice of caution screamed out that it was a very bad idea. But too eager to show off Sam, I blatantly ignored the voice, again, and continued with my question, "Would you like to drive out and meet him?"

"Right now? Seriously?" Clair beamed.

Bailey nearly knocked the table over racing to the car.

CHAPTER TWENTY-THREE

ROAD TRIP

WITH EACH STEP towards the vehicles, my
stomach knotted tighter like it knew something I didn't.
I wracked my brain for a valid reason to take back my
offer. I plunged forward.

"Let's take two cars," Rayyan suggested. "Clair,
you ride with Emily and then I'll bring you back after
we meet Sam. That way, Em can stay behind for a little
smoochie-smoochie action." She ended her sentence
with a giggle.

With my hand on the door handle, it dawned on me
that he might not even be home. What if he was still
running errands? This was stupid. What was I trying to
prove, anyway?

Unfortunately, bad ideas usually have bigger
problems to go along with them. Since it was still
raining, we obviously weren't going to walk to Sam's
farm from my house, and that was the only sure way I
knew how to get there.

"Doesn't your phone or car have GPS or
something?" Clair asked. She always had the newest of
everything.

Annoyed, I answered, "Yes, but I don't know his
address." I dug through my glove box and found a
wrinkled map. I showed them the approximate area of
Sam's farm and the road I saw yesterday while cooling

off in the pond. Tracing the lines on the map, I followed our route. "We'll take Humphrey Road off of 24. If we pass 62nd, we've gone too far."

Clair and I made small talk about the landscape that whizzed by the car windows as we sped out into the country. She was impressed by its tranquility. I showed her the samples I picked out from the hardware store and we both laughed at the idea of me becoming a country girl. She liked the suede sample best, but I was still leaning toward sponge painting. We turned our conversation to the boy at the grocery. She admitted to only knowing his name because of his name tag. She was thinking about asking him to a movie this weekend. I complimented her on her bravery.

"What are you going to do about Alex?"

Just as she finished her question, my phone chimed.

"Well, speak of the devil." I showed her the name appearing on the screen.

I pressed the read button. "Please, talk to me."

"I feel sorry for him," I sighed, "but at the same time, he's beginning to scare me. Especially since he's doing drugs."

"Yeah," Clair agreed. "I don't know much about it, but Danny said that he looked like hell."

"I heard this story about some guy who was really high on cocaine and shot up his house with a shotgun because he was hallucinating white rats running rampant all over the place." As an afterthought, I added, "It was a really nice house, with a swimming pool."

Clair looked at me in disbelief.

"My mom is a probation officer," I said, adding authority. "He was one of her convicts."

Her eyes bugged. "In that case, I guess I'd be scared of Alex, too."

A feeling I'd never felt before shimmied up my spine. "You don't think he'd go psycho, do you?"

She thought for a moment before answering. "If anything, he'd probably commit suicide, like his dad did."

I really didn't want to hear that answer either, and the thought of poor Alex left me speechless. I guessed Clair was just as uncomfortable because the silence became enormous. Finally, her phone rang. "They want to know if we're almost there," she said.

Just then, Humphrey came to a dead end and split to either side.

"What's going on?" I asked, mostly to myself. "My map doesn't show this." Grabbing the paper, I examined it again. Letting out an exasperated huff, I really wanted to throw it out the window. "Look for a street sign."

"Hang on, we're lost," Clair said into the cell phone.

Just then, a white truck came from the east and whizzed past us, traveling south. "Hey, that looked like my Dad's truck."

"Shouldn't he be at work?" Clair reasoned.

"Yeah, it wouldn't make much sense for him to be out here." I said, dismissing the passing vehicle.

Clair took back the map and stuffed it in the glove compartment. "Just chill out and follow us. We're almost there," she said into her phone.

And then we made three wrong turns.

Clair's phone rang again. It was Bailey.

"Don't even answer it." I cranked the wheel for another u-turn."She'll just complain."

Clair spoke with her eyes. They were bordering on pity.

"This was supposed to be fun," I said, hoping to improve the mood. "Too bad the rain didn't agree." Flipping the wipers up another notch, I held the steering wheel tight as I turned back onto another section of Humphrey. That's when I saw the turn off in the distance.

Please be it!

I slowed down as I approached the next left. It was a small gravel road, with grass growing up amongst the crushed rock. I was so nervous—I didn't know if I was afraid or excited.

"This looks promising," I said, finally able to smile.

As the car crept along, the sounds of the small stones crunching beneath the tires and the swish-swash of the wipers seemed to magnify inside.

I could hardly stand it. I held my breath as Clair and I searched the landscape for signs of life.

"This is it!" My heart began to thump as the familiar grassy field came into view. "This is the pond." I tapped my finger repeatedly against the car window.

Clair leaned towards me to get a closer look. I pressed the gas pedal down in anticipation of seeing the barn and house at any second. Only the darling house and barn never came.

"What the hell?" I rolled down my window, expecting a clearer view. An old dilapidated house littered the otherwise barren field. Stomping on the brakes, the seatbelts jerked tight. Knowing I should apologize, I didn't, transfixed by the structure that almost resembled Sam's home. Nearly all the windows were smashed out and the front door was missing. Wooden roof shingles sagged heavy in the middle.

Despite the heavy rain that still poured down, I got out of the car. I still could not believe my lying eyes. A noticeable grassy mound with a few scattered wildflowers offset the nearby house. It made me think of where the barn should be, if this was Sam's house. But obviously it wasn't. It couldn't be.

Lost in my own confusion, Clair startled me as she held an umbrella over our heads. "Bailey wants to know what's going on."

"I don't know." I was embarrassed and frustrated. "I really thought this was it. I'm sorry. Let's go back to Humphrey and see if there are any more roads turning left."

Clair gave me the look.

Once again, we turned our small caravan around and headed back to the main road.

"I'm sorry, Clair," I sighed, hoping to make myself feel better, and wishing she'd tell me that getting lost was normal. But she didn't.

"I'm sure we'll find it on the next turn," she said, instead.

But that didn't happen either.

The next turn after that was 62nd. We had gone too far and had run out of roads. I pulled the car over on the shoulder and got out. Clair trailed behind me, shaking open her umbrella. Rayyan and Bailey were getting out of their own car, too.

I couldn't understand what was going on. I *knew* that was Sam's pond back there. I *knew* those were the trees that led back to my home. I was one hundred

percent positive. I opened my mouth to speak, but heard
Bailey's words instead.

"He's too good to be true," Bailey sneered,
"because he *isn't* true." She laughed bitterly.

"Give it a rest." Rayyan came to my defense.
"We're probably on the wrong road altogether."

Bailey's words stung deep and I could feel my face
get hot. I had wanted so badly to show off Sam. Instead,
I ended up looking like a fool. I fought back tears of
shame.

"Seriously, I think the mystery man is the invisible
man," Bailey continued unmercifully. "I think you are
out here all alone and dreamed up this story just to have
something to talk about. To make us jealous."

My mouth dropped open at her accusations.

"The next time you scheme up some plan and take
us out for a joy ride in the pouring rain," Bailey
continued to vent, "have the sense to figure out a better
ending!"

I forgot how to speak. My cold skin made the tears
burn as they rolled down my checks.

"What is wrong with you, Bailey?" Rayyan
demanded. "It's not like being lost is a crime, ya
know."

"Yeah, Bailey. What gives?" Even Clair agreed.

Bailey held her ground with her jaw clenched tight.

I wiped the rain and the tears from my checks and
stepped up to Bailey. Stopping five inches away from
her face, I stood up tall and straight. "I don't know what
misery has come into your life this time, but don't take
it out on me!"

Bailey's hard expression broke. Taking a step back,
she slouched, and looked down at the ground. "I'm

sorry. I'm…" The rest of her sentence was lost in a sob. "Things are pretty bad at home." She looked back up at us with red tinged eyes. "Mom left Dad and is moving in with her boyfriend."

As Rayyan let out a shocked gasp, and Clair moved closer to share her umbrella, my feelings of self-pity turned to sorrow for my friend. Life just seemed to dump on Bailey.

"Why didn't you tell us sooner?" Clair asked.

I quickly remembered back to how I felt not too long ago. "Parents sure know how to screw things up, don't they? But trust me, it will work out. I never would have met Sam if we didn't move." I bent forward until our foreheads touched and made a silly grin. "I know you. You'll be fine."

At least she giggled. "I hope so," she said.

"If you ever need anything, I will help all that I can." I pulled her in next to me for a hug. Her arms wrapped around me tight.

"We'll all be there," said Clair.

"I will be fine, won't I." Bailey nodded, giving me an extra squeeze. After she thanked me, I backed away. Clair and Rayyan offered up a hug as well.

As we stood there, the wind picked up, making the rain feel like tiny needles. Clair lowered her umbrella, completely hiding her face. "Let's get out of here. It's gonna take me forever to salvage my hair."

"You and your hair," Bailey scoffed, only to add a smile. "Though it is pretty miserable out here." She headed for the car, then looked back. "It was good to get together, Em. Just be sure you get his address and other vitals the next time you see him. We'd still like to meet him."

"If I can catch my new man, maybe we can all go out some time," Rayyan added, as she slipped into the driver's seat.

"You're going to like him!" I called out, waving goodbye.

The weather no longer seemed all that cold as I stood behind my car and watched my friends drive away. I was too caught up in feeling like a complete idiot. Somehow, I'd have to redeem myself, but I'd worry about that another day.

Right now, I had to find Sam.

CHAPTER TWENTY-FOUR

THUNDERHEADS

AS I MADE MY WAY HOME from this morning's disastrous adventure, my thoughts progressed into a sick obsession. Completely mystified by my inability to find Sam's farm, I still came back to the same conclusion: I had found the right road and the correct location.

No way could I have mistaken the pond Sam and I were in yesterday. But that created an entirely new set of absurd problems: Where *was* the charming farmhouse? Or the perfect red barn with the wooden wagon parked in the front of the double doors? Buildings just couldn't up and leave.

Then I considered an alternative scenario: could I have hit my head so hard that I gave myself some mind-altering concussion?

Nonsense!

Trusting in my friend, denial, I decided to blame today's misfortune on the map. It had to be the map. It was old and out of date.

I pressed down on the gas pedal. I couldn't get home fast enough. I *needed* something that would make me feel normal. Impatiently, I flipped on the radio and searched for a jazz station. Not finding any, I shut it off. Now I was "0 for 2."

The simple process of turning into our driveway and bumping over the railroad tracks brought an immediate sense of peace. Soon, I would be in the safety of my own bed, listening to the sounds of rain coming down upon the roof. I'd relax, pull myself together, then hike over to Sam's place.

Unexpected electronic chimes from my cell phone interrupted my state of well-being; looking at the view screen, it was another text from Alex. "Call me plz."

My mind conjured up an image of a loser drug-addict. "I should probably call your *Mom*." Wishing he'd just leave me alone, I stuffed my phone back into my purse and ignored the creepy feeling of hairs rising on the back of my neck.

As I rounded the final curve in the drive, the house came into view, along with Sam, who stood beneath the sheltering over-hang. A mile-wide grin swept across my face as I saw him dressed in his standard white shirt and well-fitting blue jeans. *Country boys.* I waved at him childishly as I passed him by to park beside the house. Jumping out of my VW, I ran toward Sam.

"Whoa there, little lady." He smiled, greeting me with his hand up in a stay-back manner.

"Oh, Sam!" I wanted to throw my arms around him, but his stance kept me at a distance. "You're a sight for sore eyes."

Dropping his defensive guard, he tilted his head to the side. "I am? Why is that?"

The realization of my actions hit me broadside. No way could I confess to what I'd been doing. "Oh," I stammered, trying to invent a story. Nothing came to mind, so I settled for, "I'm just glad to see you." Then I smiled and added, "Did you run your errand?"

"Yes, I did. Thanks for asking." Sam tilted his head in the opposite direction, as if to get a better look at me. "I was hoping to find you, in case you were planning on coming over to the farm today. There isn't much to do at my place on a day like this so I thought you might like to spend the day here, instead." He smiled again. "You don't mind, do you?"

"Not at all. I'm glad you're here," I confessed. "Have you been waiting long?"

"Nope. I just got back myself."

"You were in Topeka, right?"

Sam's eyes narrowed at the question. "Yes, ma'am. Why do you ask?"

I almost asked him if he went for coffee. "You must wear popular cologne."

"What does Topeka have to do with cologne?"

"I don't know. I'm just being random." Glancing around the yard so I could avoid the you-are-weird look he was giving me, I noticed something else unusual.

"Where's your car?" I asked.

"Well, you see...I love spring rains. I walked. I know, it's odd."

"Hey, we all have our things, but wow. You're already dry. You must have been here for a while."

Sam muffled a cough. "You caught me. I didn't want come off as some creepy guy hanging out on your door step waiting for your return because I have nothing better to do."

"Um, are you?"

Ignoring my question, he asked his own. "What were *you* doing that got you so wet?" He lifted a chunk of rain-soaked hair and let it drop.

"Oh, I just got caught in a downpour." I pointed towards the door for him to follow me inside the house. "I wanted to call you earlier today, but I never got your phone number."

"Don't have one," Sam replied, following me to the kitchen.

"What? No phone?"

"No, ma'am," he replied, shaking his head. "I'd much rather pay someone a visit."

"But how do you keep in contact with people out of state?" I asked, filling the teakettle up with water.

"The postal service. I suppose I could use a pay phone if it was that important."

"A pay phone! I thought you were a country boy, not Amish. I don't think I have ever used a pay phone before. Do they still exist?"

Sam laughed. "I guess it has been a while since I've seen one on the street corner."

I couldn't remember *ever* seeing a phone booth on a street corner in my entire lifetime. "I'm going to quick change into some dry clothes. Will you please take the kettle off the stove if it starts to whistle before I'm down?"

Nodding, he headed for a kitchen chair.

When I returned, the teakettle had been moved to the center of the stove top. "Do you drink tea?" I asked while choosing a flavor from the wooden tea box. "I started drinking it for the antioxidants. Can't be too healthy, you know."

"Love the stuff, but I'll pass, thank you," he replied politely.

"I've been thinking about it, and I like living in *the now* with all the modern gadgets. I can't imagine life without a phone." I lowered the tea bag into the steaming water. "In fact, the light is blinking on the answering machine. Excuse me while I make sure it's nothing important."

"It's mighty interesting that you'd first assume the message might not be important. I think I made my point," Sam teased.

I stuck my tongue out at him and pressed the button.

"Hey, Em," my mother's voice began, "Dr. Lui returned my phone call this morning. Believe it or not, there is an actual parasite that could have entered into your bloodstream the day you fell and hit your head. She called it an... Acanthamoeba infection." Her words sounded unnatural, like she was reading something she had jotted down from a previous conversation.

I should have hit the stop button, but I was so stunned, I had to keep listening.

"She states this illness is very rare, but abnormal taste sensations and visual disturbances are both symptoms of this infection. The prominent symptom is eye pain. Do you have any eye pain?"

I became consciously aware of my eyes, and no, they didn't hurt.

"I also told her about how upset you were about Alex and the move. Maybe you're just stressed out. Stress can play tricks on your mind, too. At any rate, she thought you should come in and be seen. Your appointment is at 3 o'clock. I'll come home and then we can go together. Love you."

The message ended.

"Ha! Mothers! They say the darndest things," I said, whirling my finger at my temple, escaping into the next room.

"You're still frettin' over all that stuff?" Sam asked, following me.

How do I respond to that? *Well, let's see, Sam, I was beginning to worry that I was experiencing psychotic episodes, and after the drive out with the girls, I'm pretty certain I am. But it's nothing to worry about, honest!*

As I took a seat on the couch, Sam sat at the other end.

"Yes, I'm still worried," I said. "Surely you could hear what my mother was saying."

Staring at the coffee table, he rubbed his chin.

"Actually, I hope I do have an amoeba running around in my head. At least then I'd know I'd get better."

"I'm sorry I didn't pay closer attention the day you brought it up. You're certain your mind is playing tricks?"

"Actually, I don't know what to think. I'm most comfortable with denial." I folded my hands and tapped my thumbs together. "Maybe I've inherited my mother's paranoia, but the flowers, and your cologne—"

"My cologne? What about my cologne?"

"Don't laugh, but I taste it. Whenever you touch me."

Sam leaned to the side, widening the gap between us. "Unusual tastes, smells… even hallucinations can all be symptomatic of a number of things. Maybe you should get your well tested for heavy metals. That seems like a logical place to start."

"Lead poisoning? Wouldn't the rest of my family be affected if the water was bad?"

"I suppose so," he said, slouching. "I reckon I was just wishing." He leaned towards me with an outstretched arm, but sheepishly withdrew his comforting gesture to scratch the back of his neck.

The ends of the couch seemed to move a mile apart. I crossed my arms. "You know something that you're not telling me."

"I know a lot of things. What do you want me to tell you?"

I wanted the truth! This was the second open invitation to ask any question. I could ask him about having coffee. I could ask him about the hug that made me choke.

I could ask who his parole officer was!

"What happened to your family?" My question came off callous.

Sam scratched his nose, like people do when they are nervous. Then he took a deep breath and blew it out through "o" shaped lips.

"Ma died in a fire." His words lacked feeling. "Pa fell apart afterwards, believing he was responsible for her death. Not long after that, he took my little sister and they moved away."

"God! That's horrible!"

He gave another heavy sigh, "I'm not finished yet. Pa took Amelia back to the Goldenrod steamboat and began singing. Although it probably wasn't in Amelia's best interest, I figure that's where Pa had his best memories of him and Ma together." Sam held a blank stare.

"My sister had a voice just like Ma's. She wanted to sing too, but Pa wouldn't stand for it. Performing wasn't like it used to be. It'd turned...almost cheap.

They had heated arguments." Sam's head sunk a little lower. "Then one night, Amelia stormed off after a fight. They found her floating in the Mississippi the next morning."

I concealed a gasp beneath my hand.

"Pa died, shortly thereafter." Sam's head dropped completely. Without a sound, he took his hands and combed them through his curly hair. He looked up with a half smile and tears in his eyes.

I slid down the length of the couch to be beside him and held his hand. The sweet, smoky taste prickled my tongue. "I can't imagine being the only one left in the family…"

Sam looked deep into my eyes. Once again, searching. Searching for comfort, or understanding, or maybe rejection. "What if I told you I wasn't the sole survivor?"

His statement caught me off guard. His hand slipped through my fingers. "Who else is there?"

Sam stood up. "Never mind."

"Please tell me," I pressed.

He took a seat in an adjacent chair facing me. His expression was torn and he fuddled with his lower lip.

"Remember when I told you that things are not always as they seem?" he finally said.

I searched through my memories and nodded.

"Most of my life has not been what it seems." Sam looked down at the floor and then returned his gaze. "Against my better judgment, I am growing quite fond of you, Miss Emily. You are kind, smart and very beautiful. But age is not our only barrier."

The words he spoke about me were sweet, but they did not come across as complimentary. It sounded more like the start of a confession. Oh man! This was it. I was going to hear—

"BBRRRIIINNNGGGG!" Both Sam and I jumped. "Brrriiinnnngggg." It rang again.

What timing! "I should get it, in case it's about my appointment," I said apologetically.

"Hello?" I watched Sam stand up and stretch. Casually, he walked about, appraising the interior of the house. It struck me as odd how soft his footsteps were on the hardwood floor compared to my own, especially in his heavy leather boots.

I hung up the phone. "That was my mom, checking in on me."

"You have a great ma," he said, sitting back down, but this time on the edge of the seat. He gestured for me to join him.

Sam took in a deep breath and exhaled slowly. I could smell the sweet, musky smell in his breath. *Did he drink his cologne?*

"Emily, what I'm trying to tell you is—"

"Vvvvvrrrrr." My cell phone vibrated loudly on the wooden table.

I looked at him with disbelief, but didn't budge. "I'm sorry." *What were the odds?*

"It must be the fate of the gods," Sam said coolly, rising from his seat, again. "I can see now why you enjoy modern technology."

I looked at him uneasily. I looked at him like he was somebody who just told me that he never wanted to see me again.

"Aren't you even going to see who called?" he asked sourly.

I picked up my cell, expecting it to be another lame text from Alex. It was a text from my dad. "Love you."

"I don't know what's gotten into everyone. First my mom calls, now it's a text from my dad."

This time, Sam avoided my gaze. "The air feels like it could storm."

"I suppose you would know. You *are* the farmer." I hoped for a smile, but his lips didn't even twitch. He just stood there, looking large and uneasy.

He moved over to a window and pulled the curtain aside. "I don't like storms," he said, peering out.

"You look a little big to be afraid of the weather." I tried to sound cheery.

He just shrugged. "I should go before it hits."

CHAPTER TWENTY-FIVE

LIGHTNING STRIKES

"DON'T GO," I said, hoping not to sound too
desperate. "I've got something that will take your mind
off the weather."

The tension on Sam's face broke, but his smile still
appeared guarded. "What might that be?"

Suddenly my invitation took on a perverted quality.
I felt my temperature rise. "My guitar. Can I play my
guitar for you?"

Brown leather boots crossed the floor. "I'd like that
very much."

"I keep it in the loft. That area is just for me." I led
him up the stairs to where my guitar waited.

The loft was open to below, furnished with a couple
of wooden chairs for playing instruments and two more
that were suitable for listening and relaxing. A stereo
sat against the wall, underneath a wide window. Two
pieces of art hung on either side of the window. They
were the most treasured paintings in the house,
according to Mom.

Sam took immediate notice of them and remarked
on their creativeness. "Let me guess, fifth grade art
class?"

"This one is mine." I pointed to a girl swinging on a
tire swing. "And this one Kitty painted of herself,
playing poker with Grandma and Grandpa."

He laughed out loud. "Stop pulling my leg."

"Really. They love playing cards. And she loves to catch Grandpa cheating."

Still curious, Sam peered down the opposing hallways. "What's down that-a-way?"

"The bedrooms."

Sam's smile faded. "Is it all right that I am up here?"

I was taken back by his question. "Oh, yes," I answered, admiring his apparent reputable nature. "Thank you for asking."

"I suppose I should meet your parents, sometime," he said, looking not all that happy.

"They will like you." I smiled, walking over to my guitar resting in its stand. "Please take a seat and get comfortable." I eloquently gestured to one of the comfy chairs like I was a TV game show model.

He took a sturdy chair instead and moved it next to mine so we'd be sitting face-to-face. Despite his anti-touch attitude, I liked the way he liked to be close, and wondered what he was afraid of.

"I don't know any jazz tunes," I apologized. "Is there anything else you'd like to hear?" I picked up my guitar and strummed it just to make sure it was in tune. It was unlikely that I knew how to play any of his favorites, but it seemed polite just to ask.

"Only *your* favorite," he responded, pointing directly at me, personalizing the statement all the more.

"That's easy," I stated, but shifted nervously on my chair. I felt a bit awkward, playing my music for the first time in front of Sam.

Rhythmic sounds quickly filled the loft as I picked the notes of my musical lariat. My strumming became bold and crisp and any trace of apprehension vanished into thin air. I could tell that Sam liked my song too. He was leaning back against the chair with his eyelids closed, keeping time with gentle nods.

When my song finally ended, a crooked smile came across his face. "That song moves my soul. Does it have a name?"

"Naw, it's something I wrote."

"Hmm," Sam murmured. He continued to face me, for what seemed an entire minute. He looked to be puzzling over something, so I sat there, looking back at him, feeling rather uncomfortable.

"Will you play me another?" he finally asked.

But I didn't stop at one more. I played through my entire list of songs.

"How many years did you take lessons?" Sam asked, realizing the concert was over.

"Just one. It comes naturally for me." I offered my guitar to Sam. "Would you like to try?"

"Oh, gosh, no." He leaned back like I held the black plague. "How about your other instruments? Where are they?"

"They're in my room," I said, taking note of the heavy, dark clouds appearing outside the window. I stood up, flicked on the light switch and returned to my seat.

"Oh." Sam sounded disappointed. "I was hoping you'd get them."

"Sorry, I only play those in school."

"That's too bad. Are you familiar with Garvin Bushell?"

I was not.

"He was an incredible musician—the first to play the oboe in *any* jazz band. Then came Yusef Lateef who played both the oboe and the bassoon in his jazz performances."

"I've heard of Lateef before. He won some kind of musician's award not too long ago."

"I'll tell ya, if you ever heard either of these men play, you'd be hooked on jazz. The next time we're in town, we need to find you a recording."

"A recording? That'd be great. I actually tried to find some jazz on the radio today. Maybe we could even take in a show aboard the Goldenrod. Er, or, not. I'm sure it wouldn't make it as one of your top ten vacation destinations. I'm really sorry to have been so thoughtless."

Sam bowed his head for a moment. "What happened to my sister was really horrible, but I don't blame the ship. I can understand why Pa went back there. It created its own kind of energy." Sam's expression slowly grew. "It had the best of everything, and for its time, it was *huge*. It could hold more than a thousand passengers."

"Sam, you just light up talking about it."

"As kids, we used to stand on the furniture, pretending we were the entertainers. Pa even took us there once. Ma made us plug our ears when we passed by the vaudeville stage, though."

"Risqué, huh?"

"It wasn't for kids. Pa made me promise not to tell Ma when he let me watch the first few minutes of the show."

"No way." I was thinking he'd tell me something racy about the production, but Sam's face dropped instead.

"It'd be my pleasure to take you there, unfortunately, she's not sailing anymore." Then he stood up. A new smile formed as he took my hand, guiding me up from my chair. "You could have been a star on the Goldenrod."

Licking the taste between my lips, I asked, "What happened to it?"

Sam peered out the window again, drawing my attention to the now black rain clouds, the kind that always produced the heaviest of rains. A worried look crossed his face, but he proceeded to lead me to one of the over-stuffed chairs and motioned for me to sit.

"You'd be surprised by how quickly things can tarnish if not properly looked after. I heard she's on the National Historic List, but in rough shape." His smile faded and his eyes grew dim. "Like so many American highlights, even the Blackstone Theatre is no longer the diamond it used to be. It's been turned into a school. Times change, and with it, so do ideas of entertainment. Motion pictures changed a lot of things."

Motion pictures?

Sam's strange habit of using out-of-date words reminded me of my grandfather who used to call the refrigerator an "ice box" even though he hadn't used one since he was twelve. I cut my own smile short after noticing the lack of one on Sam's face as he sat next to me.

"I'll tell you what, big boy," I said, using a seductive May West tone. "If my new school has a drama department, I'll arrange for you to have front row seating on opening night. That is, if I get a part." I laughed at myself.

He laughed too. "That is the finest invitation I've received in quite some time."

A lull in the conversation allowed for Sam's eyes to wander. "This is a nice home you have."

I nodded.

"It sure could use some paint, though."

"Are you offering? Do you like to paint?" I asked eagerly. "I'm trying to convince Dad to put that on the top of the 'to do' list." I scanned the walls, envisioning splashes of life to offset its bleakness.

Sam stretched back against the chair, putting his hands behind his head. "I suppose I could be bribed into helping." A mischievous grin spread across his face.

"What kind of bribe?" I batted my eyelashes.

Sam's hands came to rest against the edge of his chair and he pressed his weight toward me. "Miss Emily, you could definitely get me into a heap of trouble."

I focused on his lips. They looked irresistible. I imagined myself locked inside his steel arms for a passionate kiss. The kiss I'd been waiting for.

I leaned forward so that our lips were just inches apart. "What kind of trouble might that be?"

Sam pressed his lips together hard. With the devil in his eyes, he leaned back against the chair, stretched his arms out, and finally repositioned his hands back behind his head.

I had to admit, flirting was fun; pretending you don't get it when you very well do, watching boys squirm in their chairs trying to be all cool and collected when they really want to plant one on you, but don't know if they should.

"So, your daddy owns a gun shop, huh?" Sam grinned.

I giggled.

"What makes you so sure your mama would spring me from the tank?"

"We were just talking about you being in jail," I said, then wished I hadn't.

"Me in jail?" Sam bolted upright. "You were talking? With who? I didn't think anybody knew."

Oh crap! Maybe I am glad I said it. Did he just admit to being an ex-convict? Were my fears true after all? If not his family, who did he murder?

Panic gripped my insides and twisted as I realized he was between me and the stairs.

"Relax. I'm pulling your leg." he said, easing back into his chair.

"That's not funny!" *Well, maybe it is, but...* Why I continued to ignore all the red flags I had about Sam, I had no idea. Besides the fact he was tall, dark, and handsome, and smart, and funny, and he liked me. And I *really* liked him.

"I ran into my friends this morning and incidentally, your name came up."

"Incidentally, huh?" Sam gave me the eye.

I tried to think of a way to get out of the hole I'd just thrown myself into.

"Is that all I am to you, incidental?" He obviously enjoyed his turn at making me squirm. "Actually, I saw you this morning, at the coffee shop," Sam admitted.

"What?" I was horrified at the possibility he may have overheard my failed plan to find him. "When? I didn't see you."

"I didn't want to intrude. Plus, I know what city girls tend to think about us *farmers.*"

Morbid embarrassment rushed to my face. He had overhead me. But where was he? I never saw him. Only when the man and woman came in through the front door…I… tasted him!

"Emily, what's wrong?"

What was happening to me? And why did it always seem to revolve around Sam? The now-you-see-it-now-you-don't experiences. *Am I really going crazy?* My cheeks went from hot to cold. I felt a little dizzy. Maybe I was still lying next to the stream where I fell and I'm in some coma? *Oh God, let me wake up!*

"Emily?" Sam put his hand on my knee. "Are you okay?"

The taste, Sam's taste, settled on my tongue. I looked at his hand on my knee. My heartbeat quickened. I looked at Sam. I was afraid. Overwhelmed by circumstances that just didn't add up, tears welled up in my eyes. I wanted to ask him if he was part of an elaborate dream I was having, but I knew that would only confirm that I was completely insane. I slapped my hand over my mouth to keep it shut before any sounds of panic could escape.

"Miss Emily?" Sam's expression became a mixture of emotion.

Words rattled around in my head.

Just then, a tremendous crack of lightning hit the house, shaking the structure violently. Brilliant light flashed through the many windows, illuminating the interior with a giant silver explosion. Instantly, all the color drained from Sam's body and his large frame began to flicker. A deep hum turned shrill instantly and without warning, the albino white Sam exploded into a million pieces. Its blast punched the air from my lungs.

Gulping in a fresh breath of oxygen, my hands became a barrier between reality and the horrifying world of visual hallucinations. Heavy rain began to beat down upon the roof while the sounds of thunder continued to rumble.

"Emily, look at me," Sam's gentle voice commanded.

I kept my hands across my eyes, quite certain that mental illness had taken me hostage.

"The lightning—"

"Don't say a word!" I barked. I needed to think. I pushed my hands up through my hair and felt the cool dampness of a nervous sweat. Afraid to look at him, I kept my eyes low only to notice tiny beads of water glistening over my arms, legs…everywhere. I questioned if I'd ever changed out of my damp clothes at all. Over the next couple breaths, I forced my mind to focus on what I thought I saw happen to Sam. My eyes had always been my foundation to my belief system. *People don't blow up.*

Unable to trust my eyesight, I was at an extreme disadvantage as I desperately tried to conjure a psychological reason for what just happened. *Was it possible for the lightning to enter the house through an open window, creating the appearance of Sam exploding?*

I slowly lifted my eyes to face Sam's remorseful expression.

He opened his mouth. "You're not crazy."

CHAPTER TWENTY-SIX

PSYCHOLOGICAL WARFARE

I SCREAMED IN TERROR as another strike of silver lightning flashed, throwing light in every direction. A second, more powerful wind shear ripped through the loft and made my eardrums pop. Thunder shook the house and vibrated beneath my feet.

"Emily—" Sam called out, but his voice was the wrong pitch.

Confused, as if I'd been struck by lighting myself, I peered around the loft. I was all alone.

"Emily—" the voice repeated. The echoing sounds of footsteps trailed through the house. "Emmy? I'm home."

Another intense blaze of lightning flashed, leaving white streaks in my eyesight; a voice called out to me, but it was unrecognizable. Nothing made sense. My eyes, ears, and brain could not be trusted. They were all playing tricks on me.

The voice called out a fourth time, finally sounding familiar. *Mother! My mother is home for my appointment with Dr. Lui!*

Her voice rang painfully in my ears. I shut my eyes tight, as if it would magically mute the chaos roaring in my head. I dug my nails into the chair cushions, scared to let go.

What is happening to me?

As her footsteps grew close, my stomach churned, turning on a heat that swarmed my entire body. Within the heat was fear that squeezed tight around my throat like a murderous villain shutting off my air supply. Time seemed to stand still as I heard her footsteps echo up the stairwell, one slow step after another.

"Here you are, Honey."

The touch of her hand on my shoulder made me jump out of my chair, ready to defend myself.

"Emily! For heaven's sake. What is wrong?"

In a desperate attempt to pull myself together, I took in a deep breath but it merely forced its way back out as a quivering sob. I sucked in more air, and somehow managed to hold it in. I could not admit to her what had just happened. Doing so would force me to admit it to myself. My brain raced for something to say, but everything I could think of sounded psychotic. I envisioned microscopic amoebas scurrying around my brain. I let the air out; this time, the exhale was more controlled. I knew what I had to ask.

"Did you see Sam leave?"

She gave me a worried look. "No. Was he here?"

I gave her a pathetic smile. "I didn't think so." I was beginning to think he was never here.

"Is everything all right?"

"I'm not sure."

She took my hand and led me down the steps. We walked into the sunroom and sat on the brand new love seat. Thick sheets of rain clouded the large glass windows.

"Quite a storm we're having, huh?" she asked.

I nodded.

"About Sam..."

The muscles in my back turned rigid. "What about him?"

Folding her hands in her lap, Mom looked at me with a tight lipped smile. Then the smile disappeared. "I received a phone call from your friend, Clair, this morning."

I could tell from her voice that she was concerned. But why would *Clair* call my mother? Mom must have meant to say *Alex*. Clair must have decided to do something about Alex, so she called my mom, the probation officer.

"Among other things, she said that you and your friends drove out to meet Sam today."

Anxiety wrapped a band around my chest and it hurt to breathe. Staring at Mom, I had no idea what to say. I swallowed hard.

"She said that you couldn't find Sam's house."

My ears turned hot. Clair called my mother, about *me*? Clair was more worried about me than Alex?

Enraged, I yelled, "Does she think I'm nuts, too?"

"Nobody thinks you're nuts, Emily, but people are worried," she said calmly.

"I knew it! Who else thinks I'm cracked?"

"Stop calling yourself names. It doesn't help by overreacting."

"Overreacting?!" I yelled even louder, "I'm not the one calling other people's mothers and interfering in other people's business just because they get lost!"

"Dad tried to find it too, Honey."

My mind flashed back to the white truck that drove past us this morning. It *had been* my father's truck! "Now you have Dad in on it, too?"

Mom gave me a frustrated look. "There is no farm,
Emily." She paused for a moment. "The only farm that
has ever been there burned down in 1936."

The room became as quiet as death. I sat still,
thinking of all the crazy things that I had been
experiencing. Had I been imagining the whole thing,
Sam and all? After all, he was no longer here.

Was my mind truly capable of creating an entire
fantasy out of the skeletal remains of an old shack? Did
my mind create all the beautiful wild flowers, the barn,
the steel windmill, and little vegetable garden? Mom sat
next to me, quiet and patient. I leaned back, crossing
my arms across my chest and continued to sit, and
think.

Sam, or *whatever* I was hallucinating was right. I
wasn't crazy, I was completely insane! Real people
don't blow up.

"Well then." I slapped my hands on my knees. "I
guess we better not be late for my doctor's
appointment."

Sitting in the passenger's seat of Mom's car, I focused
on her tight grip around the steering wheel. "Are you
worried for me?"

She looked over at me briefly, then returned her
eyes to the road. "No. I am hopeful."

"Why would you be hopeful?"

"Because there are things such as antibiotics, and
the practice of bloodletting was retired many years
ago."

"Gosh, Mom."

She flashed a quick grin and patted my thigh.
"Keeping a sense of humor is the best medicine anyone

can prescribe." Her hand returned to the wheel. "Life sucks sometimes. You need to learn how to roll with the punches."

"How do you cope?" I asked.

"Hmmm, first I sulk. Then I count my blessings. Remember Job? He lost everything. His children, his health, his home, but his faith never wavered. God blessed him for that and restored all that was lost."

"What about his children?"

"Job went on to have more children."

"So if I died, you'd just have another one to replace me?"

"No, silly. I would miss you terribly, but I would also look forward to seeing you again in Heaven. Besides, you're not dying!"

I had to pause and digest this information. "Why did Job suffer?" I finally asked.

"God used Job to be an example for us. We can be assured that God is in control and He knows of our good and bad times." Mom turned and smiled my way. "Even times like this."

Times like this. Times like when I visit farms that no longer exist? Times like when the guy inside my house explodes into a one hundred mile an hour wind gust?

I continued to question God's plan for me when Mom pulled into a parking spot in front of the clinic. It no longer looked like a place of healing. Its large stern exterior was perfectly symmetrical in shape. Judging. With great condemnation.

As she put the car into park, intense nausea gurgled up deep from within. Swallowing hard, I put my hand on the car handle and pushed the door open. Waiting for me at the front of the car, Mom held out her hand for me to grab. Her hand was moist.

"At least the rain has stopped," I said.

As we walked to the entrance, I spotted Dad's white truck already parked nearby.

"Dad's here."

"Yes."

A band squeezed tight around my chest. Fear and the impulse to run gripped my body. I would run! As fast as I could! Until I was somewhere safe, but where? I frantically looked around the parking lot; maybe I could grab a pole and refuse to let go. A disturbing low laugh welled up from my stomach as I pictured the evening news: *Crazy Girl Holds Self Hostage at Clinic.*

Mom looked at me with alarm in her eyes.

For a brief instant, I wished I could trade places with Job—at least he was sane!

I could no longer breathe. I choked on the air. Mother gave my hand a firm squeeze.

"I'm scared, Mom."

"Relax. It's going to be okay."

But I didn't believe it. Amoebas or not, knowing that I had lost control of my mind was more than I could handle. I was not like Job. My feet turned into heavy cement blocks. I started shaking. I leaned over and my stomach heaved. As the contents from my stomach splattered over the asphalt, I overheard my mother talking on her cell.

"John, come outside. We need help."

Still bent over, I looked up to see my father and two men dressed in scrubs walking quickly towards me. My vision was blurred from tears forced out from throwing up. Spit stuck to my lip and hung there like some disgusting drunk.

The men drew close. A surge of panic hit my body. I flung my arms wildly and pushed hard at anything in my way. Mom went flying backwards. As I was making a run for it, strong hands grabbed my arms and became tighter as I struggled to get away.

"No! Please no! Let me go!" I yelled and begged, flailing my arms and kicking my legs as hard as I could.

"Careful Smitty! She's like a wild cat," a man's voice hollered.

"A wild cat! That's *my daughter*," Dad yelled back. "Don't hurt her!"

Hands continued to grip my arms, neck, and back. Strange faces appeared all around me. Heavy bodies forced me to the ground, crushing me into compliance. People chattered all at once, but in the madness, I heard a new voice.

"Let me in!" he ordered.

CHAPTER TWENTY-SEVEN

HONESTY HURTS

"TAKE THESE THINGS OFF ME!" I yanked my arms against the tethers that restrained me to the hospital bed. I was being forced into submission from my outburst. Other people dressed in hospital garb paid little attention to me.

"Emily, dear." Mom reached out and stroked the top of my head. "You need to stay calm."

Her words stung like venom.

"Calm? You're not the one tied up, traitor!" I hated her more than anything. "You knew they were going to do this, didn't you?"

"Hold on there," Dad said, walking in the room. "The straps will come off, if you promise to chill out."

I studied Dad's face, then I looked over at Mom. She nodded. I flopped my head back against the pillow. "Fine."

Mom gave Dad a look and he proceeded to untie the restraint.

A staff member came up to Dad with his mouth open like he was ready to speak.

"Back off, Chum," Dad spoke in his gruffest voice.

I gently shook my freed wrist.

"Is that better?" Dad asked. His voice was low and even.

"Yeah." I looked around the room, which was really a partitioned segment of a larger area divided by fabric suspended from the ceiling. People dressed in scrubs pretended not to listen.

Dad looked at Mom a second time. He proceeded to free my other arm.

"We came here for an appointment with Dr. Lui." Mom's tone was quite serious. "If you're ready, I think it best to continue with that plan, don't you?"

I arched my brow, shrugging my shoulders. "I guess I'm okay with that."

Mom left through a split in the curtain, only to reenter a few minutes later with a woman and a man on either side.

"Emily," Dr. Lui greeted me by name. She had been caring for me since I was three. "Let's try and figure out what is going on with you." Her tone was friendly and upbeat. "Your parents have told me some things about your symptoms and situation; however, my colleague and I would like to get the information directly from you."

I managed a fake smile for Dr. Lui. Eyeing the man next to her, I already knew I didn't like him. He wore an expression that suggested he was superior to everyone else in the room. The longer I looked at him, the more I disliked him, and regarded his nose too small for his face.

"Why is the patient not restrained?" he asked. His tone of voice was critical, and maybe even sounding a bit disappointed.

"This is Dr. Kendall. He is one of our staff psychiatrists," Dr. Lui stated, a bit uneasily.

The man cleared his throat at his introduction, then pushed his nose higher into the air.

I saw Dad send a look to Mom. I got the feeling they didn't like him, either.

"Restraints are no longer necessary, Dr. Kendall. Emily simply panicked, that's all," Dr. Lui continued.

Kendall scrunched his face like he already disapproved about something. "So tell me, what brings you here today?"

Focusing on Dr. Lui, I told them about slipping and hitting my head on the rocks in the creek. Also about the lack of hand-eye coordination that seemed unusual for me. Elaborating on the walks with Sam, I disclosed the strange sensation that I could taste him, and how some things seemed to appear when I was with him.

"Things seemed to appear?" Dr. Kendall echoed, his voice taking on new vibrancy.

"Well, not really appear, more like not remembering them to be there in the first place."

"These experiences are limited to the times you are with Sam, am I understanding that correctly?" Dr. Kendall asked.

"At first, yes. Then today, the taste occurred at the coffee shop while I was with my friends…but, I guess I *was* talking about him."

Dr. Kendall jotted something in his notebook. "I hear that you have basically withdrawn from most of your friendships."

"I moved to a new town. Today was the first day I'd seen them since being in Silver Lake."

"Tell me your feelings about that, the move," he said.

"At first I was devastated! I didn't know how to handle saying goodbye to my social life, my senior year." *Did he just smile?*

"It sounds traumatic." Kendall's words came off coldhearted. "Did the news of moving produce any dreams about being rescued or saved?"

"Excuse me?"

"Your history involves a horrific auto accident involving your grandparents. They both died and you nearly lost your foot. As a four year old child, you claimed that a fireman rescued you; however, firefighters never arrived on the scene. Only the police."

I didn't know what to say. "I was four years old. I must have been confused."

"Tell me about Alex."

"He's a boy I used to know."

"*Others* described him as more than that." Dr. Kendall turned to face my father. "Is your daughter sexually active?"

Dr. Lui's jaw dropped.

Dad turned a little pale and said nothing.

"Herpes encephalitis can produce the type of hallucination your daughter is describing. Maybe we should screen for STDs."

The words the doctor spoke made my head spin. *Was herpes encephalitis what Mozart died from and did he just accuse me of having sex with Alex?*

"No, Dr. Kendall," Mom said with an irritated sigh. "I'm sure we don't have to worry about STDs."

"Ahh, the ever-trusting parent, Mrs. Stokes." After a brief smile, he continued with his line of questioning.

"Did you like to partake in any known chemical substances—legal or otherwise—while pregnant?

"Certainly not!" Mom snapped.

"Any instances of bi-polar, depression, schizophrenia, or other mental illness in the family?" His voice gradually increased in pitch.

Mom seemed unprepared for that question. She looked over at my father and he shook his head. "There is not," she answered.

"Dr. Kendall, if I may," Dr. Lui spoke up.

Kendall turned to face Dr. Lui directly. "Schizophrenia *can* occur without a previous family history. There is evidence of social withdrawal and clear signs of delusions and olfactory hallucinations. Additionally, this may not even be the only time she's had breaks with reality. The early childhood *dream* could very well have been the primary break…as a reaction to great stress." He spoke to Dr. Lui as if she were his student.

Ignoring the rest of us in the room, he continued with his diagnosis. "Needless to say, it's obvious the patient viewed the move as a tremendous stressor…thus creating a magical land to help deal with it." Dr. Kendall's face almost beamed. "A prescription of Seroquel should control the hallucinations and delusions."

"Are you suggesting schizophrenia?" Mom gasped. "What about depression? Bizarre things can occur when people are depressed."

Kendall's mouth flipped into a tangled snarl. "Teenagers commit suicide over broken hearts, not develop reactive psychosis!"

"Dr. Kendall!" Mom regained her professional composure. "I am quite certain you are jumping to conclusions without thoroughly evaluating my daughter's condition or symptoms. I hardly believe that a medication like Seroquel is in order."

The lines in Kendall's face went flat. "Would you prefer Thorazine?"

Dr. Lui opened her mouth to speak, only to be silenced by the palm of Dr. Kendall's hand in front of her face.

"Mrs. Stokes," Kendall began, quite condescendingly. "I'm sure it must be very stressful watching your daughter suffer like this." He looked my way, and then returned his gaze towards my mother. "But we all know that *the farm doesn't exist!*"

"Get this jackass out of here!" Dad's face turned crimson red.

"No need for temper, Mr. Stokes." Then Kendall turned to Mom. "We can run all the tests you like, but the facts won't change." With a spiteful sneer, he slipped his pen in his pocket, spun around, and strode out the door with his chin held high.

"Elizabeth, John, and dear, sweet Emily." Dr. Lui's expression was one of astonishment. "I am embarrassed by my colleague's behavior."

"Never in my life—" Dad's skin color slowly returned to normal. "What rock did he crawl out from?"

"He's new," Dr. Lui offered as some kind of apology, then turned toward me. "I am so sorry! I asked him to join me in hopes he could help, not create hysteria." She waved her hand in the air erratically to emphasize the drama.

I didn't know what to say or do. *Stupid jerk.* Staring at the gray wall, a question popped into my head. "Can I go home now?"

"We would like to keep you here overnight, just to be on the safe side," Dr. Lui replied. "The lab tech should be here shortly to draw some blood. Despite some previous rash statements, I believe we have several different options to rule out before we make any firm diagnosis."

"Will I have to go to the Psych Ward?"

"No, you will not." Sitting down on the side of my bed, Dr. Lui smiled reassuringly. "You'll be moved upstairs to pediatrics."

That made me feel a little better.

Dr. Lui stood. "I know you are afraid, but you're in good hands. Your parents love you very much."

"We're here for you, Em." Dad placed his hand on my shoulder. I felt the weight of Mom's hand rest upon my other.

Dr. Lui left, leaving my parents and me alone to talk about nothing of consequence. We all agreed the weather was nice, and it would be great to have a swimming pool, but couldn't decide who would have to pick all the leaves out of it. We talked about getting a contra bassoon before school started back up in the fall. We talked about Mom gardening and Dad fishing. We talked about everything we could possibly think of, so we could avoid talking about me, or Sam, or the fact I was currently lodging in the hospital.

We were occasionally interrupted by the hospital staff, including an elderly women who presented us with a butt-load of papers to sign so I could be properly admitted as a patient and receive treatment, a man who needed to collect a sample of my blood, the orderly who escorted us to my room, and finally a young looking nurse who identified herself as Brandy, who would be on the clock till eleven pm. Among other things, she informed us that she usually didn't work second shift, but had switched with a co-worker who wanted to attend an out-of-town concert.

"By the way," Brandy said, handing me a hospital gown. "Your dinner should be arriving shortly."

It was then I realized I should have at least packed an overnight bag.

Mom and Dad brought their dinner up from the cafeteria so we could all eat together. My parents both had spaghetti. My meatloaf was delivered just in time. We were all pleasantly surprised by the tastiness of the hospital food, and for a second, I forgot where I was.

"Where's Kat?" I asked, finishing my last bite of roll.

"Sleepover at Britt's house," Mom replied.

The three of us sat in silence with our empty plates.

"I'll bring a puzzle tomorrow for us to work on," Dad suggested.

His idea was well intended, but made my meatloaf turn over as I realized I might be in here for a while.

Silence crept in again.

"I'll call the nurse for an extra blanket and stay here with you tonight," said Mom.

Somehow the idea sounded revolting. I was becoming desperate for some alone time, to try and come to grips with life. That would be next to impossible with Mom hanging around.

"You don't have to stay. There's no sense in both of us getting a bad night's sleep."

"I can't leave you alone—"

"You heard Dr. Lui. I'm in good hands here."

Mom looked at Dad.

"It's your call," he said.

After too many hugs and kisses, Mom and Dad went home. At first, I pretended to relax by stretching out over the bed. Quickly becoming bored and very *un*-relaxed, I had some fun pushing the buttons controlling the electric bed, curious to see how high each end would raise.

That too lost its novelty.

A television was suspended from the wall in front of me, but there was nothing I wanted to watch. It would only show people suffering. No wonder I had invented Sam; I saw my life just as miserable as the ones portrayed on television. My heart ached for him.

With a deep sigh, I knew I was only putting off the unavoidable. It was time to accept the reason why I was in the hospital… to face the reality that I didn't want to admit. Strange though, the possibility of having a rare brain infection didn't bother me so much, nor did the accusation of having a true form of psychosis. Either of those two explanations for my recent strange events would be the easy part to handle.

My throat began to sting as I mournfully considered the idea that my greatest source of joy was not real, and would soon come to an end with the remedy of my illness.

Bailey was right again. I was in love with someone who was too good to be true.

CHAPTER TWENTY-EIGHT

THE INTERNET

ALTHOUGH IT WAS LATE in the evening, I found myself restless and awake. Maybe I was afraid to fall asleep—afraid Sam would not be a part of tomorrow. I scanned the room and found comfort in a small piece of artwork hanging on the otherwise gray wall. It reminded me of Sam; he was my artwork in an otherwise gray world. He had brought so much beauty into my life. What would I do without him? Holding back the tears, I pulled the covers up to my chin.

Still not ready to end the illusion, I returned to the memory of playing my guitar for Sam; the last place I'd ever see him. Ignoring the freakish parts, I concentrated on his smiling face while I played my song for him. This memory helped ease the emptiness I felt, yet at the same time, intensified the pain crushing down upon me.

Just when I was about to call mom and ask her to come back, it dawned on me she said something about a communal computer in a nearby waiting room. Perhaps I could use it? I pushed the red call button located on the side of my bed. Brandy, the young nurse, arrived a short while later.

"Do you need something?"

Obviously I did, that was why I pushed the button, but I let it go. "Yes, I was wondering if I could use the computer out in the waiting room?"

"Hmm." She pressed her lips together. "Let me check your chart for restrictions."

Hearing the word "restrictions" caused me to stiffen.

Brandy disappeared out the door and returned with a clipboard full of papers. Her pointed finger zigzagged across the board as she silently skimmed through the pages.

"This area of the hospital is rather quiet tonight. I don't see why not," she finally said. "I'll still be able to observe you from the nurses' station."

Observe? While her nursing verbage made my skin crawl, knowing I had something to keep my mind occupied seemed to take an invisible weight off my shoulders. "Where is it located?"

Tossing the chart on the foot of my bed, she turned around and faced outward toward the hall. "It's down the east corridor," she said, pointing to the left. Then she turned around to face me again. "Can't be more than twenty feet. You won't miss it. There's a small visitors' kitchenette directly across the hall. Help yourself to some hot chocolate, tea, or fruit juice if you like. You might even be able to find some crackers."

"Wow, thank you!" I responded in earnest.

"We even have a bathrobe for you to wear." Brandy walked over to the tiny closet and gave the sticky door a mighty yank. "These hospital gowns can be a bit drafty," she said, giving me the, you-know-what-I-am-talking-about-look while fanning her rear end.

I grinned, thinking how glad I was that I didn't respond sarcastically towards her first comment. She was quickly becoming a huge asset at making my time here more like a hotel stay rather than a dungeon lockdown.

"I just *love* helping people," Brandy said, handing me the robe. "That's why I became a nurse."

"I can tell," I said. "It shows."

"Thanks. If there's nothing else, I'll be on my way then. Enjoy the computer." Brandy smiled, and then left to go about her own business, forgetting my patient chart still at the end of my bed.

I thought of her as friendly, but not very professional. Just as I was about to call after her, it dawned on me to take a look at my chart for myself. I snatched it up like a misbehaving toddler. My name appeared at the top, naturally, but what was *next* to my name in bold red letters made me choke on my own spit: "SUPERVISION REQUIRED."

What? Supervision? Like Brandy really has to observe me?

I scanned the first paragraph that simply contained my demographic information. "Admitting Circumstances" followed. "The patient presented as a hysterical white 17-year-old female exhibiting severe visual and olfactory hallucinations. Patient was agitated upon arrival and behavior increased into aggressive physical outburst. Further fits of violence may be treated with Ativan prn. Patient admits to a marked deterioration in social networks prior to hospitalization. Depression may be present, but not likely to manifest current symptoms. Diagnosis: Rule out Schizophrenia."

"What happened to the little creatures scurrying around inside my brain?" I asked myself. "The report didn't even mention anything about me falling or hitting my head." I thought that was why I was here, to be evaluated for an infection, or a concussion…or something!

I skipped down to the physician signature. It was signed Dr. Richard Kendall. Bastard! I wondered if people called him "Dick." He didn't even mention me hitting my head! I hated that piece of crap more than ever! Stupid idiot! The idea of ripping up my chart crossed my mind, but I decided that would only give Dr. Kendall more evidence of violence, so I returned it to the hook outside my door.

After slipping on the yellow hospital robe, I continued to internally bash "Dick-face" as I plodded down the hallway for some hot chocolate, a keyboard, and a chance to clear my mind.

The dust had already settled from pouring the chocolate mix into my styrofoam cup. It took me a while longer to realize where to find the hot water. Stirring my heated beverage, I marveled over the simplistic pleasure of preparing my own hot cocoa. If nothing else, being strapped down to a hospital bed let me appreciate firsthand what I normally took for granted. *That* was one of the most disturbing experiences, in my life, *ever.* But then, I've been having more of those lately.

Reflecting on the day's events, I thanked God, believing that my illness would be cured. I had to admit, it wouldn't be so bad to stop second-guessing myself as insane.

And then I apologized to God for lying. I didn't want Sam to go away.

Stirring my cup reminded me of coffee, which quickly progressed to Clair. I couldn't understand how she could have betrayed me. Or was it a true act of friendship? I didn't know. I was so confused.

Across the hall, I spied the components of a computer arranged on top of a large desk. Another colorful piece of artwork hung beside the desk brought another wave of remorse. And emptiness. Would every flower I see, real or painted, remind me of him?

Aside from myself, the area remained deserted. Many of the overhead lights had been dimmed, making the small table lamp on the desk stand out. Settling down in front of the computer, I wondered what to do next. It was easy to avoid social networks. Although I had plenty of interesting things going on in my life, I certainly didn't want to share, and I hoped none of my friends would be so thoughtless as to post our mishap adventure on the Internet. Unwilling to look, I sat in the chair, staring at the blinking prompt.

My knees shook nervously under the desk; my fingers hovered above the keyboard. The word finally filtered through my subconscious: Goldenrod.

I quickly typed the word and hit 'enter.' My stomach tightened; I felt like a stowaway child in a candy store, about to be had.

Many different hits popped up instantly with brief descriptions. Scanning the first article, I began to read: "*It was built in 1909...the last, largest, and most luxurious showboat designed for the Mississippi.*"

I could almost see Tilly and Garret performing on stage in front of a large audience that applauded joyfully as they sat in extravagant red velour theatre boxes.

Scrolling down the page, a current photo displayed a badly neglected vessel, desperate for paint and some

TLC. In fact it was junk! How could such as magnificent craft rot so quickly? It made me angry to think that such a historic part of our past was rotting away, just like Sam had mentioned.

"Sam."

Scrolling back to the top of the page, I continued reading the article.

"Hmmm."

The story continued, but not in a way I had anticipated.

"In 1910, there were twenty-one riverboats touring the Mississippi River. By 1928, this number dwindled to eleven. With popularity plummeting and already in need of repairs, she was moored at the St. Louis riverfront in 1937. The magnificent Goldenrod was the last showboat—"

"What? It stopped sailing in 1937?" I wondered aloud. "That doesn't make sense. It had to be a typo. Sam said—"

I sat back roughly in my chair. The wooden joint creaked under the abrupt pressure. Why was I doing this to myself?

An internal war raged within my very core, where one part of me tried to accept that Sam was a figment of my imagination, while the other part of me fought to keep him alive. I did not trust Dr. Dickhead Kendall or his theory of schizophrenia. Sure, I had been upset by the move, but enough to create an entire fantasy world? I knew I used my fair share of denial and repression. But psychotic?

But then, how else could I explain all the bizarre things about Sam? People don't blow up in lightning storms.

Frustrated more with myself than anything else, I went back to the main search page and clicked on another site for the Goldenrod. Skimming over the story, I read the same basic information. I decided to try a third site. The heading confused me: *"Ghosts of the Prairie."*

At first I thought I had the wrong page, but then I caught sight of the familiar boat, the Goldenrod. Intrigued, I scanned this article quickly for something to catch my eye. *"...haunted by a young girl."*

My pulse quickened. I continued scanning the article for pertinent clues. *"She had been nicknamed Victoria. Legend tells of a widower raising his daughter. The girl was found floating in the harbor. She had been brutally murdered...the attackers never found. The father died shortly thereafter."*

My arms fell to my sides, useless. I looked up at the ceiling for some kind of reassurance. I felt my pulse quicken. Could this be Sam's sister? How could I make this up?

"Miss Stokes?"

Startled, I nearly spilled my cocoa.

"Finding anything interesting?" Brandy asked, looking as cheery as ever.

"Oh." I repositioned myself in front of the screen. "Not very."

"Is that the Goldenrod?" she asked, pushing me aside to view the monitor.

My stomach dropped. How could she have known? I dreaded what she might add to my file after catching me obsessing.

"They made a movie about that back in the '80s,"
the nurse continued. "It was on T.V. a few nights ago.
Did you see it, too?"

"Oh?" I replied, glad she was not spying on me, but
feeling quite ill about it being made into a movie.
Maybe I *had* seen it.

"I wished I lived in that era. People seemed happier
then."

"Yeah." My stomach hurt. Maybe that's how I
knew about the boat.

"I actually stopped by to give you these." She held
up a tiny paper cup. "It's time for your meds."

"Meds? I wasn't told I would be receiving any
medication. Are the blood tests back?"

"Not yet." Brandy smiled kindly. "The lab probably
won't report anything until morning. The doctor
ordered this late this afternoon and apparently the
pharmacy had been busy today. But now that the
prescription is here, I need you to take it."

She extended the paper cup in her right hand and
held up a plastic glass of water in her left.

I immediately regretted sending my mother home. I
didn't want to take the medicine, but I didn't want to
put up a fuss and appear violent either, so I swallowed
the pill without quibbling, then thanked her out of habit.

"By the way, what was it?" I asked, handing the
empty cups back to her. I'm not sure why I asked; about
the only medicines I was familiar with were Tylenol
and Midol.

"Seroquel. And it's a pretty high dose so it's going
to make you sleepy." After crumpling the paper cup,
she put it inside the larger plastic cup and then threw it
all in the desk-side wastebasket. Starting down the

hallway, she added "You should probably head back to your bed shortly."

"Okay," I mumbled, not really paying attention because I was more interested in my next search. Turning back towards the monitor, my muscles tensed with apprehension. Maybe fear. I had a mystery to solve: finding the theatre where Garret met Tilly.

Before I could find out if there was a movie about that too, I first needed the name of the theatre. It was easy to recall "Sam" telling me about his parents. I pictured his face, smiling, and his eyes twinkling, as he described his parent's first encounter to me. Unfortunately, I only remembered it took place in Chicago.

"Chicago Theatres" only led to movie theatres.

After fifteen minutes of searching, I was growing exceedingly impatient and the meds were kicking in. My eyes kept fogging over and I was ready to call it quits when I found it. *"A History of the Merle Reskin Theatre: The Blackstone Theatre."* Sam had called it the Blackstone.

A quick search proved that there had never been a movie made about the Blackstone Theatre. My heart started pumping faster, knowing I couldn't have had pre-knowledge about this place.

An interior photo of the theatre showed a magnificent French architectural design all in gold. Gold velvet curtains, gold chairs, and gold carpet. More gold accents trimmed the beautiful woodwork. Once again I became envious as I imagined what it would be like to perform on such a grand stage. Memories of my own past performances in the school auditorium transformed onto the stage of the Blackstone.

My short-lived burst of enthusiasm gave way to eyelids growing heavier by the second. I forced myself to read on, in hopes I could prove I wasn't crazy after all. And to prove Sam *was* real.

"The Blackstone Theatre became a leading center for drama soon after it opened on New Year's Eve, 1910."

My body froze. My eyes pained. Surely there could not be *two* typos. I squeezed my tired eyes to clear the fog.

"*1910.*" Sam's mother performed on opening night.

It couldn't be. I hit the back arrow on the screen repeatedly until the Goldenrod flashed up on the screen. I scanned the page for dates through squinted eyes.

"*Built in 1909. Moored in 1937.*"

I clapped my hands over my eyes, shielding myself from the horror on the computer.

They were right. Somehow I was inventing Sam.

Unable to deny the facts any longer, a terrible pain grew inside me, much like a knife plunging into my heart with each beat. Desperate to end this misery, I slid my hands aside to allow another peek at the screen; forcing the truth into my mind. Sam was nothing more than an imaginary friend.

I willingly shut my eyelids to see him in my mind's eye and love him one final time. It was time to say good-bye. How I adored his twinkling eyes, his incredible smile, us swimming together. The vision progressed to the two of us walking in the field...talking. That was the part I'd miss the most.

A thin stream of tears spilled upon the desk; my thoughts vacillated between anger and denial. Sleep called commandingly, yet I struggled to keep myself awake. I pinched the tender undersides of my arms. Hard. I pictured him sitting on our couch in his jeans and vivid white shirt. I smiled because he *always* wore jeans and a white cotton shirt.

I wondered what he would have told me this afternoon had the phones not rung, *and had he been real.*

Sam spoke of surviving. Would the great psychoanalyst, Dr. Sigmund Freud, simply interpret this as an elaborate way to remind myself that I am a survivor? Is that why I couldn't hear his footsteps on the wooden floor? Does this explain why the water remained calm when he swam? Because he wasn't real?

The words on the screen and the questions in my head continued to blur. Why did I create such a tragic life for him? Opening night, 1910. Does strength come from tragedy? Moored, 1937. Not the sole survivor, 1936.

Suddenly, clarity pierced through in the fog. The fire. The dates. Of course, it does make sense. I know what Sam had to say.

I had to tell! I had to call home. I couldn't keep my eyes open. The medicine was too strong. I struggled to keep my head off the desk. I had to tell…

…Sam…

…the lightning…

….I understood. Sam… didn't… survive.

CHAPTER TWENTY-NINE

WAITING

WAY TOO MANY HOURS had passed since the last lightening strike. Far more regrets were yet to come. It became obvious to Sam that Emily was not coming home anytime soon.

His heart ached as he tried to imagine what it must have been like for her. He further rebuked himself as he openly called himself a coward: out of fear to protect Emily, he had set her up. He had lost his chance to confess his existence to her. He wasn't even sure if she would ever want to see him again. Worry began to mix in with fear and guilt.

The nightmarish flashbacks continued to pound his thoughts. A thick line of self-criticizing obscenities concluded each re-run: by the time he had pulled his molecules together, the woman's voice had already called out a second time—the same voice he had heard on the answering machine. Her mother, no doubt, home to take her to the appointment.

If she was at the hospital, it was far too risky to wander the halls looking for her. Death always lingered there.

The deeper Sam thought, the worse the scenario became. The sun had been gone for over an hour when her parents finally arrived home—alone. Panic swarmed him like a thousand angry bees.

He knew that eventually, Emily would come home. He'd just have to wait it out. Only there was one problem: he couldn't wait at the house any longer. He had to leave.

CHAPTER THIRTY

DR. KENDALL

"**H**OW IS THE PATIENT responding to the medication?"

It was early morning. Far earlier than any doctor's rounds normally occurred. However, this was not a typical morning, nor a typical patient. Dr. Kendall was excited! He had been waiting for a patient like this since he first entered medical school. Richard Kendall thrived on mental illness.

Still disappointed he had not been accepted as Director at the Larned State Correctional Facility for the Mentally Ill, his ultimate goal was to some day work with the most disturbed people in the U.S. Until that time, he would be forced to continue his practice here at the hospital, where he was already bored with lonely and overworked wives who drank too much wine as a means of solace.

But not this patient. She was great! Active and vivid hallucinations… just the thought of it made him smile. *Maybe she'd go ballistic again. It was awesome…to the point of wickedness.*

"Take a look for yourself. She's drooling," a nurse uttered to the doctor's question.

Crinkling his nose at the RN, Dr. Kendall bent down and spoke too loudly in the patient's ear. "Emily, can you hear me?"

Emily's eyes fluttered at the sound of the voice. Her head jerked sporadically as she tried to lift it off the pillow. She licked her lips like she was preparing to speak, only to release a small sigh no louder than a whisper.

"How are you feeling today?" the doctor asked.

Again, Emily tried to lift her head off the pillow. It bobbed for a moment before falling back upon the pillow.

"Don't try to move, honey," the nurse said, patting Emily on the shoulder. "Just talk, if you can."

"Sam—" Emily's voice cracked. She licked her dry lips again. Peering through squinted eyes, Emily opened her mouth a second time. "Sam is real." That being said, her head flopped to the side.

"Still delusional." Kendall smiled broadly. "Let's continue with drug therapy, although I'd like to increase the dose to one hundred milligrams."

Hearing something like a gasp, Dr. Kendall eyed the nurse. "Did you say something?"

She cleared her throat. "No, sir, just a tickle." Just as she picked up a pillow to fluff it, the room's telephone rang.

"Hello?" she answered. "No, this is her nurse…Good morning, Mrs. Stokes. Yes, Emily is here, but the medication she is taking has made her quite drowsy…seventy-five milligrams of Seroquel…Oh no, it wasn't Dr. Lui. It was Dr. Kendall. He's in charge. Would you like to speak with him?"

The line went silent in the nurse's hand. "That was Mrs. Stokes," the nurse said, putting the phone back in its cradle.

"I gathered that," Kendall huffed.

"She sounded pretty upset."

"Parents usually have a hard time accepting psychiatric diagnoses. She'll come around."

"It's really sad, isn't it?" the nurse said.

"What is?"

"She might be pretty if her hair were combed—and wasn't drooling." The nurse paused for a breath. "She's so young. Schizophrenia is such a cruel twist of fate for any person. She's got her whole life in front of her! It might very well be spent on medication and frequent trips into the hospital."

Dr. Kendall crossed his arms. "Do you have a name?" he asked the nurse.

"Nancy. Nancy Roberts."

"Life is what you make it, Nancy Roberts. You see sadness. I choose to see opportunity. Research opportunity. She could make me famous." Kendall reached in his breast pocket and pulled out a pen. His smile grew wider as he turned for the hall; his thumb clicking the end of his ballpoint. "I'll update the patient's chart."

It took about an hour for John and Elizabeth to arrive at the hospital. Sitting in the parking lot, Elizabeth turned to John and finally spoke, "I don't think I can go in there."

"Why?" asked John. "What do you mean?"

"I don't think I can go into the hospital." Elizabeth paused as she searched for words. "Something is wrong. There's no reason why Emily shouldn't be able to answer the phone for herself. I'm going to walk in there, freak out, and get arrested." Tears began to well in her dark eyes. The tissue she had concealed in her hand now lay tattered in her lap.

John grabbed his wife's hands and pulled them to his lips. "Mrs. Stokes, you are the bravest, smartest woman I know." He kissed her hands again. "I have seen you on the witness stand, and that Kendall character is no match for you."

Elizabeth smiled, tears rolling down her cheeks. "Thank you." Pulling her hand free, she retrieved the tissue in her lap and held up a piece of the shredded fiber. A sorrowful giggle escaped from under her breath as she wiped the tears away with her own fingers. "I love you."

The two sat quietly for a moment.

"I am, because of you," she said with gratitude.

John smiled through closed lips. "We are, because we are." He paused a little longer, then gave his wife's hand a final squeeze. "Ready?"

Emily's parents made their way through the hospital and took the elevator up to her floor. Elizabeth made a point to stop at the nurse's station.

"Oh, good. You're here just in time," the charge nurse stated, peering over a stack of papers. "I need you to sign the consent form."

"Just in time for what?" John fired out as a bad feeling crept over him.

"They are preparing to transfer your daughter over to Parkview."

"Parkview!" Elizabeth took a step back to catch herself from falling. An intense wave of nausea pulled the blood from her face.

John looked at Elizabeth, then at the nurse. "Where and what exactly is Parkview?"

"It's the psychiatric hospital, sir." The nurse seemed more than a little apprehensive as she tucked her hair behind her ears. "I'm sorry, I thought you had been informed of this decision."

The hairs on the back of John's neck began to rise. Elizabeth's brow furrowed. "No, we were not informed. Who made this decision? Dr. Kendall, I presume?"

"Let me check the orders." The nurse grabbed the top chart off another stacked pile.

Not waiting for the nurse to find an answer, Elizabeth stormed off toward Emily's room. Anticipating her daughter's condition, Elizabeth stopped cold as an unsightly mess confronted her eyes. Her mouth dropped open as she stood frozen in the doorway. She glanced at John, only to confirm he was seeing the same thing as she. As reality set in, they both rushed to the bedside. Heaped and bent, Emily lay motionless. Her long hair was tangled and stuck to her head; she was breathing though her mouth, taking rapid and shallow breaths.

"Oh dear God!" Elizabeth reached out her shaking hand and combed through a few of the snarled stands of her daughter's hair. "What have they done to you?"

"Let me assure you, Mrs. Stokes," a man's voiced boomed out from behind the couple. They each whirled around to stand face to face with the enemy. "We are providing the very best medical treatment money can buy."

"Kendall, are you responsible for this?" John pointed to his unresponsive daughter.

"Don't worry yourself. It's just a mild side effect from the medication."

"You call this *mild?*" John's tone was sharp and accusing, his eyes were wide with horror.

"It takes time for the patient's body to become acclimated to the drug dosage."

"Where is Dr. Lui?" Elizabeth asked with undertones of suspicion.

"Her specialty is in Pediatrics, mine is in Psychiatry. Therefore, your daughter is under *my* care."

"So when are you going to start caring for her?" John snapped.

"What about her blood work? I would like to see her lab results," Elizabeth demanded.

Dr. Kendall puffed up his thin chest like a rooster ready for battle in an illegal cockfight. "Of course you would, and you may see them. However, just as the truth was revealed yesterday, the truth still stands today! You said it yourself, lady. The farm doesn't exist. Nor do any little amoebas swimming around in her blood." Leaning forward, Dr. Kendall narrowed his weasel eyes as he intruded into her personal space. "Welcome to schizophrenia, Madame!"

John clenched his fists. The skin over his knuckles turned white. His arms began to shake as he let out a low growl that continued to grow in intensity.

Elizabeth looked on as her husband launched toward the doctor. Powerless to stop what might come, her eyes grew wide as she expected her husband to rip the doctor limb from limb. It all happened so rapidly, yet it seemed to occur in slow motion. Kendall backed against the wall and stiffened as if to prepare himself for the assault. The doctor's hands flew up to shield his face as John closed in on him. Just before their bodies were about to collide, John took a swift sidestep and simply brushed the doctor's shoulder with his own as he passed by on his way out the door.

The doctor's eyes opened. "Well, then." Kendall cleared his throat. "I see you are the rational one in the family."

"I wouldn't make any assumptions if I were you, Dr. Kendall. You're still standing."

The doctor turned his nose up in the air. "Point taken." Taking in a large breath, he held up his boney finger. "Let's get back to the issue at hand."

"Excellent suggestion," Elizabeth barked. "Why is our daughter being transferred—"

"Simple. Parkview specializes in serious mental illnesses."

"Only you haven't demonstrated she has one."

"How so?"

"You have failed to conduct any psychological testing, whatsoever."

Kendall tugged at his collar, unbuttoning it.

Elizabeth sensed she had struck a nerve.

"There simply was no time."

"Liar!" Elizabeth yelled.

"Oh good woman, you must believe me," Kendall offered. "I worry for her safety, just like you. I have an oath to protect all my patients."

"At this point, you'd better worry about protecting something else," Elizabeth warned.

"Like his career?" John called from the hall.

Elizabeth muffled a laugh while the doctor let out a small huff.

"I see we have started the day off on the wrong foot." The doctor back peddled. "I will cancel the transfer orders and Emily will remain here for further observation. Admittedly, I *was* disappointed to see her go." He put his hands behind his back and stood up tall. Hearing no objections, he continued, "You may not like my vigorous treatment for your daughter, but I have witnesses that can testify on my behalf."

"Witnesses? What kind of witnesses?" John walked slowly back into the room.

"The nurse, last night. After giving your daughter her medication, she documented Emily speaking hallucinatory gibberish. Then again this morning, a second nurse heard Emily distinctively repeat the name 'Sam,' and 'He's real.'"

John thought he caught Kendall about to roll his eyes.

"I'm sure it must be difficult for you." Kendall looked at Elizabeth, then to John. "But any patient suff—*experiencing* hallucinations is serious, and requires serious treatment. We will begin psychological testing as soon as possible. In fact, an interview with the two of you would be a wonderful place to start. You can provide us with any other concerns you may have, or if you have noticed any other unusual behavior."

"Yes," Elizabeth agreed. "That would be a good place to start."

Kendall's expression changed to mild pleasure. "Refresh my memory. Is there any history of mental illness on either side of the family?"

Elizabeth and John looked at each other.

"No," John answered.

Kendall's head bobbed, as if making a mental note to himself. "All right then, if neither of you have any further questions, I'll begin the orders." Without waiting for a reply, Kendall took out his ballpoint pen and began clicking the top as he proceeded to the nurse's station to complete the necessary paperwork.

John opened his mouth to speak.

"Don't even waste your breath," Elizabeth whispered.

"I think it would make me feel better," John whined.

With a heavy exhale, his wife smiled. "Vent if you must, but I don't want to hear any cuss words."

"That vile sack of horse apples doesn't know his head from his tail feathers."

"Feel better?"

"No. Well, maybe a little."

Elizabeth grinned as she collapsed in a chair.

"Let's start the day over with a cup of coffee," John suggested.

"Perfect! I'll go to the cafeteria," she agreed. "But first, I need a hug."

Elizabeth found a comb in her purse and began the tedious work of unsnarling Emily's hair. As she worked, she sang silly songs, like the ones they would sing together when Em still wanted to be pushed on the swing set.

John flipped on the television and found a golf game. Regrettably, the action was not near thrilling enough to divert his fearful thoughts about his daughter. He doubted even front row, center court seats at a KU game would be thrilling enough. For the first time in his life, at least that he could remember, John was afraid. He was afraid for his smart, beautiful daughter.

What if? What if she never gets better? What if she gets worse?

John picked at an old scab on his knuckles where he had cut himself while building a bird house. Then he looked at his daughter. His baby. It seemed like only yesterday she was still too small to ride a bike. John fought hard to stop the sting in his eyes and throat. Refocusing on his knuckles, he noticed the wound was bleeding again. He went to the nearby sink and washed away the blood. His thoughts drifted to Kat and how much he loved her, too.

Grabbing a paper towel, he wrapped it around his knuckles and then returned to Emily's side. As the man of the house, it was his job to protect his family. But how does a man battle this? Letting out a sigh of discouragement, he wished he could trade places with his daughter.

A knock came from the outside of the hospital room. "May I come in?"

Elizabeth rushed over to greet Dr. Lui. "Tell, me, Yia, what is going on?"

"Oh, please forgive me. Once again I feel the need to apologize for that insensitive—*man*. He has absolutely no bedside manner."

"Never mind him." Elizabeth waved her hand in the air. "Tell me about Emily." The two ladies sat down in faux leather chairs arranged in front of the room window. "Kendall said he had witnesses."

"Let me start with the lab results. The blood work all came back negative. Liver and kidney functions are in normal range. General blood counts look good and there is no evidence of parasites or other infections. Emily is healthy. But—" Dr, Lui momentarily broke eye contact. "The lack of physical causes implies the hallucinations are all formed up here." Dr. Lui pointed to her head. "We can do an MRI scan of her brain, but I truly believe that the results will be negative as well. Emily's hallucinations are very detailed and that simply is not indicative of head trauma."

Elizabeth lowered her head and wept. Dr. Lui reached out her hand and placed it on Elizabeth's knee. John walked around from the other side of the room and knelt down beside his wife.

John gently took his wife's face in his calloused hands and began dabbing her tears. "Have faith, woman."

Elizabeth took the paper towel from her husband and fumbled with it in her hands. Then with an exasperated huff, she looked up from her lap and held the towel in the air. "You gave me your used, bloody paper towel?"

Heat flushed John's face. His voice was sheepish. "It's all I had handy."

"I'd say it's *your* head that needs examining!" Elizabeth exclaimed.

Dr. Lui laughed. "You two were made for each other. But if you're ready, I'd like to continue."

Without a third chair, John continued to crouch beside his wife in preparation for what Dr. Lui had to say.

"It's difficult to speculate what information we would have gained from a psychological examination had it occurred yesterday. The purpose would be to reveal how the delusional theme might cross over into various psychological areas of functioning and thinking patterns. At this point, now that drug therapy has begun," Dr. Lui's face wrinkled in disappointment, "it is best to get Emily stabilized and then proceed with the mental exam."

"And the witnesses?" John asked in curiosity.

Dr. Lui's brow furrowed. "Both the third shift nurse last night and the nurse currently on duty heard Emily speaking of a 'Sam.' He is believed to be the boy she described living at the farm."

Both Elizabeth and John nodded simultaneously.

"The purpose of the medication is to stop the hallucinations altogether," Dr. Lui stated.

"So, as long as she talks about Sam, the medication continues?" John asked.

"Yes."

"What if that doesn't work?" John looked over at his daughter, lying in bed.

"Anti-psychotic medication is the number one method of treatment."

John cringed hearing the word psychotic.

"In some cases, when the psychotic features are associated with depression, other measures are necessary and work with fairly high results and low risks," Dr. Lui finished.

"Like what?" John asked naively.

"I really don't think it will result in that—" Elizabeth tried to end the conversation.

"I'd like to know," John interrupted.

"ECT," the doctor spoke clearly.

John, still crouching beside his wife, held a blank expression on his face.

"Electro-convulsive therapy."

"What?" John nearly yelled. "I sure as *hell* don't like the words *electric* and *convulsion* combined into the same word."

"John," Elizabeth hissed.

"It is a relatively simple technique where they hook small electrodes up to the patient's scalp—" Dr. Lui began.

"And electrocute someone until they flip out into a seizure?" John took a defensive stance near his daughter. "No frickin' way is anybody going to do that to my daughter!"

Visions of his daughter's entire body shaking uncontrollably on some metal bed with smoking electrodes taped to her head and the burning flesh under each buzzing pod charged with ample electricity…was more than he could handle.

"Mr. Stokes," Dr. Lui tried to console, "no one has even begun to consider that technique. It is far too early in the treatment stage for that. I only brought it up because you asked."

The doctor stood and faced John, who was regaining his composure. "I know that this is very difficult for you. Mental illness can be an extremely difficult diagnosis to accept." Dr. Lui's posture relaxed and she tried to smile. "Perhaps you two would like some time to be alone with Emily."

"That would be appreciated," Elizabeth replied.

The doctor left, leaving the two parents alone with their drugged and unresponsive daughter.

"It was almost like she was on *his* side," John sneered as he doubled-checked the hallway for snoops and ears.

"But she's not. *She* said it with compassion."

"Oh, Izzy." John reached out for his wife, returning inside the room.

"Have faith, man."

CHAPTER THIRTY-ONE

CALAMITY

AFTER SPENDING A QUIET DAY with Emily, John and Elizabeth drove to the other side of the city to pick up Kat from camp. Their thoughts were collectively divided between the relief of knowing that Emily would continue resting throughout the night, and the preoccupation with the only clear word Emily continued to speak, "Sam."

Elizabeth was the first to break the silence. "I'm not sure what I find more disturbing. The diagnosis, or for her to be so in love with someone that doesn't exist."

"In love?" John asked skeptically.

"Oh yes," she sighed. "I tell you John, you should have seen her walk in the kitchen door the first night that Sam came to be. She was utterly and entirely enamored."

"I thought people had hallucinations about aliens, or God talking to them—not about falling in love," he said.

"I only know general information pertinent to schizophrenia, but I'm still not convinced that is what she has. I don't think she's had the symptoms long enough to warrant such a diagnosis. Plus, we just don't have that kind of mental illness in our family history."

"Suppose the jackass is wrong. You brought up depression before... She really liked that Alex kid.

Maybe I should have been more accepting of him when he showed up on our doorstep the night we moved."

"Stop second guessing yourself."

John patted his wife's thigh. "I still remember the day you walked into my gun shop, looking for a pistol to protect yourself from that nut-job down in Wichita."

"The BTK serial killer," Elizabeth recalled. The corners of her lips curved up. "Instead, I found you—a far better alternative to a handgun."

His face soured. "Up until today, I believed I could keep my family safe from any danger."

"John…." His wife's expression was soft and compassionate. "Emily is not *in danger*."

"Damn it, Elizabeth, you know what I mean," he said, smashing his fist atop the dash.

She slunk back in her seat. "I do now."

"I'm sorry," he said, still driving with one hand. He glanced at Elizabeth. "I am out of my realm here. I grew up watching Westerns, for Pete's sake; I learned that all a man ever needed in life was an accurate six-shooter and a new wagon wheel." John shook his head, laughing at his own simplicity.

"I cannot tell you how thankful I am that you are the man in my life." She reached over to hold her husband's hand. "Nearly every day I meet men who are in no way qualified to be fathers, which is probably why their children are on probation. Our children get good grades, are active in extra-curricular activities—you have done a wonderful job."

"But I feel so helpless. I don't know what to do, Izzy."

"Just be there for her. Tell her that you love her, no matter what."

"I don't know." Feelings of inadequacy lingered on. "John Wayne was a hell of a gun fighter."

Elizabeth gave her husband's hand a tight squeeze. "That may be true, but John Stokes is a hell of a father."

Kat waved erratically as her parents pulled up at the camp entrance. Running lickity-split across the grass, she stopped herself with a crashing *thunk* against the driver's side car door. "Can I go to camp next week, too? There are still openings!"

John looked over at Elizabeth. "What a great idea!" Getting out of the car, he gave Kat an extra big hug. "It's good to see you, Honey. Let's go get the 4-1-1 from the registration desk."

She and John returned a few minutes later.

"I'm in!" Kat announced to her mother, still seated in the car.

Elizabeth smiled enthusiastically, but once on the road, it didn't take Kat long to pick up on the unusually tense atmosphere. Both of her parents were strangely quiet, yet overly doting at the same time. They seemed to hang on every word she said. Kat was calculating the probability of getting a dog if she were to ask for it when she noticed the car was headed for home, instead of the hospital.

"Why aren't we going to see Emily?"

"She's resting," her mother replied.

"So? I still want to see her."

"Well, it's more like sleeping, actually."

"Sleeping?"

"Yes, the medication she is taking makes her very tired," Elizabeth continued.

Kat sat quietly in the back of the car, heading in what she thought to be the wrong direction. Finally she spoke up. "Emily is really sick, huh?"

"In a way, yes."

"What's wrong with her? And don't sugar coat the facts. I can handle the truth."

Although the words were not intended to be funny, she saw her parents smile.

"The truth, huh?" her Dad echoed back, glancing at her reflection in the rearview mirror.

"Yes, Daddy, I want the truth. The whole truth and nothing but the truth, so help you God."

"I wonder where she gets *that* from?" John peered at Elizabeth from the corner of his eye.

Ignoring the implied accusation, Elizabeth proceeded to explain Emily's condition. "Emily is not sick in the way most people get sick." Elizabeth cranked her body around as far as possible in order to face Kat. "It is not like an ear infection where we go in and get a prescription to make us feel better. It's more like a malfunction.

"There are many different chemicals that make our brains work correctly. For example, my personal favorite is serotonin. One of the duties of this chemical is to make us feel happy."

"Is that what's wrong with Em?"

"She has different chemicals that are not working properly. Emily's mind is making stuff up and right now, she can't tell the difference between what is real and what her mind is imagining."

Kat blinked.

"Remember when you were younger, and you used to pretend that you were Jane of the Jungle?"

"Yes—"

"Well, Em doesn't know she's pretending."

Kat's eyebrows wrinkled as she scowled. "What is she pretending?"

Elizabeth shifted in her seat. "About the farm, and Sam."

"Sam!"

The conversation ended, and Kat became very still and quiet as she thought over all the things Emily had recently told her about Sam.

"Kat?" Elizabeth checked over her shoulder. "How about if you choose a game the three of us can play tonight after dinner?"

She knew to expect popcorn and a game on Sunday night, but tonight was not Sunday. It was Friday. The offer intended to bring comfort only gave her a stomachache.

"This is horrible!" Kat said beneath her breath. "The doctors have obviously made a mistake."

Although Kat never claimed to be an expert at anything, there were a few things she was quite certain about. Take monsters for example. She was sure there were no such things as monsters that lived under the bed. The reality of Santa, on the other hand, was questionable. But after her father produced digital prints of Rudolph, the theory of the jolly man in red seemed a bit more reasonable. And the tooth fairy. Kat knew to expect a visit from her on nights she had a tooth fall out. That was a no-brainer.

Then there was Sam. He wasn't a monster. Or some fabricated character. Deep in her heart, Kat knew Sam was real, and she had to find him.

Early the next morning, Kat dressed herself in comfortable clothes for hiking. Then she grabbed a small notebook and two pencils, and stuffed them in a floral designed purse.

"I'll need these," she said to herself as she grabbed a handful of hair ribbons and stuffed them in too.

Satisfied she had everything from her bedroom, she held the purse out at shoulder height and examined her choice. "Still room for water and a snack."

Just then, her stomach rumbled, reminding her she'd better not skip breakfast. After all, food was important for thinking and today, she was Private Detective Stokes, in search of a missing person. Slinging the strap over her shoulder, she headed down for a bite to eat.

Despite her intense excitement, Kat resisted running down the stairs as fast as she could. She could not risk raising suspicion in her parents. Each step was a deliberate thump as she made her way down the steps.

"Look who's up and already dressed," her mother greeted her.

Kat smiled at her mom, who was pouring cream in her coffee. After closing the refrigerator door with her foot, Elizabeth planted a kiss on Kat as she walked by.

John looked up from yesterday's newspaper with his own coffee cup, still steaming. "My goodness! She even has a smile."

"It's not that big'a deal that I'm up." Kat tried to downplay her early morning rise and hide her floral purse at the same time. "It's not like I have plans or anything."

Sitting at the table next to her father, Kat tried to sound nonchalant. "I sure am hungry."

"How about some bacon and eggs?" Elizabeth suggested.

"With hash browns!" Kat's eyes shone brightly. "And some orange juice, too?"

"You are hungry," John remarked, setting his paper aside. He looked pointedly at his daughter. "What kind of mischief are you up to today?"

Kat's whole body flashed hot and she thought she was going to burst into flames. *He knows!*

Kat swallowed hard and looked at her father's face. It looked normal.

"Oh, not much," she said in her most unenthusiastic voice. "I was just thinking about counting how many different kinds of birds I could see in the woods today. Have you talked to Em yet?"

"She's still sleeping," Elizabeth said, pouring the shredded potatoes into the frying pan. "Birding sounds like fun."

Kat's empty stomach knotted in fear that her parents might like to go along. That would be disastrous! "Yeah, I think *I'll* have fun. What are *you* two up to today besides visiting Emily? Watering your flowers, and rearranging the garage?" she added quickly.

"The soil is dry, that's for sure. And the weeds...."

"Actually, the garage is pretty clean already." John sat up tall in his chair.

Kat's eyes bugged and she held her breath. She just knew he was going to ask to go along.

"How about we go fishing later after I visit your sister?" he asked.

In great relief, Kat slouched against the backrest of her chair. Then she put on a chipper smile. "Later might be possible. Unless Mom says I can visit Em."

"Okay, then." John picked the paper up off the table and opened it with a firm shake.

Kat silently congratulated herself on successfully eluding her first obstacle—getting out of the house without being followed. Then time dragged.

She looked on with agony as the second hand on the wall clock made another full sweep. Breakfast was taking too long. Valuable time was being wasted!

Hurry up, Mom! Clues are probably disintegrating as I sit here. Everybody knows from TV shows that it's next to impossible to solve a case after it turns cold!

Another minute passed.

Kat began to fidget with her bag. She double, then triple checked its contents, making sure she had everything she would need. She considered skipping breakfast altogether, but decided against it only for the fact that she believed the vitamins and minerals would help her to think more logically, like a super sleuth.

In the middle of Kat's preoccupation with saving the day, her thoughts returned to her sister. "Why does Em sleep so much?"

"She's on some pretty powerful medicine," Elizabeth replied.

"It *makes* her sleep?" Kat asked. "How can she get better that way?"

"I don't know," Elizabeth sighed, wiping some stress off her forehead.

"Don't worry, Mom," Kat spoke up. "Everything will be okay."

"Spoken like a true Stokes," Elizabeth said, placing the plate before Kat.

Breakfast was worth the wait. Kat's hunger pangs vanished and her good mood returned. After putting her dirty dishes in the sink, she asked her mother for a bottle of water, grabbed her own snack, and placed them both into her bag and zipped it shut.

Just as Kat was about to leave, a mixture of *scary-excitement* filled her little body. It reminded her of the feeling she got when she would inch closer to the front of the roller coaster line. Hesitating, she turned towards her parents, still at the kitchen table. Placing her hand over her heart, she cleared her throat and declared, "Mom, Dad, I love you!" With a flamboyant wave, Kat sent a shower of invisible love towards her parents before disappearing out the door.

"Stay close," her mother called from inside.

Crossing her fingers, Kat replied, "I will."

Taking a secure hold of her purse, Kat prepared for her secret mission. She recalled seeing her sister emerge from the south edge of the yard, next to the bird house she and her dad put up. Standing underneath the tiny house, she scanned the depths of the forest. Trees, trees, everywhere. Kat searched for some kind of landmark. Nothing stood out. She kept searching.

"Ah-ha!" She spied a cluster of poplar trees, growing unusually close. She quickly appreciated her dad teaching her about land references during their many fishing trips.

Kat locked her eyes on her target. Upon arrival, she unzipped her floral bag, reached in and pulled out one of the ribbons to tie it around a branch. She smiled as she stepped back to admire her well-formed bow. Next, she retrieved her pad of paper and one of the pencils. Flipping the notebook open with exaggerated flair, she wrote a small numeral "one" followed by a period, then, the word "home." On the next line, she wrote the number "two" followed by a period, and then the words, "three trees."

Kat slapped her notebook shut with the same dramatic flair and placed the objects back into her purse. Once again, she searched for her next landmark. Kat continued this process two more times until she reached the stream.

Reaching for another ribbon to tie onto a shrub near the water's edge, the call of a hawk caused Kat to look upward.

"Oh my gosh!" she gasped in astonishment.

However, it was not the hawk that seized her attention.

Her hand opened and the ribbon fell to the ground unnoticed. Her fingers traced the words carved in the tree. She read the message aloud, "This way to Sam's." Kat's eyes drifted north, following the arrow below the message. After a brief moment of silence, Kat burst into a celebration dance.

"Oh yeah, oh yeah," Kat sang and jumped and spun around. Then she did what seemed most logical.

"Ssaaaaamm!" she yelled as loud as she could, then looked around for an approaching person. Much to her disappointment, no one came forward. At least she had the arrow to follow.

As Kat continued on her mission, she enjoyed splashing through the creek, and delighted in seeing some new species of birds. It was fascinating that the feathered creatures didn't seem to be bothered very much by her occasional calling; she only regretted not bringing her bird book along.

She knew her brilliance of the ribbon idea far outweighed the neglect of a book, so with determination in her heart, she made her way up the stream, tying brightly colored ribbons as she went. Unfortunately, with Kat's focus on so many different things, she didn't have time to notice that the sun was gliding across the sky much quicker than she could tie ribbons.

Meanwhile, back at the house, Elizabeth kept busy. This was her chance to pull out every last sorry-ass weed and reclaim her flower garden. She never wore gloves while gardening; she liked getting her hands dirty with the dark soil. She believed it strengthened the bond between her and the flowers. Maybe this idea was a little weird, but she didn't care.

She found it hard to ignore the knots in her stomach and the sense of dread and urgency. She tried to convince herself that everything was fine, and to enjoy the beauty unfolding in crisp shades of red, delicate pinks, stunning yellow, deep purples, and bold orange, but somehow her tears still managed to fall upon the ground that held budding flowers. With a firm grip around the handle of her spade, she stabbed at the weeds even harder.

As Kat meandered the countryside and Elizabeth contemplated perennials, John had long since arrived at the hospital and was now sitting next to his daughter, who remained motionless. The steady rise and fall of Emily's chest pulled John into a trace-like state to the day he took the training wheels off Emily's bike. He wondered how the years passed by so quickly; although much taller, she was still his little girl.

John felt such a pain in his heart that he could no longer look at his daughter. It was like a form of torture in a living hell. *Why did this have to happen?*

Diverting his eyes, John looked at the book he'd brought along. He stared at its cover for a long time before finally speaking.

"I'm sure you've already read this one, but I found it in your room, so I'm pretty sure you like it." John opened the book cover and flipped to the first page of the first chapter and began reading aloud.

About the time John reached the middle of chapter nine, a lady dressed in a brown uniform entered the room holding a kitchen tray. He glanced at his watch. It was half past noon. He gave the nurse a puzzled look as she carried it in. She simply shrugged and set the tray and its contents down on the bedside table.

Removing the dented metal lid covering the main entrée, John picked at the vegetables intended for Emily with the fork.

"She hates cooked carrots," he called out after the woman, already gone. Hungry, he took a mouthful.

Continuing to read aloud and chew at the same time, the phone rang and interrupted him mid-sentence.

"Hello?" John answered, then swallowed.

"I can't find Kathryn," a distraught voice responded from the other end of the line.

"What?" John asked, unsure he understood his wife's words correctly.

"Kathryn. I can't find her."

"She's missing?"

"I made lunch over an hour ago. I've been calling for her, but she's nowhere to be found!" Elizabeth's voice trembled.

A heavy sigh filled the airwaves as John thought about his next move. His stomach churned as he dare not ask aloud, *what next?*

"Tell me what to do, John. I, I just can't—"

John quickly went through a mental list of things his wife did to relax. To suggest a bubble bath would warrant a divorce. "Pour yourself a glass of wine. Just one! Then keep calling out to Kat in case she can hear you. In fact, get a radio and play it, *loud*, out on the deck."

"I can do that," Elizabeth responded in a tone that still sounded stressed.

"I'll be home as soon as possible." In his rush, John almost hung up the phone but changed his mind. "Izzy?"

"Yes?" she answered.

"I love you!"

"Hurry home, man."

John slammed the phone back into the cradle. He didn't know why all this crap was happening to his family, but he was going to do his best to protect them.

With his thoughts already out the door, John leaned over the bedrail and kissed his eldest daughter's pale cheek good-bye.

Emily moaned at his touch. Her eyes batted, trying to open. "Daddy—" her voice whispered.

John froze as he heard her voice. Feelings of intense happiness turned to panic as her words continued.

"Help me."

A giant vice grip wrapped around John's heart and squeezed. Pain darted outward like the venom from a giant widow spider poisoning his system. He stood there, immobilized–and hoped he wasn't having a heart attack. He looked at one daughter, laying there. He thought of his other, lost somewhere in the woods. He imagined his wife, crying. The mash of words and faces racing through his head fell hard upon his shoulders.

Desperate, he bowed his head. *God, protect my family!*

A tremendous urge to grab his daughter's body and run like hell darted through John's mind. John leaned back over the metal bedrail. "Stay strong, Em! It will get better."

Emily moaned and her head fell to the other side. No matter how hard John tried to convince himself, it seemed wrong to leave his daughter after she asked for his help.

But what was a man to do? What else could he do in this circumstance? Emily was safe, here, in the hospital, wasn't she?

The contents of his stomach rose abruptly. He swallowed hard. Bile burned the back of his throat and left a sour coating in his mouth. John turned the faucet on in the bathroom. Not waiting for the water to turn cool, he cupped up a few sips of water in his hand and swished out his mouth.

Returning to his daughter's bedside, John gave his daughter a second kiss. "I love you, Emily. I'm sorry, but I have to go."

Emily did not stir this time. Her eyelids remained closed.

"I'll be back!" he promised.

CHAPTER THIRTY-TWO

THE RESCUE

HOW COULD I HAVE BEEN SO FOOLISH?
Kat sat in the tall grass, scolding herself. *I'm nothing more than a complete idiot!*

Kat buried her face in her hands and broke down into uncontrollable sobs. *Why didn't I turn back around when I ran out of ribbons?*

Already weary from the miles of travel, Kat crumpled under the exertion from crying. Fretfully make-shifting a grassy pillow, she laid her head down to rest. She thought it might also be a good time to say a little prayer.

"Dear God—"

A distinct noise in the grass caught Kat's attention and her eyes shot open as she listened.

Silence.

She heard the sound again. It sounded almost like...maracas, like she used in music class.

Pushing herself up with her hands, she couldn't tell which direction it came from. Slowly twisting around, Kat eyed what was making the sounds a few feet behind her. Before she could consciously think the word, her small frame started shaking violently.

Rattlesnake!

Coiled in the grass, Kat saw the unmistakable rattles sound its warning. Its jaw was set wide and the sharp venomous fangs were fully exposed. Ready to strike, Kat knew an escape was impossible.

As she began mentally preparing for her death, a shrill call sounded out of the bright blue sky. Outstretched wings drew back and a rusty-red blaze dive-bombed the reptile. Large, sharp talons snatched the reptile in its return to the sky. In awe, Kat looked on at the wriggling snake dangling from the hawk's grip, both shrinking in the distance.

When the figures were no longer visible, she looked around the tall brown and green grass and wondered how many more snakes were in the area. An internal ache reminded Kat of her mother and father. She was such an idiot! A second round of tears began to fall.

"Excuse me," a deep, gentle voice glided down upon her broken spirit.

Looking up towards the cloudless sky in the direction of the unfamiliar voice, Kat hushed her sobs and wiped her nose on her shirt. A large man stood over her, looking down, partially blocking the sun.

"May I help you?" A residual sob marred her unwarranted question.

The man laughed. "No, but thank you. I was actually wondering if I could be of service to you."

"I doubt it," Kat answered with a sigh.

"Oh? And why is that?"

"I'm looking for somebody."

The man stroked his chin. "And I had the silly notion that you might be lost."

"Actually, I'm lost, too." Kat's slumped over in discouragement.

"Well then," the man spoke, "I'm glad to have stumbled upon you."

Kat looked up to see his hand extended in front of her face.

"I happen to know this area better than anyone else. This was my playground when I was a youngster."

She grabbed the man's hand and stood up, taking a second look around the field. "Where's the swing set?"

"I'm old," he said. "We swung from tires when I was little."

As the two set out across the prairie, Kat asked, "Do you know where I live?"

"No, but I know it's not here. The only things that live out here are rattlesnakes and field mice. There isn't a house around for miles."

"Oh," Kat muttered; her past encounter still fresh in her mind.

"So, how is it that a lovely young lady such as yourself has gone and wondered off so far from home?"

"I was looking at birds."

"Birds! I thought you said you were looking for a *somebody*."

"I did," Kat insisted. "I don't know where the person lives exactly, so while I was walking, I was also looking for birds."

"Naturally!" the man exclaimed. "You remind me of my little sister."

"I do?" Kat asked enthusiastically.

"She had a lot of spunk."

"But she doesn't now?"

"Doesn't what?" the man asked.

"You said, 'had,'" Kat pointed out.

The man stopped abruptly and looked down at Kat. "Little girls ask too many questions."

Kat looked the man square in the eyes. "And you're immature for your age."

The man chuckled and began walking again. "Tell me. Who is this person you are looking for?"

"My sister's boyfriend."

Once again the man stopped abruptly. He eyed her up and down. "Boyfriends! Birds! This all sounds mighty fishy to me. Hold out your arms. Do you have a suitcase?"

With her arms outstretched like a tiny scarecrow, Kat giggled and shook her heard no. "I didn't run away, if that's what you're thinking."

The man took her purse and looked inside. He handed it back to her after zipping it shut. "Look here, Missy. I think it's time for a little heart-to-heart." The man crouched down on his knee to be at eye level with the little girl.

Kat examined his face carefully. "You're not as old as I thought you were."

"I'll take that as a compliment, but enough of me. Why are you out here in the middle of nowhere?"

Kat hesitated for a moment. "They say my sister is sick. That is why I'm looking for her boyfriend."

His eyes narrowed.

"They put her in the hospital." Kat's eyes begin to burn as a prelude to tears.

"Who did?"

Giant drops fell from Kat's eyes. "They say that Sam is not real."

With a shocked look on his face, the man nearly tipped over. After hastily recovering, he took hold of Kat's small hands in his own. Looking her squarely in the eye, he said, "You must be Kitty."

Looking up under wet eyelashes, she gave him a puzzled look. "How did you know that?"

"I'm Sam."

Kat's face became void of expression. Then with a burst of laughter, Kat lunged toward Sam to give him a giant hug, "I knew you were real!"

"Stop!" Sam yelled.

Kat's bony frame landed with a thud, flattening the tall prairie grass. "Hey! Why did you do that?"

"It wasn't on purpose, Kitty," Sam tried not to laugh. "Let me show you something." Sam looked around and picked up a small rock. Crouching, he held it in his hand, palm side up.

Kat looked at him, unimpressed. The next thing Kat witnessed made her eyes bug. "Whoa! Do that again!"

Sam picked up the same rock, held it in his hand, palm side up. Then magically, the rock fell through Sam's hand.

"How did you do that?" Kat was astounded.

"So, you think it's cool? You're not creeped out by it?"

"Not at all. Can you teach me how to do that?"

Sam chuckled, "I hope not."

"Seriously, how did you do that?" Her eyes beamed with curiosity.

"Kitty, do you believe in ghosts?"

Kat's expression turned to confusion, followed by a shade of white that erased all the lines in her face. Goosebumps rose on her skin. Her heart beat faster.

"Hold on there, little lady," Sam's gentle voice soothed. "You had the courage to find me—"

Keeping her eyes fixed upon the figure in front of her, she managed to gain control of her erratic breathing. Slowly, she extended her arm to touch his body. She tapped her finger against his white shirt. She swallowed. Kat pressed harder and her fingers entered into his chest cavity. "Does it hurt?" she asked as she continued to shove her entire hand into Sam's chest.

"Not at all."

Kat wiggled her fingers. "You feel like a cloud."

"That's 'cause I'm made out of water. Now stop that, it tickles."

Kat pulled out her hand and examined it for any sign of change. Seeing none, she stepped back in order to view Sam in entirety. Finally, without warning, a huge smile spread across her face as she lunged toward him a second time. "You're real enough for me!" Kat laughed out loud as she threw her arms around Sam's wide shoulders, careful not to crash through him a second time.

Sam returned the hug.

"Enough, already," she spoke with a fake I'm-getting-crushed accent.

Apologetically, he released his prisoner. "You don't seem to be allergic to me."

Kat gave him her best you-are-weird look, "No–"

"Never mind," he replied, standing upright. "Now let's get you back home."

"How can you be made out of water?" she asked, securing her purse over her shoulder, preparing for the long walk.

"*You're* mostly water," he replied.

"You don't have skin to keep it all together," Kat noted.

Sam scratched his head. "I'm like a glass of ice water. My skin, so to speak, is like the ice cubes floating on the top."

"But you're not cold."

"Besides temperature, another difference between ice, water, and steam is how fast the atoms move inside each molecule. I slow the atomic movement to achieve 'skin,' but since I'm not really frozen, I won't crack like ice."

"Oh," Kat replied, still processing this information. After a moment, the shimmer in her eyes turned dark. "Sam, we have to hurry. They think she's crazy." Her lip began to quiver.

A sad smile swept across Sam's face as he reached for her hand. "Fear not, little lady. We'll save your sister."

Kat managed a hopeful smile, and the two new friends started off across the countryside.

"So, how long have you been birding?" Sam asked.

"Since I've been at the new house. There aren't many city birds."

"How about I teach you some bird calls? You know how to whistle, don't you?"

"Gosh, I'd love that!" she said, imagining calling in all sorts of birds. "How many do you know?"

His eyes whisked the sky in thought. "About fifty."

Time passed and the scenery changed from grassy fields to woodland. Kat's legs had moved past the point of rubber and she was sure they would never feel normal again.

"You were a long way from home." Sam noted.

Kat looked up at Sam. "I'd do anything for my sister." Just then, she pointed to a red bow. "That's mine."

"The ribbon?"

"Yes, I tied them around the tree so I wouldn't get lost."

"I see you get your skills from your sister."

"I can tell we've returned from a different direction. There should have been blue and green ones first."

"So you know where we are?"

Kat unzipped her bag and took out her notepad. "This is one of ten red ribbons." She continued to study her notes and her surrounding. "I think there will be four more red ribbons followed by a slew of yellow ones. We're getting close to home."

"Your tracking system is a little more impressive than Emily's…" Sam's head dipped low. He fell silent.

She occasionally snuck a peek at Sam as they walked along the stream's banks. She could see the pain on his face.

They had passed several yellow ribbons when she finally spoke. "We're almost there."

"Yes, we are." He turned his ear toward the west. "I can hear music."

"Music? They're having a party?"

"I reckon not, silly. I'd imagine it's so you can hear your way home."

"I wonder how long I've been gone?"

"What time did you leave?"

"This morning, after breakfast. What time do you think it is now?"

Sam looked at the sun. "Four o'clock?"

"Oh, heavens! They must be frantic. Dad is probably organizing a search party." Kat began to run.

"Kat, stop!"

Her head lurched forward from the abrupt halt. Catching her balance, she spun around.

"I don't always look this way." He gestured to himself.

"And?" Impatient, Kat began walking again.

Sam reached out and grabbed her by the shoulder. "The more people I'm around, the harder it is for me to maintain a body form."

Kat didn't get it. "Why are you telling me this? I gotta get home!"

"Because I don't want your parents to go berserk when I meet them!"

Unable to understand Sam's concerns, Kat mindfully tugged on Sam's hand as she led him past the engraved tree. "Don't worry! Both my mom and dad are 'with-it' kind of people."

"I hope you're right," Sam grimaced.

As the two approached the backyard, Sam cautioned Kat to slow down as he scanned the area for people. No one was in sight.

"They must be inside," Kat whispered as they reached the sliding patio door. "And remember to smile. You'll look friendlier with a big smile."

"Whatever you say," Sam said, standing up tall. "Here goes nothing…"

Kat grabbed his hand and looked up at the man, who looked more like a giant than a sister's boyfriend.

Elizabeth and John were inside, waiting for the local sheriff when the doorbell rang alerting them of his arrival. "I'll get the door," John called out to his wife, who was busy making a fresh pot of coffee.

Elizabeth was setting the coffee mugs onto a tray when something blocking the kitchen patio glass door caught her eye. "Johhhhhn—" she called out in a strained voice. "Apologize to the sheriff. Kat is home."

As John bid the man in uniform good-bye, he puzzled over his wife's strange reaction to the good news of their daughter's return. Quickly entering the kitchen, John came to a screeching halt. Before him was a sight he could not comprehend. His eyes darted back and forth from the patio door to his wife. Standing just inside the open patio door, was his daughter, smiling, holding the hand of a...giant...flickering on and off like a dying flashlight. His wife, now fainted, lying on the floor.

Sam leaned over and whispered in Kat's ear, "I think that went well."

"Hi, Daddy," Kat said, beaming with pride.

A staring, speechless John went over to aid his wife as she attempted to get up from the floor.

"I'm sorry for, um, startling you folks." The giant looked down at the floor as he struggled for words; his six-foot, four-inch muscular frame still hazing in and out. "But Kitty here tells me that Emily is, well, in the hospital. I'm here to tell you that... I'm Sam."

John, who was perched on one knee, fell back onto his hind-end in slow motion, pulling Elizabeth over with him.

"Please don't act like a couple of idiots and embarrass me in front of Sam!" Kat fussed. "I told him that I had cool parents."

"Ease up, little lady. I'd imagine I must be a sight to see."

"That you are," Elizabeth finally found her voice to speak. "Please excuse us." She stammered as she crawled off John and proceeded to wipe imaginary dirt off her pants.

John was still staring but had managed to close his mouth.

Still unsure what to say to their unexpected guest, John and Elizabeth both stood in the middle of the kitchen waiting for their senses to digest this revelation. John was close to forming a coherent sentence when his eyes grew wide with alarm.

"Emily! Oh dear God! We have to get Emily!"

Elizabeth clutched her husband's arm. "What is it, John?"

Fear ripped through his body, cutting off the ability to speak.

Elizabeth increased her hold on his arm. "Speak, man."

His thoughts zipped back to the last words Emily spoke to him. He regretted leaving her all the more. "We've got to get Emily and bring her back, now!"

"What's with the urgency?"

"Don't you see? Sam's *real*!"

John's panic invaded Elizabeth. "All right! We'll leave now. But what are we going to do with Kat?"

The two parents turned and looked at their youngest daughter whispering something to the giant.

"We can't bring her along!" John exclaimed.

"She's too young to stay home alone."

"Maybe we can leave her in the car. People leave dogs in the car."

"In the car? Come on!" Elizabeth groaned.

John smacked himself in the forehead. "You're right, bad idea."

Elizabeth's hand shot up to massage her temple with her thumb. An idea popped into her head. Making eye contact with John, she glanced over to Sam without moving her head. She repeated the movement until John picked up on the idea.

"You want to leave her with Mr. Strobe Light?!" John asked in a voice all too loud.

Elizabeth let out an exasperated sigh, "You have a better plan?"

Kat jumped up and down. "Oh, goodie!" Clapping her hands, she turned to Sam. "Will you *pleeease* babysit me?"

The two parents looked at Sam. John rolled his eyes. "Fine."

"Sam," Elizabeth asked, "would you mind staying with Kathryn while we rescue our daughter from the hospital?"

CHAPTER THIRTY-THREE

AN ACT OF KINDNESS

"EMILY, YOU HAVE TO WAKE UP,"
a voice whispered in my ear.

"Hmmm?" I mumbled.

"Listen carefully."

Hot breath tickled in my ear.

"I didn't give you your last dose of meds. I realize some strange stuff has been going on, but that Dr. Kendall... he's the crazy one! You've got to get out of here. As soon as you feel strong enough, you must leave!"

Silence followed.

With closed eyes, the warning circulated in and out of my head, urging me to wake up, wake up, get up. But why?

"He's the crazy one...you must leave!" the voice repeated only in my head.

Who was crazy?

And where should I be going? I was too tired to be going anywhere. I just wanted to roll over and curl up with Bunny. I loved Bunny.

Instead of dreams, I heard the echoing voice: "Emily, wake up."

My eyes opened to slits.

The voice annoyed me like a tiny gnat, buzzing about my ear and interrupting my sleep. Yes, it was only a gnat. My eyes closed again. *Go away, gnat. I want sleep.*

"No meds," the gnat said.

That was ridiculous. Insects can't speak. Maybe someone was here.

I opened my eyes far enough to see. Nothing looked familiar.

"He's the crazy one…you must leave!" the gnat continued to speak.

Annoyed, I took a swat at the gnat, but only managed to slap myself in the chin. Although painless, it seemed to jar some sense into me, and the idiocy of a talking gnat became evident.

I wondered where I was. Ruthlessly tired, the room swirled terribly as I tried to rise. My arms and legs seemed to weigh an impossible thousand pounds. Then I started to remember….

Of course! I was in the hospital. Strange events revisited my mind. But who did the voice claim crazy if it wasn't me?

The name fell from my lips. "Kendall!"

"He's the crazy one," I repeated with the voice.

Once again I fought to keep my eyes open. I hated this place.

Paranoia crept into my thoughts and I feared for my safety. Somebody knew something. Something about Kendall.

Yet, why would someone warn me of danger only to leave me in no shape to do anything about it? And who? I thought back to the voice: *I didn't give you your last dose of meds.*

Someone risked their job for that bit of information. An insider, but why? And who would leave me in this condition? It took a minute more to register. Then it seemed obvious. Brandy.

My tired arms couldn't even begin to reach the phone. Each futile attempt exhausted me even more. As the room grew dim, I knew I didn't want to find out what kind of sick plan Kendall had in store for me. I had to get away. At least I had to try...

...my eyes opened again. Crap! I'd fallen asleep. I wondered how much time had passed by.

I looked around. Nothing had changed. Yelling for help would only make a scene—I'd end up with a shot in the arm, rendering me unconscious and vulnerable. Ensnared in torment, I cursed Kendall's name while I waited for the medication's disabling side effects to wear off.

The clock's slender red second hand glided across the face in the expected circular fashion; except that it moved too fast. I could only hope I had enough time to escape before whatever awful plan could be implemented. I wondered how long it'd been since my last dose of medicine.

With any attempt to raise my head, the room spun uncontrollably. Foolishly, I sent out ESP messages to anyone who might come to visit. The second hand had just completed another full circle when two unfamiliar men entered my room.

Time had run out.

CHAPTER THIRTY-FOUR

AN EMPTY ROOM

JOHN STOMPED ON THE ACCELERATOR. The needle passed the eighty mph mark.

"I'm worried too, but let's be sure we make it," Elizabeth said, wringing her hands.

John didn't hear his wife. He was too busy mentally rehearsing all the different ways he could apologize to his daughter for leaving her in the hospital.

The white truck barreled down the highway. A blanket and pillow lay in the back seat.

"I'm such an ass." John spoke up. "To think I actually believed I was helping my daughter."

Elizabeth reached out for John's arm. "It's not your fault. Nobody knew the truth. Even Emily was convinced she was hallucinating."

John looked starkly at his wife. "Kat knew the truth."

"Yeah, but she still believes in the Easter Bunny."

"You're missing the point, Izzy. Emily asked me straight out for my help. And I left!"

"When?" Elizabeth's voice cracked.

"Just after you phoned about Kat missing. She was only mumbling, I thought—I don't know what I thought. Somehow, she must have figured it out… and I abandoned her."

"For Pete's sake John, we didn't know! You drove out to the farm yourself."

John pressed his lips together and his forehead creased. "How will we ever make this up to Emily?"

Elizabeth shook her head. "We can't. But hopefully, she will forgive us, anyway."

John thought back to his days of playing hockey. He remembered the first time he broke someone's nose during a fistfight and wished for a similar meeting with Kendall.

Tearing into the hospital parking lot, John came to a screeching halt, occupying several stalls of the first row. The elevator seemed to take forever as John repeatedly jabbed the button with his thumb. Finally, the elevator opened with a ding. John took his wife's hand and boarded.

Entering Emily's room, John immediately noticed the vacant bed. His breath stopped short. "What the hell?"

Elizabeth peered in the bathroom and shook her head.

"Maybe they saw improvement and took her out for a walk," John said, searching for a positive scenario.

"If she was awake, she'd be calling," Elizabeth replied. She turned and left the room. John followed his wife to the nearby nurses' station. An unfamiliar nurse sat behind stacks of paperwork.

"May I help you?" the nurse asked, almost like she expected something unpleasant.

Elizabeth's eyes were focused on the nurse's name tag. "Yes… *Jenna*, you can. Where is Emily?"

"Emily?" the nurse echoed back, wrapping her fingers around her badge.

"Yes, Emily Stokes. Our daughter, who should be in room 308." Elizabeth thumbed over her shoulder.

"I-I'm sorry, but she's not here," Jenna stammered.

"Where is she?" John asked, his tone accusing.

The nurse seemed to shrink. "Across town at Parkview."

"What? Transfer orders were canceled!" Elizabeth yelled.

"Not this again!" John's temper flared.

"She wasn't transferred. She's obtaining out-patient services. She just left," said Jenna.

"How long ago?" Elizabeth demanded.

"Minutes. W-w-while Mr. Stokes was here this morning, he signed some papers authorizing additional treatments." The nurse held up sheets of white papers, maybe as some sort of proof, or to deny responsibility.

John's thoughts bounced back to a homely nurse interrupting the story he had been reading to his daughter. She handed him a stack full of papers to sign. "Just file fillers" were her exact words. "It was a whole pile of papers. I read the first few—"

Elizabeth's eyes flashed. "I can just see Kendall burying his damn treatment papers in the middle of something else."

John's stomach tightened. "What exactly did I authorize?"

"Dr. Kendall requested Emily take part in an experimental procedure he's developing for sudden onset of psychotic symptoms. It's called TMS."

Elizabeth blinked like she was in pain. "What's that?"

"Trans-magnetic stimulation," the nurse replied. "It uses magnetic currents to stimulate certain areas of the brain."

John felt his skin turn cold.

Elizabeth reached over the counter, grabbed the phone and thrust it at the nurse. "Put in a call to stop it," she ordered, then grabbed her husband. "Run."

"Are there side-effects?" John asked as they took off down the hall.

"It's *her brain* we're talking about," Elizabeth screeched as she pounded on the elevator door. "I don't want anybody doing anything to her brain!"

John scoured the halls. "The stairs!" he yelled, yanking his wife's hand.

Racing down the steps, Elizabeth huffed, "We can't be late."

"Don't even go there," John said, over his own breaths. "We'll make it."

This time, when John got in the truck, he didn't let off the gas until they skidded in front of the Parkview entrance doors. John and Elizabeth sprinted towards the admissions desk hollering for directions.

John made it to the attendant first. "Where's the brain lab?"

"Excuse me? Please calm down, Sir, or I'll have to call for security."

"Where is the damn lab?" John pounded his first on the desk.

"Sir!" the receptionist threatened.

"John, over here." Elizabeth tugged her husband's sleeve, guiding him in a short sprint down the corridor. "I once had to pick up one of my parolees here." She gasped for breath as she stopped in front of a directory. "We'll find it ourselves."

"Look." John pointed an unsteady finger to the white letters inside the glass covered directory. "Let's try the third floor."

The lit numbers above the elevator door indicated the lift was at the top floor. "Can't we get a bit of luck today?" John growled as he searched for the stairwell door.

Running up the first set of stairs seemed easy.

"I'm out of shape!" Elizabeth wheezed as they raced past the second floor. Half way up the next stairwell, she began to falter. "Oh, God, please don't let me have a heart attack."

"Are you serious?" John took his wife's arm and helped propel her up the spiraling stairs.

"I hope not, but I think this is the third floor," Elizabeth heaved in exhaustion, then fell against the door while trying to open it. John supported his wife with one hand as he held the door open with the other.

Elizabeth scanned the hall from right to left. "I don't… think this…is it," she puffed.

"Up or down?" John asked as he inched further into the hall.

"I…don't…know," she said on the verge of a sob.

His stomach suddenly burned like it was full of molten lava. His fists clamped shut. He turned his face upward and his voice boomed, "Help us…please?"

"Hey, you!" A staff member poked his head out from a room down the hall. "Keep it down."

John returned the unfriendly look. "Hey yourself. We're looking for the…" he looked to Elizabeth.

"TMS," she said, her hope returning. "The suites for the TMS procedures."

"It's up on the next floor," the man replied. "Hey, wait—"

"Thanks man," John called over his shoulder as the two dashed back for the stairwell.

Racing to the next level, John reached the doorknob first. Adrenaline-rich muscles yanked the door with excessive force; the door opened too far and bounced off the wall, slamming back onto John's face. A gash broke open beside his left eye. Blood poured out like a water faucet.

"Aughh—" John let out a husky howl, slapping his hand over his wound.

Elizabeth frantically scanned the barren area for anything that could be used as a bandage. "I'll find a bathroom."

"Give me your shirt," John demanded.

"What?" Elizabeth's eyes went wide.

"You women wear four layers nowadays, for Pete's sake! Give me your damn shirt."

Elizabeth ripped off her blouse, sending buttons flying. She wadded it up and handed it to her husband.

John stuffed it on his face. "Now, let's go," he said, pushing Elizabeth into the hall.

A heavy set of silver doors just started to close up ahead. Above the access, a sign read: "Treatment Suite." A smaller sign attached to the door stated: "Authorized Personnel Only".

"I can make it." Elizabeth took off running.

She made it, just in time to hear the lock click.

"No!" she wailed, desperately groping the door panels. There were no handles. "This place is a nightmare! We can't get in."

"Oh, I think we will," John muttered, pounding on the silver metal door.

Elizabeth turned toward her husband and winced at the sight of the saturated blouse.

"Don't worry about me," he said.

"It looks bad."

"It's a cut, Izzy. Don't worry!" John repeated.

Trying to dismiss the gruesome sight, Elizabeth pointed to a scanner located next to the door. "We need an access badge."

"We need a good lawyer." John resumed pounding on the door. "Let us in! There has been a terrible mistake!"

"Let us in! I need my Emily," Elizabeth pleaded.

"Step aside!" a voice of authority sounded from behind them.

Both John and Elizabeth whirled around to find none other than Dr. Kendall.

Flames burned John's cheeks. "You!" John growled. "You sick bastard! You are responsible for this."

"What is the meaning of this outburst?" Kendall asked harshly, his arm flailing in the air.

"We've come for our daughter. Take us to her now!" Elizabeth demanded.

"That would be difficult," Kendall replied.

"At least stop the procedure," John demanded.

"I can't." Kendall stepped back, away from the bloody shirt. "It hasn't started."

Elizabeth's knees went weak. "What kind of a game are you playing, anyway?"

"No game. Let me reassure you, I fully believe this treatment is in her best interest."

"Nonsense!" Elizabeth said. "Why else would you hide the authorizations? I tell you, I've had to deal with types like you more often than I'd like to remember, but you definitely top them all!"

"And what type might that be, Madam?"

"One who derives power by lording over those who truly have no power. Your pompous attitude is only a poorly disguised cover up of your true feelings of inadequacy. In layman's words, Dr. Kendall, you suffer from Small Dick Syndrome!"

An eavesdropping orderly stifled a laugh as he held ajar the double doors. "You folks must be Mr. and Mrs. Stokes. We've been expecting you. Excuse me Dr. Kendall, but would you like to show the Stokes' in, or should I just bring them back?"

Kendall scarcely acknowledged the question as he dismissed them all with the slight of his hand.

"Follow me." The orderly gestured; his friendly voice added a calming effect to the situation.

"How in the hell can they call this a 'suite'?" John asked, rereading the posted signs on the wall.

Elizabeth pulled him past.

"It looks like you'll be needing some stitches," the orderly stated, looking back at John. "We can't do that here, but I can arrange for transportation over to the ER."

"Thanks, but no thanks. I've got my truck."

The orderly acknowledged John's response with a worried nod.

John scanned the surroundings, which were gray and dull, except for the orderly, who was dressed in green scrubs. He felt uncomfortable in the dimly lit area and it occurred to him that he stepped rather quietly, as if avoiding capture.

The orderly led them through a second door where a padded table dominated the room. Behind it, stood a nervous looking woman dressed in a white lab coat, fiddling with the linens in her hands.

"Our daughter: Emily Stokes. Where is she?" Elizabeth asked.

The woman glanced over at the male orderly and then back at the couple. "She never arrived. I got a call from security not too long ago."

A hot flash zipped through John's body. He didn't know whether to be alarmed or relieved. "Where is she?" he asked.

"I'm afraid I can't answer that. It seems that she disappeared sometime during her transfer," she replied.

John looked to Elizabeth. She stood motionless, her eyes transfixed on the floor. Finally, she looked up and met John's eyes.

"This is good," she said.

CHAPTER THIRTY-FIVE

THE FUGITIVE

I PRETENDED to be asleep the moment the men entered my hospital room.

"A-1 Transporting Service. Here for Emily Stokes," one of them said.

"She's knocked out, Ted. No need for introductions."

"So she is," Ted replied.

At the mention of a transfer, my mind raced with all sorts of awful scenarios. The gnat's warning popped loudly in my ears: *Get out as soon as possible. Dr. Kendall is crazy.*

Heat flushed my body.

"Not like that," the other man snapped. "Put the gurney on this side." Sounds of scuffling feet stopped as something jarred against my bed.

"Can I help you fellas?" I recognized the voice...the young nurse, Brandy. I considered grabbing onto her.

"Naw, we got it." Ted spoke up.

"You two taking her over to Parkview?" Brandy asked.

"That would be the plan," the bossy one stated.

A hand rested upon my leg. Maybe it was Brandy's.

"I wish she didn't have to go there. It's no place for a girl like this," she said.

"Why not?" asked Ted.

"It's not our decision," the bossy one snapped. "We work for a transport company and it's our job to transport this patient. Now, excuse me. We need to be on our way."

After being lifted and bumped onto the other bed, I silently thanked Brandy for the little information she had just given me. I gathered that whatever awaited me at Parkview was what I needed to avoid.

In no time at all, I was being rushed down the hall towards a place where I should never arrive. The high pitch screech of a squeaky wheel became my solace knowing its silence meant something worse. I tried to concentrate, to come up with a plan, but with each curve we rounded, the only idea that grew stronger was my fear.

I needed help.

But I only had *me*.

Forcing aside my darkest uncertainties, I knew I couldn't arrive at Parkview. Somehow, I had to escape; denial wouldn't work for me this time. An escape. Yes. I'd sneak away during the transfer.

A gust of hot air signaled our passage through the automatic doors. An engine idled nearby.

The screeching wheel went silent. I could scarcely breathe.

"Open the door," the bossy man said. A draft of chilled air mixed with the humid air outside.

Faster than I thought possible, I was inside the vehicle. Only the doors didn't shut.

"I'll ride in back," Ted said. The rear end of the vehicle sagged as he stepped aboard.

My plan was doomed.

"Just ride up in front with me," the bossy partner replied. "She's not going anywhere. Let's eat our burgers before they get completely cold."

"Yeah, I hate stale fries," Ted agreed. The back of the vehicle bobbed upward.

The doors closed, leaving me unaccompanied.

All at once, a huge weight seemed to rise off my chest. Opening my eyes for the first time since leaving my room, I found myself in the back of a no-frills cargo van. With my head off the pillow, I realized the vertigo was nearly gone and I started to believe I might actually pull this off. Eyeing the door latch, it looked simple enough to operate; a quick turn and I'd slip out. But I couldn't allow myself to get too excited. I wasn't free yet.

Not knowing the intended route, I considered it best not to wait too long. Too bad Brandy didn't mention how long the trip would take.

The van started to move. One of the men switched on the radio and cranked it up. Better still.

I easily unbuckled the safety straps, and keeping low, rolled off the bed and crouched on the floor. The intense feel of cold steel beneath my feet made me gasp. Unnoticed by the two men, I edged to the far rear of the plain metal van.

I was ready. My hand gripped the door latch. At the next stop, I'd do it.

Or the next.

With no windows in the back of the van, I was flying blind. The loud music playing up front prevented me from hearing any outside noises. Double whammy. At least I had my wits.

It took a while for the van to come to a second stop. When it did, I made the commitment. Twisting the handle, I pushed the door open a crack and hoped for the best. The intersection looked deserted. Quietly, I gathered the back of my hospital gown, slipped out the back of the vehicle and gently pressed the door closed.

Checking for gawking pedestrians, I skirted to the sidewalk and watched the A-1 transport vehicle drive off as the light turned green.

I was free.

Glancing down both paths of the sidewalks, a frown crossed over my face. *Now if only there were still payphones on the corners!*

Unfamiliar with the lower side of town, I continued south in hopes of finding a main road, or at least something other than housing. It couldn't have been more than two minutes before I heard a squad car tear around the corner.

My heart lurched to my throat. *They're on to me!*

With only half a block between us, I dove into the middle of leafy shrubbery, not expecting a yard on the other side. I landed in what squished like dog poop, but I was so afraid, it didn't really matter at this point.

The police car raced past without slowing.

Were the cops really looking for me…a fugitive? What would they do to me if they found me?

I waited for my heart to recover. Then I wiped my hand in the grass. Taking to my feet, I snuck around the landscape and peered down the sidewalk, wondering where I could find a phone.

A siren blared in the near distance. Something was going on. I fled back to the safety behind the bushes as two more police cars zipped past. They headed in the same direction as the first. Maybe to Parkview.

I made it as far as a Chinese restaurant when the patrol cars returned and started trolling the streets. If any were K-9 units, I'd be had for sure. I scrambled to the back-end of the building and wedged myself between a dumpster and a small privacy fence to wait it out. The sides of the dumpster were plastered with layers of old food and slimy grunge; the fence, with splinters. The smell of rancid oil clung to the air. I held my breath and hoped my pounding heart wouldn't give me away. The crackle of a police scanner gave away their location. I envisioned a uniformed officer peering out an open car window.

And all the means of discipline strapped to his belt.

Fear and worry filled my head. *What if the cop is having a bad day? What if he has anger management problems? What if he shoots me?*

The K-9 dogs never arrived and eventually, the sounds of the scanner moved on, allowing me to make my next move. I had to find a phone. For the first five minutes I walked with a limp because my right leg had gone numb from squatting in such an awkward position. For the next five, I wondered where the cops went, and what was living inside the grease smeared all over my hospital gown.

After the wind picked up and blew the back of my robe wide open, I considered it might be better to take my chances with the cops. I'd surrender with my hands up. I was tired, every pebble I stepped on stuck to the bottom of my bare feet, and I smelled like an old egg roll. Then I spied the clothesline.

I felt a bit like a creeper, sneaking into the back yard. The clothes were worn, boys, and the pants were way too big around the waist, but at least I was rid of the hospital garb. As I stashed the robe in a neighboring trash can, it occurred to me there might me a drugstore on Gage. Gage was only three blocks away.

"Excuse me," I said to the girl behind the counter at Walgreen's. The way she looked at me made me very self-conscious; I went for my hair and felt muck on the back of my head. Something must have rubbed off while I hid behind the dumpster at the Chinese restaurant. I gave the cashier a polite smile. "I'm part of a church group. We're raising money for homeless people by pretending to live like one." I thought it was a pretty good excuse for looking like I did.

The girl appeared to be about my age. "Oh, yeah, I think I heard about this. It sounds like fun. I should have signed up."

"Do you think I could use the phone here?" Whoever designed the building placed the entrance parallel with the main street. A squad car traveling too slowly caught my eye. I pressed closer to the counter.

The girl's eyes traveled to the road and back to me. "We're not supposed to let anyone use the house phone," she said.

"Please, I really don't feel well. I'd like to call my parents for a ride."

The girl thought a moment more. "Make it quick." She handed me the phone. "My boss is in the back."

I dialed Mom's cell number. "Don't freak out. I'm okay. You're where? Who's getting stitches? I found clothes… At Walgreen's, the one on Gage …I'll be waiting."

I handed the phone back to the girl and tried to hide behind a rack of greeting cards beside the automatic front doors. Ignoring the cashier staring at me, I looked out onto the sun creating its final glory for the day, casting florescent orange rays into gray-blue skies. Tears spilled down my face. It was over.

I was already half way out the door when the yellow taxi pulled into the lot. Mom barreled out the door.

"Emily! Oh, thank God, Emily!" She proceeded to give me a hug, much like the kind that Kat gave.

My baggy pants nearly fell off in the process.

"I'm so sorry," she finally added.

"It's okay."

She held me out at arm's length for a visual inspection. Then she embraced me again. "How are you feeling? Ew, you smell terrible."

"Thanks, mostly tired. No worse for wear."

"My dear, sweet Emily. I can't imagine…"

"Let's just get out of here. I think the cops are after me." I expected her hug to loosen, but instead it tightened.

"It's not you. The cabbie told me that someone robbed this very store earlier today."

And to think I was afraid of the good guys!
"What's with the cab, anyway?"

"Your dad needed the truck to drive back over to the hospital to get his stitches," she said, still holding me.

"Shouldn't *he* have taken a taxi?"

"You know your father," she said. And then just stood there. "I can't seem to let you go." With a tiny huff, or maybe a laugh, she gave me another kiss on the forehead. "Are you hungry? We can hit a drive-thru." With a bit more struggling, she finally managed to break an arm free to open the cab door. Climbing in after me, she left no room between us. Settling in, her arm wrapped around my shoulders and I laid my head to rest.

The cab pulled up in front of the hospital and I could see Dad waiting just inside the emergency entrance. Even from inside, I could see the large gauze turban wound around his head and left side of his face.

"It's my Sunshine!" he said, emerging from the waiting area with his arms outstretched. Wrapped in his arms, I felt warm and loved.

"Your face. Does it hurt?" I asked, letting go.

"Still numb." He poked his finger into his cheek.

"It looks bad. How many stitches?" I said.

"It's just a little scratch. Twelve," Dad replied, looking a bit proud.

"Twelve?" Mom shrieked.

"Did Brandy call you and tell you to come?" I asked.

"Who's Brandy?" Dad asked.

"A nurse. I'm not really sure, but I think she decided not to give me the medicine any more. Could she get into trouble for that?"

"The only one who's getting in trouble is Kendall." Dad's face twisted.

"I'd like to thank her, if she did," Mom added.

With my Dad's head wrapped in a gauze turban, and blood on my mother's clothes, I wondered what all I'd missed. Making sure no one else was near, I leaned in closer to my parents. Copying me, we formed a tight circle.

"You didn't leave him in an alley somewhere, did you?" I whispered.

"Emily James Stokes!" Mom barked.

Dad laughed. Then it started. "There's a man who should have never been allowed to practice medicine. I. Tell. You…I'm getting a lawyer and—"

"Thanks for coming to get me." I wrapped my arms around his waist. His tirade ended. "You too, Mom."

"Thank yourself, Em. I'm not sure how you managed to get out of the hospital unnoticed, but they'll be talking about you for years!"

I managed a smile. "Where do we go from here?" I asked, still clinging to my father.

"Home, I suppose," he said. "Unless there is something else—"

"So, do you still think I'm crazy?" The words brought about a sudden wave of nausea.

"Oh, honey!" Mom sighed. "We never believed you were crazy. Kendall's diagnosis was convenient, but it didn't make sense. Dad and I talked about toxins… concussions. We knew something wasn't right, but didn't have an explanation."

"That's right. Do *you* know you're not crazy?" Dad asked with a candid laugh.

Relieved, I finally had the courage to let go. "I figured it out just before the medication arrived. What changed your minds?"

Mom's brow rose in a bewildered gasp. "Kat brought Sam home."

I thought back to the last time I had seen him. *Explode.* I thought about all the things I discovered on the Internet about his parent's history. "What did you think about Sam?"

My parents looked at one another.

"I think we were hoping you could tell us," Dad said.

I didn't want it to, but my face cringed anyway. "I think I'm dating a dead guy."

CHAPTER THIRTY-SIX

RESUSCITATION

THE LAST THING Alex did was grab his chest and fall to his knees.

For a long time, there was nothing.

Then, he heard *her* voice.

CHAPTER THIRTY-SEVEN

REGRETS

STILL JUST A COUPLE OF YARDS from the hospital entrance, Dad shook his head, like he was trying to assemble some logic in his thoughts. "Let's get out of here. That is, if the truck is still here. I'm pretty sure I left the thing running."

As he put his arm around me to leave, a shrill siren announced an incoming ambulance. Flashing red and blue lights beamed off the top of the vehicle. Moments later, the ambulance came to an abrupt halt inside the adjoining admit shelter.

Although I knew it was impolite to gape, it was the natural thing to do. I scurried back to the entrance and I pressed my nose against the glass to avoid the glare.

The emergency team worked quickly, and soon a gurney holding a body was hoisted from the back of the ambulance. I inched farther down the window to get a better view.

"That's Alex!" I exclaimed as my curiosity turned to horror. I couldn't take my eyes off the stretcher.

"Are you sure?" asked Dad.

I didn't answer. Instead, I searched for a passage way into the ambulance entrance to see my first love.

"Alex!" I barged into the middle of the commotion. He was pale, even gray. He had an oxygen mask strapped around his mouth. Hoses seemed to be connected everywhere. For the first time in a long time, I saw his steel-blue eyes. Glazed and unresponsive, they looked like death.

"What are you doing here?" a large EMT asked, shoving his face before mine.

I froze, believing I was in trouble. I stared at his mouth, waiting.

"You know this boy?" he asked.

"Yes. Yes, I do. He's Alex Hibbs." A new kind of fear I'd never felt before ran through my entire body. "What is wrong with him?"

"We got an anonymous call. He OD'd in the park. Probably meth," the man said loudly over the organized confusion. "Are you family?"

Wide-eyed, I shook my head.

"Stick around. You can tell us how to reach his family." The EMT brushed past, pushing Alex farther into the hospital and out of sight.

All became quiet, but the chaos lingered in the circulating red and blue lights that bounced off the walls, the windows, and even my skin. Mom and Dad appeared first, followed by an obese woman with a wobbly gait.

"My name is Wanda Greenberg." She held out her thick black hand. "I'm with Social Services. Are you willing to give us some information?"

"Is he going to die?" I asked.

"Frightening, isn't it? People just don't realize what they are getting themselves into." Wanda's lips squished to one side in a frown. "So, are you still willing to give us some information on the young man?"

"Of course." That was an easy decision.

We followed Wanda as she waddled past the admission desk. With each step I took, I thought less about her weight problem and more about Alex. Guilt began to pile heavy upon my back: why had I been so mean to Alex? Why didn't I call him back? Why? Why? Why! All he ever did was care.

Halfway down a long corridor, we stopped in front of an open door. A shiny gold name plate was glued to the wall beside the doorjamb. Her name appeared in plain white letters.

Wanda extended her arm. "Please take a seat."

Sitting behind her own desk, she assumed an expression like she had done this before. "Were you with him?"

My eyes went wide.

"Where you the one who dialed 911?"

"Oh, no," my words came out in a nervous laugh. "I just happened to be here, at the hospital, with my Dad," I said, pointing.

Her shoulders relaxed. "Then I'd like to start out by saying how glad I am that you are willing to get involved!" Wanda leaned forward and folded her hands on her desk. "That young man sure is lucky to have a friend like you."

Friend? Did she actually have to go and say the word "friend"? As if my guilt wasn't bad enough? Accessory *to his problem was more like it.* "Is he going to be all right?"

"Honey, let me put it to you this way." Wanda's eyes grew large and her head bobbed from side to side. "If you were a prayin' girl, I'd start right away. If he makes it through the night, he'll still have plenty more hurdles to jump over as he battles *this* demon."

I hid my face in my hands.

"Oh mercy! What's the trouble here?" Wanda asked.

"Our daughter used to be…quite fond of the boy," Mom offered as an interpretation.

"Oh, I see." Wanda leaned further over her desk. "Chin up, honey. You did the right thing. This act of kindness will not soon be forgotten."

All I could manage was a scowl.

CHAPTER THIRTY-EIGHT

LIFE AFTER DEATH

I COULDN'T SHAKE the image of Alex's unfocused eyes. They were so…void. He looked dead. After giving Wanda the information she needed, my parents and I began the drive home. Despite the warm night air, I wrapped myself in a fleece blanket I found in the back seat.

Without making a conscious effort, my thoughts wandered to an English essay I had written in Mrs. Johnson's class my sophomore year. My topic had been about death. I discovered that more people die from heart disease than any other cause of death. I read that being crushed by a war elephant was rated among the manliest ways to die, and I learned that falling into a vat of aspheric acid would be one of the most painful ways to die.

I wondered how Sam had died. I wondered if Alex was going to die. I wondered how old I'd be when I died.

It wasn't often that our truck was silent, but Mom and Dad looked as exhausted as I felt. About halfway home, I realized the truck had been quiet for too long. "Where is Kitty?"

"Home," Mom replied.

"Alone?"

"With Sam," Dad said.

His simple reply made me pause. "You trusted Sam with Kathryn?"

My parents gave each other an evaluating look. "Sometimes," Mom offered, "circumstances make choices for you."

"Huh?"

"We believe Kat went out looking for Sam. Somehow, she found him. That's gotta count for something," Dad said, finishing Mom's thought.

They continued sharing the story of how Kat showed up with Sam. I laughed at the funny parts. Mostly of the fainting, the flashing, and the name, Mr. Strobe Light.

"Who'da thunk she could have pulled it off?" I asked, mostly to myself. It was too easy to get caught up in the annoying part of my sister.

"I'd say we have *two* heroes in our family," Dad added, still chuckling.

My smile gave way and the ache in my gut increased to the point of being noticed. "Are either of you mad at me or Sam?"

Silence.

"Confused, bewildered…it never occurred to me to be angry," Mom said. "Are you?" Her eyes were on Dad when she asked the question, but I thought the question was intended for me.

I considered the last time I had seen Sam. He had exploded into a million little pieces. It had been terrifying. But no, I wasn't mad.

"I'm just glad we have you back safely!" Mom said finally.

Dad pulled the truck in front of the garage door. The engine idled loudly for a moment before he killed it. He twisted to face me. "Are you ready?"

I shifted in my seat and the pungent smell of eggroll filled my nostrils. It made me shudder.

It was a strange homecoming, from a strange outing. I knew that Kat would be excited to see me— alive and unscathed. She would no doubt get a running start and nearly break my neck in a violent hug…. But what about Sam? How would he react? How should I react? My heart thumped. I wanted to wait outside until I felt the joy of being in love. Right now, I felt fear. Or exhaustion. Or, I don't know what.

Outside the truck, I frowned at the clothes I'd stolen off the clothesline. I couldn't be sure what made me feel worse: stealing or my appearance. Then I noticed the dust and dirt that had seeped up between my toes. I looked up in time to catch Mom's eyes as they finished their assessment.

"At least your braids look nice." Mom said, tugging one. "I've got some blush in my purse." She dabbed my checks. "And lastly…" she retrieved a tube of lip balm and traced my lips.

"That feels good." I rubbed my lips together.

"I think that's as good as it gets." Mom smiled her endearing smile.

"Emily—" Dad stepped closer. "You have been through a lot the past few days. No one expects a Beauty Queen to walk through the door. I am just thankful we completed our mission today…bringing you home safe and sound. But, just to let you know, even after everything, you'd still give any contestant a run for their money if you showed up for a pageant looking like this."

"Thanks, Dad." While his words brought some comfort, I still felt scared about seeing Sam. "You go in first."

Dad paused to unwrap his turban, leaving a rectangular bandage taped to his face. With an exaggerated smile, he opened the door and walked in the house. "We're home."

Kat was already waiting by the door. "Yeah!" She went to give Dad a hug, and then her eyes went big. "Whoa! Your face!" She put her fingers over the gauze covering Dad's stitches.

"It's all cool," he said. "It looks worse than it really is."

Kat's eyes shifted back and forth from the covered wound to me. Satisfied he was safe, she came bounding for me. "Emily, you're home!"

As Kat took her last leap, her arms opened wide and I braced myself for the ferocious hug.

"I knew I could find him, Emmy!" she continued, speaking too loud. "I found him and brought him back home!"

"Thank you, Kitty." I lowered her back to the floor and fluffed the top of her hair. "You are my hero."

"Hey! You guys had Chinese food without me. No fair!" she whined. Tugging me by the hand, Kat led me through the kitchen. "Come in and see him."

The harder Kat pulled, the slower I walked. Angry hornets buzzed in my stomach. The skin on my arms and back turned hot. I stopped under the archway to catch my breath. Stalling, I glanced over my shoulder to see my parents a few steps behind me.

"What are you waiting for?" With a giant yank, Kat pulled me into the adjoining room. I entered with a loud thud. "She's here!" Kat squealed, maintaining a smile from ear to ear.

Regaining my balance, I saw something that made me stop and stare.

"Hello, Emily." A tall, transparent white cloud hovering near the sofa began to drift across the floor to our side of the room.

Straining, I recognized facial features that resembled Sam. The body, if I could call it that, was scarcely defined. White wispy curls gracefully trailed from its edges and back. "Sam?"

"Yes!" Kat blurted out, unable to contain her excitement. "Isn't this cool? He can get tall, short, thin, fat, disappear, and even fly!"

"Where's your color?" I managed to ask, even though my thoughts were several stages past bewilderment. I looked back at my parents again. "Do you believe this?"

"No," Dad answered.

"The sun has set," Sam explained. "I use the color spectrum from the sun to maintain a colored form."

I was reluctant for further conversation, occupied by my appearance, but curiosity overruled. "You look like a cloud—"

"That's 'cause he's made out of water!" Kat squealed, still very charged.

Sam passed something of an arm in front of his unformed body. Feathery edges trailed freely as he moved. "Yes, the gravitational pull of the moon... it messes with my atomic cohesion. You should see me during a solar flare!" Sam joked, but his smile quickly faded. "I guess this is one downfall of being a ghost."

I heard it. He said it. *Ghost.*

"What else affects your appearance?" Dad asked.

"Mostly the weather, sir." Sam drifted closer to my father. "My molecules have little cohesion of their own. Like this, I am slightly heavier than air. But, I have learned a technique to artificially produce— it's really not important."

"Go on," I heard myself say.

Sam turned toward me, but kept his distance. "I gain density by absorbing water and energy from my surroundings, much like a developing rain cloud. It takes a lot of solar energy to fully form, to pick things up, or…" The white wispy floating Sam looked at my sister, who was bouncing on her knees on the couch. "To hold your hand, Kat."

Sam moved slowly in my direction. He had no feet: only whiteness that tumbled upon itself like waves coming into shore. "Obviously, there are some things that I cannot compete with. Actual raindrops or standing water is much too heavy. And as you saw firsthand, Emily, lightning is not my friend, either." He looked at me apologetically before swooshing toward me. His quick movement left a thick trail of mist that caught up to him seconds later.

"I am so sorry if I scared you, Emily." The edges of his body turned to a rippling state of flux. "I can't even begin to imagine what that was like, seeing me burst into pieces."

Once again, I thought back to the loft. I remembered the odd dampness I felt on my skin. It had been Sam—a raincloud— exploding.

"By the time I pulled myself back together," he continued, "your mother arrived. I panicked." Pain filled the lines in his visible features. "I waited for a while for you to come back, but you didn't." He paused and his milky-colored eyes searched mine. "I finally returned to the farm, hoping you would come to me."

"Why didn't you just stay here?" Mom asked next.

"I couldn't. I was no longer an invited guest in your home. If an uninvited spirit dwells for too long, it attaches to the house. That is how hauntings occur."

Dad grimaced.

"Emily…" Sam turned back towards me.

A terrible sorrow appeared in the shadows of his face. His pale white lips opened farther.

I could tell he was about to tell me something heavy, something important. "Not now," I said. "Not yet. Let me shower and put on some real clothes. I'd like to look presentable." Then I made a hasty exit.

I was appalled by my reflection in the mirror when I flicked on the light in the bathroom. Steam soon billowed out above the shower door and the smell of wildflowers filled the air.

With my hair wrapped up in a towel, and another around my body, I wiped the condensation from the mirror in a circular motion. A small smile formed on my lips. My internal mood rings weren't green with grief or melancholy tan. They were blue. I was home safe and Sam was waiting for me downstairs; that's all that really mattered.

I grabbed my toothbrush and toothpaste and gave my teeth a well deserved cleaning. As the paste began to foam, I wondered what God thought of us hosting a ghost downstairs in our living room.

After combing my hair, I went to my bedroom for some clothes. I also wondered why Sam was still on Earth. Dressed in comfortable lounging clothes, I looked in the mirror once again. This time, I approved.

"There she is," Dad commented from the sunroom. My family, plus Sam, sat around the glass topped table. All eyes turned toward me, and I felt a bit tense, kind of like making a stage entrance, rather than walking inside my house. "Sam was just telling us about the day you showed up at his farm."

"Yes." Sam's form rose in what appeared to be a standing position, except that he was standing within the center of the chair.

Mom gave Dad the look and whispered, "I'm a sucker for old-school charm."

"I'd pull out a chair for you, Emily, but—" He held up his two wisps of arms.

Dad quickly stood and fumbled for a chair beside Sam. "Sit here, honey."

As I took my seat, I checked the window to see if Sam cast a reflection, and he did. What that meant, I didn't know.

"You know, John," Mom chuckled. "You could learn a thing or two if you pay attention."

"I hope you remembered to brush your teeth," Kat blurted.

"You look beautiful!" Sam seemed unashamed to say in front of my parents.

I'm sure I blushed and for a moment, all I could see was Sam. It was good to see him, even as a ghost. But as my heart found its rhythmic pattern, I felt my stomach tighten, watching his translucent figure vary in a constant state of flux.

"Perhaps it's time to let you two have some quiet time," Mom said as she stood up from the table.

"It's past your bedtime, Kiddo." Dad directed his statement at Kat as he pushed in his seat.

"Awh," she whined. "I don't want to go to bed."

A familiar routine, Mom took hold of Kat's arms and proceeded to pull her off the chair.

I looked over my shoulder to see my sister's limp legs sprawled out behind her as Mom dragged her away. "Little sisters are so annoying."

"At times," Sam said. "She reminds me of my sister."

"Your sister!" Hearing him speak of her reminded me of the story I found on the Internet.

CHAPTER THIRTY-NINE

GOOSEBUMPS

"WHAT IS IT?" Sam asked

I chewed my lip as I debated if I really wanted to tell him the story I had uncovered on the Internet. "What ever happened to your sister?"

"I already told you the story." His voice lost its natural ease, making me wary. "What is it?" he asked.

"You mentioned that uninvited spirits become the kind of ghosts that haunt places?"

"Yes, I did. Why?" he asked, leaning in towards me.

"It's like they become trapped?"

"What do you have to say, Emily?" Crossness scratched his voice while his white billowing edges turned jagged, flickering wildly like flames in a fire.

Seeing this reaction, I stiffened and felt a thick layer of fear crept over me. "Don't hurt me."

The flickering stopped. He closed his eyes and let out soft meditative hum. Once again, his edges softened and rippled gently like an easy breeze. His torso, appearing much like a shifting fog, stirred gracefully.

"Don't be afraid of me Emily. I will never harm you." His arms absorbed into the sides of his body and reemerged out front. "I give you my word."

Was that the reason for my apprehension? Could I be afraid of my...boyfriend. My ghost boyfriend?

A wispy hand came to rest on top of mine.

At first, I thought I'd been zapped by electricity. I jerked in my chair. Still unsure of what just happened, I examined my hand. Unintentionally, my mind zoomed back to the pricker bush in the woods…the tiny kiss he had given me there. It didn't hurt, it felt…

"What just happened?" I asked.

"I apologize. I didn't expect it to be so strong. I should warn you, at night, my touch can be…very intense."

"I…I don't understand." Surprise and fear muddled what felt to be sexual pleasantries.

"With your permission, I'd like to show you something."

In my heart, I trusted Sam, but this request only seemed to make me feel worse. I felt my stomach tighten even more and I wished I knew what I was afraid of. I pressed my lips together until I had the courage to say, "Okay."

Sam replaced his hand upon mine and immediately I felt the heat, the tingling, and the complete pleasure. The sensation worked its way up my arm. "Sam, this is…wow!"

"Do you like it?"

"Ah, um, yes."

Unexpectedly, Sam whooshed directly at me.

Upon impact, my chair slid back from the table in a wild jerk. With a great gasp, my body heaved forward as Sam passed through my very core. Goosebumps speckled my entire body. As chills ran down my spine, the heat of fire spread across my skin. The formless Sam swirled around me like a trained cloud of smoke and I could barely restrain myself from calling out in pleasure, knowing my parents were still in listening range. Much too quickly, my body became spent.

As if he knew I'd had enough, the white spirit swirled higher into the air, stretching out twice his normal height. Nearly touching the ceiling, it made a sudden arch and darted across the top of the room, before finally settling back into a subhuman form hovering within his chair.

I was still trying to catch my breath as Sam started to speak.

"Emily, I apologize for whatever pain you have had to suffer because of me. And I know I should be sorry that I came into your life, but I am not. I have been a lost soul, wandering the land for many years, and for the first time in my life, I feel complete. The last thing I want is for you to be afraid of me."

I couldn't tell if his expression was one of hope or worry.

"At least now you know that I can make you feel good, too."

"Did we just have sex?" I asked, short of breath.

Sam's expression remained guarded. "Did you like it?"

"I don't know. No. I mean, yes, I did like it, but I was hoping to stay a virgin until I married. At least older." I was so flustered I didn't know what I was saying.

"I swear on my honor. You are still a virgin." Sam said. 'I'd feel guilty tarnishing your reputation so soon." He placed his feather-weight hand over his translucent chest.

"But you plan to corrupt my innocent youth?" I huffed, still catching my breath.

"Corruption is such a harsh word." Sam's body glowed for a brief second like it received an extra boost of energy. "I'd prefer to think you'd be a willing partner because you wanted me."

"I would want you, but what just happened was…a little overwhelming." I reached out to touch him, just to double check if the sensation was still there. Instantly, another rush of pleasure spread over my hand. It was so intense. I pulled back. "Does this always happen?"

"Only at night." Sam replied. Creases developed where his forehead ought to be. "But, you sound disappointed. I had hoped you'd like it."

"No, it's not that," I continued to stammer, still awed by the whole thing. "I'd simply like to know if a normal hug is possible, too."

"You're sitting here with a ghost and asking about normal?"

Laughing at myself, I had to confess, "It's a bit confusing not knowing what to expect."

"Here I'm trying to impress you and instead I come off as difficult." Sam's torso swooshed and swayed for a moment before encasing me in a see-through hug. "Here, maybe you will like this better."

Heat penetrated into my muscles, instantly melting my body tension into nonexistence.

"It's like being in a sauna." Then came the moisture. Just when I was about to tell him I'd need a towel if it lasted much longer, a thought occurred to me. "How can you change your physical state so easily?"

The hug ended quickly. "It's not as easy as you might think. It takes a lot of energy to spark, like boiling water without a heat source."

"Spark?"

Sam's hue brightened momentarily, like there was a sudden surge in electrical voltage. "Silly ghost terminology. It's not important."

"Is that how you describe the, intense…feelings when we touch?"

"Something like that."

"Can other ghosts do this?"

"Emily, sparking is something I'd rather not get into at this time, unless it's me doing it to you," he said, with his pale eyes twinkling.

"Maybe I could handle a little more sparking." I leaned forward and for a moment, I thought he was going to kiss me. Instead, he turned a brighter shade of white and flew out of his chair. He buzzed across the ceiling and ricocheted off the walls. He was moving so fast, my eyes only registered a white trail. The room seemed to fill with some kind of energy, and I found myself smiling. The next thing I knew, Sam had me encircled in a white rope of mist.

Goosebumps returned to my flesh and I shivered in pleasure. Blushing, I looked for Sam's face, but there wasn't one. "But not here," I whispered as loud as I could, not to alert my parents. It felt incredible, but the last thing I wanted to do was start moaning out in ecstasy. "My parents are in the other room."

The circling motion stopped and the form of a human quickly took shape, settling back into the chair. "Yes, I should take you back to my place for a little privacy."

I was coming to the conclusion that sparking was kind of an all or nothing deal. "Does that feel good to you, too?"

"You have no idea." The form of Sam leaned back in his chair to relax, but then sprang forward. "I'm so happy I found you."

His statement took me by surprise. "Wait a minute. I was the one who found you."

His form dimmed and small flickers erupted across his edges. "Actually…" It took him a bit too long for him to finish his sentence, "I saw you on your deck before you ever came to me. I heard your guitar and I followed the music. It was so beautiful."

"You were spying on me? That's how you knew I lived by the railroad tracks?"

"It wasn't intentional."

Maybe I was too tired, or too trusting, but his words sounded sincere to me. I found myself a little flattered and cast my eyes on the table.

"After seeing you," he continued, "I schemed of ways to meet you, and low and behold, you came and found me. Destiny! I tell you."

I looked Sam straight in his milky-white eyes. "Do you really believe in destiny?"

Keeping the close physical proximity between us, he replied, "Some days I'm not sure what to believe in. But I do know that right now, I almost feel alive."

Almost alive….

His outer edges thinned and lengthened, curling up and over like an ocean swell. I caught myself listening for the sounds of a crashing wave as I considered the possibility of destiny. Could there really be a master plan that includes a ghost? Dismissing my immediate concerns, my heart filled with warmth. "I'm glad you're here." Then I yawned.

A momentary increase in Sam's hue seemed to indicate he was pleased. "Me too." A brief smile crossed his face. "However, it's late and you must be tired, but before you go to bed, please tell me what you know about my sister."

The question kindled new alertness. "I don't think it's good, Sam."

"What makes you think you know about her anyway?"

I explained my findings of the Goldenrod while at the hospital.

"If that really is Amelia." Sam shook his head. "She's messed up."

"Isn't there anything you can do to help her? It's crazy enough that you are here, but to have both you and your sister still on Earth…what are the odds?"

Sam's body ruffled. "My poor baby sister."

I tried to sound encouraging. "There has to be a reason."

"Not that it'd be a good one."

Seeing Sam's expression made my heart ache. It was foolish on my part, but for a moment, I thought I could console him. Then I considered I had never died, lost my entire family, or learned that my sister had become…demented?

"I'm sorry to be the one telling you this." I reached out touch him. To comfort him. The part of him that I tried to touch scattered like homemade clouds at the children's museum. It made me feel even sadder.

"No one ever said life would be fair, huh?" Then with movement so sudden it made me jump, Sam swooshed through the back of his chair and twirled up toward the ceiling. "You know what's one of the coolest things about being a ghost? Flying!"

I tipped my head back to watch him glide through the air. "I wish I could fly."

After a few more twirls and loops, Sam effortlessly floated back to his chair and the contours of a man began to take shape. "It's absolutely wild…but it doesn't even compare to the things I've had to exist without."

Once again, I couldn't even begin to comprehend what it was like to be dead, but nodded out of respect and tried to imagine….

"What are you thinking about?" Sam asked, bringing me back from a deep thought.

"*Prelude to a Kiss*," I whispered.

"What about it?"

"Can that really happen?"

"I'm no expert, but I'd say a drifter might be able to steal a body."

My arms shot around myself in a safety hug. "Steal it?"

"I wouldn't worry about it, Miss Emily. It only happens when the original body is compromised in some way, like when your grandpa was having surgery."

"Is that what you call your kind? Drifters?"

"I reckon not. Those were some unlucky people who died before their time, and now they're forced to wander the Earth, waiting. For me, it was my time. I'd be a Marmion."

"Marmion? You mean to tell me there are different kinds of…ghosts?"

"Oh, yes." Sam sighed. "Our appearance, abilities, and what side we're on, sets us apart from each other."

"What *side* you're on?"

Sam thought a moment. "In your photographs, have you ever noticed small specks of light? Sometimes, it's not reflections. They're party crashers."

"Party crashers?" I blinked and cocked my head.

"Look at them closely. I'm sure you'll find tiny glowing specks of light. Ghost hunters call them orbs. Actually, those things were never human. They're demonic."

A buzzing stirred in my stomach. "Stop! This is just too much. I can handle you, but I can't handle ghost hunters or a room full of demonic partiers, okay?"

Sam pursed his snow-colored lips. "I suppose I should be more considerate of your feelings. I'm just so dang happy that you know…I want to share everything with you."

"I know," I said, curving over into a slouch. Looking at the reformed hand I tried to hold earlier, I used my finger to trace alongside its edges. "I do want to know everything about you and the way you experience life, but not all in one night." I paused for a yawn. "You are an amazing man with extraordinary tales. That is one of the reasons why I like you."

Sam raised his head and smiled. "So it's not just for my radishes?"

"Sam Easley, you are a rascal!"

Sam's deep laugh comforted my soul.

Excusing another yawn, it was getting difficult to ignore the pains of being completely exhausted. At the same time, I didn't want to leave him. "Before I go to bed, tell me one thing. How old are you, Sam?"

"Well, that depends, doesn't it?"

"On what?"

"If you go by my last birthday or if you continue counting from the time I died."

His response rang absurd in my ears. My question seemed more so. "How old were you when you died?"

"Nineteen."

"You're not as old as I thought. When did you die?"

"In 1936."

A shudder of remorse rattled my upper torso. "That was a long time ago, yet you seem so… unaffected by it."

"Miss Emily, I've been dead longer than I was alive. *This* is normal to me."

"I guess that makes sense. Do you remember dying?"

Sam's body flickered. "It's getting late. Let's send you off to bed and we can talk some more tomorrow."

Accepting the hint, I rose from my chair. "I wonder if my parents are still up?"

"I'm pretty sure I saw them slink off to bed some time ago." Sam also rose from the table, wispy edges trailing slightly.

After I pushed my chair back into place and reached for his chair, I felt an unsettling in my stomach. "How wrong are we to be doing this?"

"That's not what I was expecting to hear," he said.

"That's not what I was planning on saying."

"But you worry."

"Of course I do, Sam. But now it's more than about you being legal adult age."

"You were really worried about that, seriously?"

"Yes and no. I mean, you're such a gentleman; sometimes I think my thoughts are worse than yours. I absolutely adore your country charm. And I think you are extremely attractive when you have a body —"

"But could you love me, like this?" Sam drifted effortlessly beside me.

Again, I noticed how his translucent form swirled and fluxed, offset by the outer edges rippling like a tail fin in the water.

"It's not a question of could, but rather should," I responded.

"Do you want me to leave?"

"Of course not!"

Perhaps in error, a random white wisp brushed against my bare arm. Letting out a quickened moan, I jerked back, reacting like I'd been zapped. "This is just not fair!"

A wicked smile crossed Sam's face. "But you like it."

"Of course I like it. That's not the point."

Sam shrunk to match my height. "Could you love me?"

My chest tightened. He said the L-word twice now. He wanted to know if I could love him. Love Sam. Love a ghost, or a Marmion, or whatever he called himself.

"I don't know if there is a thing called destiny that controls the whole universe, or if I'm making the worst decision of my life, but there's one sure thing I do know right now and that's the moment I laid eyes on you, there was no turning back. You were all I thought about in the hospital."

Sam's chin dropped. "Oh, Emily, I'm sorry."

"I'm not! I do love you. I've loved you from the beginning."

Under normal circumstances, it would have been the perfect time for a passionate kiss. Instead, Sam let out a loud "Yee-haw!"

His form became long and brilliant, stretching several inches above me. Arching back, the faceless figure dove forward with unexpected force, plunging deep into the middle of my chest. Bright light filled the room and seemed to be coming out of my own body. The rays of light turned solid, cracked, and disintegrated into a dense white fog. Under its own power, the fog started spinning wildly around me, 'round and 'round like a small white tornado. My arms felt like they were attached to marionette strings as they rose by an outside force. The wind whirled in my ears and lifted my hair high into the air. Nothing was frightening about it in the least. It was amazing!

I closed my eyes to continue the joyous burst of ecstasy as the sultry flavor of Sam exploded through my senses. The taste was suffocating yet intoxicating at the same time. "I love you, Sam Easley!" I called above the windy whirl. Reopening my eyes, I found myself levitating several inches above the carpet.

CHAPTER FORTY

NATURE OF THE BEAST

IT NEVER OCCURRED TO ME to ask Sam what his plans were while I slept last night. I simply left him at the bottom of our stairs and said, "Good-night."

Waiting to fully recover from the sleep-induced grogginess, I knew this day would be perfect, spending its entirety with Sam…and not worry. I further allowed myself to relive an unbelievable dream filled with whispers that made me giggle, touches that made me want more, and hugs that made me feel the special powers of love hidden inside…all leading up to the incredible, breath taking Kiss!

Too bad I woke up before the kiss actually happened. Not that it really mattered. I'd get a real one soon enough.

I took time getting ready. I wanted to look delicious, and smell delicious. Finally approving, I headed for the steps. I could already hear two men talking in the kitchen, presumably Dad interrogating Sam.

"With some creativity, I probably could, sir."

"Could what?" I asked, barging into the conversation.

There they were, sitting at the kitchen table, acting, and looking, like two normal human beings, except that Sam's color faded at my presence. Sam rose from the table, just as he had done the night before. Not to be outdone, my dad stood up too. My eyes immediately traveled to the gauze bandage on his face.

"Good morning, Miss Emily." Sam tipped his head in the greeting.

"Wow! A standing ovation." I didn't know what else to say.

"Just good manners," Sam replied.

"Nauseous," Dad groaned and sat back down.

"Well, I like it," I snapped. "It makes me feel important."

Rolling his eyes, Dad stood back up and motioned to a chair. "Please join us."

"I'd like to stand. But the two of you may be seated." I felt a little foolish. "Do I say that?"

"Something like that," Sam said.

Dad grumbled, sitting down, again. "I can already tell this isn't going to work out in my favor. To tell you the truth, I've really enjoyed women's rights. Shoveling, mowing—"

"Dad—"

"You look beautiful!" Sam remarked. "How do you feel?"

"I feel great, thank you. So, what were you two talking about?"

"Men stuff," Dad was quick to answer, shifting in his chair.

"What kind of '*men stuff*'?" I teased.

"Your dad wants to know if I'm capable of having sex." Sam watched Dad's reaction, and seemed to thoroughly enjoy the squirming.

I wanted to crawl under a rock. "How could you?"

Sam reached out his muscular arm and hooked my belt loop. Once again, the familiar sweet, smoky taste settled upon my tongue. He pulled me in close against his side. "If I had a daughter as pretty as you, I'd be worried about the same thing."

"Ha!" Dad barked, slapping his hand on the table.

It was my turn to roll my eyes. With minimal force, I broke free of Sam's grasp and headed for a packet of blueberry oatmeal.

"Tell me truthfully, Dad. Are all men pigs?"

"Yes!"

"Were you a pig before you met Mom?"

"I reserve the right to not incriminate myself. On the other hand, your mother knew well in advance exactly what kind of a package deal she was getting."

I tried not to imagine parental sex as I filled the teakettle up with water when a new thought occurred to me. "Do you eat, Sam?"

"No, Miss Emily, I do not."

"That ought to save you a ton of money!" Dad laughed at his own joke.

Sam leaned back in the chair and gave his muscular body a stretch.

Wow, he looked good. No, great.

"I reckon *that* is one of things I miss the most—being able to eat. I have traveled from shore to shore, smelling the most appetizing food you could ever imagine. But that's all I can do, is smell."

Hearing this, I was glad I used my best perfume.

Dad's reaction was quite the opposite. "That sounds horrible! A cruel form of torture no less."

"What foods do you miss the most?" I asked.

"Mmm! Deep south crawdads, roasted spring sweet corn, cheese curds, ice cream, a big thick steak. I've seen far more styles of food than the ones I ate growing up on the farm. I've never tasted a pizza, for example."

"That's very interesting, that you can smell," Dad observed.

"Actually, it's pretty amazing," I corrected. "Sam is very unique. Most…people…like Sam, never develop the kind of abilities he has." My chest puffed up in pride.

"Well, I guess that answers my question of why we don't run into spirit life forms more often," Dad said.

Sam shrugged his shoulders. The conversation lulled.

"Emily, it might be wise to take it easy today." Pushing himself away from the table, Dad stood up. I waited for him to say something more about yesterday, or something about something. "Now, if you two will excuse me, I'm going to get started on my chores." Dad pecked a kiss on my cheek before leaving the kitchen.

With each step Dad took, the deeper Sam's color turned. "Does that always happen?" I asked. "You fading and whatnot."

Sam shrugged again. "It's a by-product of being dead."

His words made me shudder. "Call me faint of heart, but could you not describe yourself as dead? I get this image of a zombie…eww!"

Immediately, Sam lifted his arms to a classic zombie pose. His handsome face turned to a blank stare. "Must… get… the pretty…blonde."

"You're not very scary with your body intact."
Pushing away his zombie grasp, I reached for a spoon.
Sam's arms dropped and his eyes twinkled. He
leaned over and whispered in my ear. "I could give you
gruesome."

My spoon became a miniature sword. "No! I'm
here to inform you that I will not find a rotting zombie
man either attractive or desirable."

"I guess that means you're probably not willing to
engage in a little sexual horror role-playing then, darn."

I shook my head and rolled my eyes. "Where do
guys come up with this stuff? Pigs. All pigs."

Sam laughed. "That doesn't seem quite fair. Last
night you were calling me a gentleman. It seems to me
that the only difference between you and me, is that I
openly communicate my sexual desires." After a smug
expression, Sam took a relaxed pose.

"Oink."

"All right then, since you don't like my idea, what
would you suggest we do today?"

My smile suddenly felt too large for my face. "Just
be with you." I took the kettle off the stovetop and
poured the steaming water over the small dried oats. "I
should also visit an old friend who is ill."

"That's a nice gesture." Sam paused, and then
added, "Who is he?"

My mouth dropped open as I searched for
something to say. "Who said anything about a 'he'?"

"If it were a female, you would have used her
name."

"An almost boyfriend." I fessed up.

"What's ailing him?" Sam seemed far more curious
than jealous.

"Drugs." A mental picture of Alex's creepy, glazed eyes flashed in my head and I quickly pushed aside the image. I focused on my oatmeal and stirred it until it resembled gooey paste.

"There's a poor soul who's got it worse off than I. You best be careful being around the likes of him."

"Come on, Sam. You'd compare yourself to him?" I hopped up on the counter to eat.

"Emily, I have roamed the streets. I've witnessed the spectacular and I've viewed the disturbing. Drug life can be *very* disturbing."

I was surprised by the depth of conviction Sam felt toward the effects of drugs. "Sam?"

"Yes?"

"Do you think you are closer in mental age of nineteen or seventy?" I spooned another bite of hot cereal.

A deep belly laugh rose out of Sam that seemed to shake the room. He approached the counter where I was perched and wedged himself into the intimate space between my legs. Sweet musk burned my tongue.

"I have experienced many things in my extended lifetime, but I feel no older than a boy. And this boy happens to be smitten with the likes of you." Sam took his index finger and softly traced the lines of my lips.

I thought of *the kiss*. Would I finally get my romantic kiss? In the kitchen?

"Miss Emily, I hope you are right." Sam said with a sigh, as he pulled me tight against his chest. My arms wrapped around him, bowl in one hand, spoon in the other.

"About what?" I asked. Heat began to consume my body.

"That if your Pa has me arrested, your Ma will come and bail me out."

I pulled back and giggled at the thought of Sam behind bars. "All you'd have to do is disappear."

"I wouldn't hide."

Pondering Sam behind bars, I had a new question. "If someone took a picture of you, would you show up?"

Sam's eyes deepened. "Why? Would you like to make a dirty movie?"

"You wish! Actually, I was thinking more of a mug shot for your police file." I gave him a shove that allowed him to stay wedged between my legs.

"I just like to talk tough." He flexed his muscles for added flair, and then stepped back on his own.

I stuffed another spoonful of oatmeal in my mouth hoping to conceal the smile that might reveal my dirty thoughts.

Sam walked the length on the counter, then turned back to face me. "But seriously, now that we're alone, I have to talk to you."

I wanted mush. I was going to get…explanations, or confessions.

"Last night, you told me of your concerns about being together. Well, a part of me is also very worried. It's time I came clean."

I stiffened. His brow creased momentarily. He walked back over to me, in steps that resembled pacing. Lifting my chin with his finger, his lips parted. "Let me start off by saying that you are beautiful, smart, fun. What I have to say is very difficult and… well, I am risking a lot to be here with you."

The oatmeal in my stomach suddenly turned to lead. "What kind of risks?"

"I suppose since I'm declaring my love for you, I'd better tell you everything."

"What exactly do you mean?" I leaned back to see his entire face.

Sam took a large step back. "Do you believe in Jesus?"

I crossed my legs and nodded. "Ahh…"

"With all the religions in the world, which one do you think is right?" He seemed embarrassed by his own words.

"That's a curious thing to ask. Where are you going with this?"

"Immediately after the accident, I didn't realize I was dead. It was confusing, and loud, and then I saw this creepy-floating-person-creature thing coming my way." Sam shifted his weight from toe to heel, and then side to side. "That's when I realized I had passed on, but from the looks of *what* was coming my way, I didn't think it was planning on taking me to Heaven."

"You're going to Hell?!" I shouted and hopped down from the counter. Bowl and spoon scattered.

Sam took a step closer. "Shh! You don't have to advertise it. It's not something I'm very proud of, you know."

"What kind of a sicko were you to deserve Hell?" I clutched my blouse, concealing my heart.

"Emily! Look at me. I'm not some demented ghost wreaking havoc in your house."

"I trusted you. I thought you were a nice guy!"

"I *am* a nice guy! I'm not trying to fool you, Emily. I'm trying to be honest."

"So, why are you going to Hell, Sam?"

"I don't know, but I must have done *something* wrong. Maybe it was the candy I stole from Mr. Wilkins' Mercantile when I was six, or the time I beat up Tommy Snodman when he didn't really deserve it, or—"

"You're going to Hell?"

Sam shrunk a little more. "Stop saying that."

"Did you actually see it?"

"No, only the Grim Reaper. I'm pretty sure it's him who takes people to Hell."

I began to understand Sam's reality. Maybe. I leaned against the counter to think. "Can't you say a prayer or something?"

"I've been on my knees plenty of times, but nothing happens. No angels, no shining light of redemption, no nothing. I don't know what to do except to keep running whenever I see the Gate Keeper coming my way."

My own measly problems seemed insignificant as I listened to Sam's story. "Oh, Sam!" I reached out and grabbed hold of his beautiful white shirt and pulled him close. I pressed my face against his chest as hard as I dared. His touch brought immediate comfort. And the sultry taste of smoke. "I can't stand the thought of some creepy Angel of Death stealing you away from me."

"I didn't tell you this to make you fret, Miss Emily. I just thought you should know."

"But you just said…" I looked up to see his face.

"I have been avoiding Hell for a very long time, and I certainly don't plan on going there now that I have you in my life."

I let out a sigh. "Promise?"

"Promise."

His hands replaced the fear that burdened my shoulders. I closed my eyes to let the peace sink in. His lips pressed down upon my forehead. In a perfect fit, his hand cradled the back of my head and he pulled me in for another hug. Although I was far from being an expert, I could tell this was not meant to be a kiss of passion, but protection.

As he took a step back, he scooped up a lock of my hair only to let the entire length glide through his fingertips. "How about if you call the hospital to see if your friend is accepting visitors?"

"You wouldn't mind?"

"It's obvious the kid needs a little support right now. Make the call."

I hopped off the counter and Sam sat back down at the table to wait patiently. It didn't take long to look up the number in the phonebook and place the call.

"That's strange." I placed the phone back into its charger.

"What is?"

"He's already gone."

CHAPTER FORTY-ONE

SETTLING IN

"**H**ELLO, EVERYONE." Kat's greeting was obviously directed more at Sam than me as she brushed past and stood directly in front of him, cranking back her neck to get a full view. His color softened.

Any further discussion of Alex would have to wait for later.

Sam tousled the top of her bed-head hairdo. "It's about time you woke up. The sun's been up for hours."

"It's summer vacation!" Kitty defended herself. "Besides, nine o'clock is not that late." She studied Sam's face for a moment. "You look cooler at night," she spoke with opinionated authority.

"You don't say," Sam replied. "What do you think, Emily?"

"I happen to like both versions of you." I shot my little sister a snub look.

Holding a coffee cup in her hand, Mom walked into the kitchen for a refill.

Sam's body faded in and out. We all stared.

"Does that hurt?" I said.

"Not in the least," he said. "It's like the moon last night; your bodies interfere with my illusion of a normal human form during the day."

"So your cohesion is based upon gravity?" Mom asked.

"And the specific charge of every atom I come into contact with. Imagine forcing gravity to make molecules do something they normally wouldn't do on their own."

"Sounds a bit complex," she replied. "How about your color?"

"That comes from the light rays I absorb from the sun. It's not as technical as keeping form. First, I increase my density by combining my water molecules with additional oxygen molecules. The drawback of being water is that it holds a neutral charge, which translates into—"

"Stop," I groaned. "You're hurting my ears."

Mom laughed.

Sam placed his left hand upon his transparent chest. "Forgive me, I forgot my audience. I'll try and speak *farmer*, so you'll be able to follow me."

My knuckles locked on my hips. "Farmer-schmarmer. I'm familiar with the periodic table, but if you want to discuss splitting atoms, maybe you should find Sheldon Cooper."

"Who?"

I was too embarrassed to tell him the smartest person I knew was actually a TV character. "My subject of choice is history, but I know enough about farming to stand on my own two feet."

Sam crossed his arms in front of his chest. "Tell me then. What do you know?"

"Okay." I paused long enough to conceive a question. "Tell me the difference between farmer and agriculturalist?" I looked to Mom for a bit of encouragement. She zipped her lips closed with her fingers.

"Nine letters," Sam replied.

Caught in my own trap. "Humph. That's not what I meant. How about farmer and grower." *They each have five letters.*

"I like farmer," Kat spoke up. "It reminds me of little chicks and baby cows."

A shady grin crossed Sam's face. "Stand aside, Miss Kitty. Your sister's throwing out fightin' words, and I'd hate for anybody to get hurt in the cross fire." Then he turned toward me. "So, you want to play rough, do you?" Sam challenged. "Let's try cultivating occupationalist on for size."

"Cultivating what?" It didn't become any clearer with my head tipped to the side.

Mom chuckled behind me.

"Cultivating occupationalist! I can cultivate your minds with a biology lesson!" Sam laughed loud and held his fist out to Kat for a celebration fist bop.

"I don't get it," she said, instead.

Sam's shoulders dropped.

"Strike one for the farmer," I said dryly.

"Can't win 'em all," he moaned.

Mom raised her coffee cup in the air. "I found your lesson to be very informative and compelling. It's been a pleasure." Then making her exit, Mom sent me a wide-eyed gawk as she headed out the kitchen door.

"It's really not all that complicated," he called out after her. His color hues brightened with her departure.

"Where do you learn all this stuff?" I asked, somewhat bewildered.

"At the universities. I can attend any class I want," Sam replied.

"Wow, no SATs or GREs." I sighed longingly.

"Hey!" Kat began to jump excitedly side to side. "Could I enter Sam in the Science Fair? I'd get a blue ribbon for sure!"

"I don't think so, Sport." Sam's words brought Kat to an immediate stop.

A frown replaced her smile. "Awh, why not?"

"Oh, my gosh!" I spouted. "Could you imagine the tabloids? We'd be overrun with reporters. Our lives would be ruined!"

"We can't have that," Dad exclaimed, entering the kitchen with his own coffee cup in hand. "We need to come up with a plan to avoid all suspicion."

Sam's large frame turned semi-transparent as the colors faded in and out again.

"Where did you come from?" I asked, surprised to see him.

"The dining room. Izzy and I are comparing paint samples. I hear you want to paint your room green."

"Yes," I said, remembering the feeling the color green gives me. "It's just so…everything. I'm totally in love with the country!"

"Hmph!" Kat muttered beneath her breath. "I didn't realize that Sam had changed his name."

Sam laughed.

I flicked Kat on the shoulder. Ignoring her whining about child abuse, I turned to Dad. "Remember to take her with you when you leave."

"You can tape the samples on the walls," Dad said to Kat. Her eyes sparkled as if he'd promised a gallon of her favorite ice cream. I wondered if I was that gullible when I was her age. *Probably.*

Drawing closer to Sam, I had a nagging question that needed to be answered. "Explain this to me. You were at the coffee shop, right?"

Sam's body began to flicker even more. "I saw you sitting there with your friends. I thought it'd be kind of fun to crash your party, but then, it seemed wrong, so I left."

"Young man!" Dad said, refilling his cup. "You continue to impress me. I would have stayed and listened."

"Don't get too impressed, Sir. I'm just an ol' country boy at heart."

I pressed the tip of my nose up, giving a quiet snort meant only for Sam's ears.

Dad must have heard it. A devilish grin spread across his face. "Is that so? I distinctively remember you saying that you can't stay formed in direct water. Perhaps it's time to trade my shotgun in for a garden hose."

"Dad!" I yelped, as my cheeks began to burn, trying to stop the visualization in my head.

"Mr. Stokes." Sam stood up tall and proud. He towered over the entire family. "I am very fond of your daughter." He took in a deep breath, expanding his chest creating the effect of a brick wall. "I will do my very best to keep her a virtuous woman."

It was difficult to know if my Dad had insulted him, or if Sam was just playing along.

Kat looked amongst the three of us. "You guys are weird! I'm going to find Mom." Kat left, stomping her feet in exaggerated disgust.

Reaching for a banana, Dad asked, "Did she ever get anything to eat?"

I shook my head no.

Plucking a second one from the bunch, he balanced it on the top of his mug and returned his attention to Sam. "All kidding aside, I'm not sure any of us have half a clue what we are getting ourselves into, especially the two of you." Dad pointed his banana at Sam, and then to me. "You are in uncharted territory, a new frontier."

"Dad—"

"Don't 'Dad' me, Emily. I am very serious. This will affect every part of our lives. Even the small things. How do you expect to go out on a date?"

"We'll just stay home."

Dad gave me the look. "What about when all your other friends want you to join them? I don't want to be a kill-joy, but this is not going to be easy for you, or the rest of the family."

Just when I thought he was going for the kill, his body language softened.

"Don't get me wrong, I approve of Sam. I'm just saying it's going to be a challenge."

"Thanks, Dad." My arms wrapped around him tight.

"I love you, Pumpkin." Then he took a step back, he gave me a tight-lipped grin and a nod of the head. His eyes turned to Sam. "She's my baby." A look of warning accompanied the statement.

Sam nodded.

"Good." In a surprising burst of energy, Dad turned to enter the adjoining dining room. With a ridiculous looking shuffle, he started his exit, continuing with a cheery little hum.

Sam and I looked on as Dad walked through the house conducting the air with the banana.

"He didn't even spill his coffee," I said, mildly embarrassed by what I'd just witnessed.

"I like your family," Sam said, returning to normal consistency.

"That's a relief!" A laugh escaped from a secret hiding place. "I have to admit, we have fun with our weirdness."

The kitchen became quiet. Finally.

"Tell me something about yourself, Sam." I couldn't imagine ever growing tired of saying his name.

"What do you want to know?"

"Everything!"

He flashed his white teeth in a generous smile. "You already know a lot about me, actually. I've already told you about how my parents met, the cotton plantation in Louisiana, my life here in Kansas. What else do you want to know?"

"What have you been doing the past, how many years?"

His voice became empty. "It's been lonely, Emily." He reached out and hooked my waist, pulling me off the counter.

"Don't you ever talk to anybody?"

"Naw. We live mostly like nomads. Over time, the concept of relationships fade away."

"Maybe that's what's supposed to happen."

Sam's brow rose.

"It would be creepy if dead people started knocking on the front door, wanting to come in and socialize."

"I s'pose so. Except for those orbs. They're nothing but mischief makers."

"Kinda like you," I teased.

Sam moved directly in front of me. His fingers combed through my hair, becoming tangled at the ends. He pulled my hair to one side and examined the snarl. "Do you think I am creepy?"

His question made me smile. "Not as creepy as the kiss Zachary Melcomb gave me in seventh grade."

"Who?" Sam asked, his face full of surprise.

"All kidding aside, I said it last night and I'll continue saying it: I'm really glad you are here. It was a scary ride getting to this place—"

Sam cringed. "I am so sorry, for everything that happened."

"It's not your fault, Sam. And who knows, maybe we wouldn't be together if it happened any other way. I truly believe things happen for a reason." *Maybe I do believe in destiny.*

Traces of worry melted from Sam's face and were replaced by such utter happiness. "You are an amazing woman, Emily."

His words nearly took my breath away. They way he said them with such authenticity. And the way he looked me in the eyes. It made my heart dance with joy.

"Do you want to get out of here?" I asked, with ulterior motives in mind, mostly about *kissing* and how wonderful I knew it would be.

"Where would you like to go?" he asked.

"It's a nice day for the farm." I batted my eyelashes.

"It would be nice knowing your daddy isn't nearby waiting with the garden hose."

As my laugh eased into a sigh, and my gaze dropped, my attention was drawn to Sam's hands resting on my hips. They nearly circled the entire circumference of my waist.

"You have big hands!"

"I know!" Smugness crossed Sam's face.

I blushed, and wondered if he was privy to the "size of hand" rule the girls used to laugh about in middle school.

Without dwelling, Sam hooked my arm in his. "To the farm."

CHAPTER FORTY-TWO

WRONGFUL HALLOWS

ALEX STASHED HIS JEEP in the distant woods and walked the open prairie on foot. Stepping inside the doorless entryway, he threw his belongings on the table which sent a flurry of dust into the air. A common gray mouse scurried across the floor and disappeared between the floor and the bottom cupboards.

Inspecting his arm, Alex unwound the bandage that held his IV in place. Ignoring the pain, he peeled off that last bit of sticky tape and methodically pulled out the long tube that had been inserted the night before. Blood spewed from the tiny hole. In a quick panic, he grabbed for the pile of gauze and wrapped it back around his wound.

Taking a seat at the table, he rummaged through his backpack and took out the box of cupcakes he had stolen from the Walgreen's the day before. He was hungry, but needed a fix first.

With business taken care of, he grabbed the package of cupcakes, tore open the end of the box and shoved one in his mouth. While chewing, he reminisced about the days when he and his father used this old abandoned Easley place as a hunting shack.

When everything was still good.

Returning to the backpack, he fished around until he found a small wooden picture frame and set it on the table. "Don't worry, Emily. I'm going to get my shit together. I *will* be a great man for you."

CHAPTER FORTY-THREE

THE KISS

I WAS FINALLY GOING TO GET IT. After years of dreaming about it, and a few more years of running from it, I was finally going to get my kiss. And not just any old kiss. The kind of kiss that makes you weak in the knees and your heart skip a beat, that leaves you breathless and your head in the clouds, all at the same time.

"What are you thinking about now?" Sam asked.

"Oh," I stammered, realizing both sides of the riverbank were full of flowers. More than I ever thought possible. "Do you do that?" I asked.

"What?"

"The flower thing." I snapped off a cluster of tall yellow flowers as we walked past on our way to the farm.

"Yes. For you," he said with a childish grin.

"How do you do it?"

"It's not as easy to explain as electonegativity, mostly because there are no words to adequately describe the scientific property—"

"I give up. Just speak *farmer*."

"Memories," he blurted.

"What does that mean?"

"Just like you and me, the Earth also has memories. If it existed, I can reproduce it."

"No way! How did you learn to do that?"

"I discovered it by accident. I actually learned how to reproduce other things before I figured out how to make myself appear."

Sam remained quiet as we walked, perhaps allowing me to conceive another intelligent question. "Can you reproduce an elephant?"

He laughed. "No, it has to be something that was actually part of the environment at some point in time."

"How about a dinosaur?"

"First of all, I think those memories might be too old, but secondly, why would I want to?"

"Yeah, just because you can, doesn't mean you should. I don't know what I was thinking. That was the kind of question Kat would ask."

Sam looked down at me, an eyebrow raised.

I pointed to my hair. "I am entitled to use it as an excuse, occasionally."

"That might work if Kat's hair were blonde too, but she's not. I just think it runs in the DNA."

"No one likes a smart ass."

"You do."

I stuck out my tongue.

He laughed harder.

The old stump beside the stepping stone bridge came into view. "Is Jedd real?"

"Ah, my good friend, the badger." The corners of Sam's mouth turned up. "Yes, he's real."

"I am so envious of you." The words were out of my mouth before I was even aware I had been thinking them.

Sam stopped abruptly. "Don't let yourself be fooled. I will share everything I have with you, but it is *you*, Miss Emily, who is truly the lucky one."

Me? What could I possibly have that made me so lucky? I was a senior in a new school, with no friends. There was nothing special about my life…Of course, life.

Grabbing Sam's hand, my tongue began to tingle with his sweet, musky taste. I could hardly wait for a kiss. My palms started to sweat just thinking about it.

As we took to the stone pathway that crossed over to Sam's side of the woods, unexpected memories crushed my happy thoughts. Vivid flashbacks of me standing in the rain with my friends accusing me of making up Sam stung the back of my throat. My legs stopped functioning half-way across the creek.

"What's wrong?"

"What does your house look like?" My voice cracked midway through the sentence.

Sam's face filled with sadness. "Ahh, I s'pose you are referring to when I'm not there?"

"Is it…falling apart?"

"It's been vacant for a very long time, Emily. Since Pa left."

I dropped Sam's hand and began to run. I needed to see the decrepit farm.

Bounding out into the open field, I came to a dead stop as I looked upon the land as it had appeared to me that horrible day: empty except for the crumbling abode. For the first time since arriving home, the reality of my recent experiences hit hard.

I heard Sam come to rest a short distance behind me.

Staring over the field, my mouth opened and out came something of a confession. "While in the hospital, my greatest fear wasn't about being crazy. It was about the farm... *of you* coming to an end." Tears clouded my vision before falling down my face. "I kept trying to come up with a logical argument for why I should be allowed to continue with my delusions."

In a giant step, Sam came before me and fell to his knees. He took hold of my hanging arms and looked up at me with tender eyes. "You don't have to be afraid any longer, Miss Emily. That nightmare is over."

I knew without doubt that Sam was indeed my protector. My heart began to pain at the amount of love I felt for him.

"It's gonna be all right, Emily. I promise."

Rising to his feet, Sam wrapped me in his massive body. The force of his chest pressing against me was stronger than I expected, and I nuzzled my cheek against him. Basking, I welcomed his scent as it filled my senses, ignoring the burn deep inside my lungs. The hug that I desperately needed last night was finally mine. I felt its power, and it felt good.

"I love you, Sam Easley."

"I know," he whispered.

The hug continued. A warmness spread over my body and I never wanted him to let go.

"Do you taste me, too?" I finally asked.

"I can't taste, remember?" Sam replied.

I thought back to our previous conversation. "You know, that doesn't make much sense." I looked up to meet his eyes, hoping I didn't insult him. His smile told me I had not.

"The rules are definitely different in the afterlife. I'm just glad I can experience most things." He inhaled deeply, and then added. "You smell as lovely as a warm apple pie."

"Really? I could have sworn the bottle of conditioner said *Wild Flowers.*"

Adding a bit more pull into the hug, Sam said, "If you're auditioning for stand-up, you'd better sit back down."

"Well, I thought it was funny."

Sam took a step back, still holding me in a distant hug. My arms fell short, so I placed my hands on top of his.

"Remember the first time you tried to hold me and I started choking?"

"Yes," he said, "and actually, I'm wondering why you aren't choking now."

"I still feel it. It's just not as strong." Just then, I noticed that the sunshine really did shine through his body. "Why is that?"

He pulled free and stroked his chin. "It seems like you are the only one who experiences it. Plus, the response is weakening..."

"Wouldn't that be a good thing?"

"One thing I've discovered about being dead is that consistency is good."

"And we're not."

Rubbing the back of his neck, he started pacing. "It makes me imagine a lowered resistance, or maybe even tolerance."

"Huh?"

"I must ask myself, 'Why would Miss Emily's body be less responsive to mine?'"

"I am still not grasping the bad part of this." I was too focused on kissing and hugging without the coughing.

His pacing stopped. "The universe is made up of things that attract and things that repel. We've changed from repulsion to attraction, which leads to connecting, like atoms."

I looked at Sam to see if he was joking. His face was serious. Taking a firm stance, I threw out my last doubt about him. "Do you promise me that you are not trying to steal my body?"

His gaze narrowed. "First of all, this ol' country boy is not into cross-dressing. Secondly, there are a lot of things I would like to do to your body, and stealing it is not on the list."

I looked at Sam. He looked at me.

I batted my eyelashes. "What kind of things?"

Sam grinned and stepped closer. "Oh, girl. The way you tease me. But seriously—"

How his flirting stopped short created a spark of panic in my stomach. His solemn expression made it surge. "How bad could it be?"

"If my hunch is correct, we'll have to live with very strict rules."

"Rules? I'm in high school. I'm not afraid of rules! Tell me, Sam. What can be so bad?"

Staring off into the distance, his shoulders rounded before turning away from me. I wanted to go to him, but resisted. With his back still towards me, he finally spoke. "I can still remember the day I died, like it was yesterday."

I covered my gasp of sorrow a bit too late.

"The rain had stopped coming. Everything was hot and dry. It was the summer of 1936 and Kansas was deep into the days of the Great Dust Bowl. I still remember going outside in the daytime, and the air was so thick with dirt that it looked like the middle of the night instead…. Luck saw to it that we had a deep well, so we were able to keep a small garden growing, the one that you and I planted.

"Pa started making gin during the Prohibition and even though the ban was lifted in '34, he kept on distilling just 'cause so many counties in Kansas remained dry. Plus life was hard for a lot of folks, being it was also the time of The Great Depression an' all. Pa thought it neighborly, and gave most of his moonshine away on Friday nights at the barn dances.

"It was a Sunday morning, and Ma went out to the barn to fetch something before church you see, and the next thing I knew, the entire barn was engulfed in flames. Everything was so dry. By the time I got there, Pa was hunched over Ma. I ran into the barn to untie the horses. The last thing I remember about being alive was seeing the roof come down on me."

His tragic story was out. I had finally heard the ugly truth. Again, I had the urge to go to him. But I waited.

"Our situation is complicated. It could be very bad for you." His eyes narrowed. "At first, I couldn't figure it out, but now it all makes perfect sense. You taste the smoke that filled my lungs."

I responded with a blank stare.

"Are you familiar with the part of the wedding ceremony, 'and the two shall become one'?"

I nodded.

"That refers to the union of spirits. The consummation creates the thread that binds two creatures together. Our souls are trying to connect."

"But we're not getting married. We haven't even had sex yet!"

"Apparently that doesn't matter. Something's different."

Ideas buzzed around my head. Nothing made sense. "What would be so awful if they joined, anyway?"

"I'm dead." His eyebrows rose to a fervid stare.

"So? Married people die all the time. I don't understand the big deal."

"The big deal is that I'm *already* dead. Once the thread is sewn, it's very difficult to break. You just have to believe me, Emily. If the Gate Keeper finds me, he could take you to Hell with me!"

Unexpected information overload. An icy chill spread up my arms and down my spine. My body began to shudder and I hopped around as the willies crawled upon my skin like tiny spiders. Wildly, I brushed my arms to rid myself of the imaginary arachnids.

Sam laughed. He laughed loudly, from his belly.

"I'm glad my doom can bring you amusement." I looked at him with great annoyance.

He stopped laughing, but his grin remained sharp. He tried to conceal it with a phony itchy-chin cover up. Finally, he just pinched his lips shut.

"Stop it!" I stomped my foot.

"Come on, Miss Emily. Watching your reaction was funny."

A new bend in life revealed itself to me. "Perhaps I should get comfortable laughing in the face of death."

"I wouldn't feel as bad about it if I knew I'd take you to Heaven." We both shared a forced smile until Sam's expression turned south. "It was never my intention to put you in harm's way, but we have to be realistic. This is serious stuff! Loving me could be the ultimate death sentence for you."

"But this is only a theory. You could be wrong."

"Do you really want to take the chance?"

A drawn-out exhale gave me time to think. "I think so."

"We're talking about Hell. It's forever."

"But you're not sure. Besides, I don't believe that God would send you or me to Hell!"

"What makes you so sure we're playing on God's playground?"

His comments were starting to piss me off. I didn't want to deal with it anymore. "Then we'll just have to figure out how to get there."

A faint smile crossed his lips as his brow relaxed. "You continue to surprise me." He stepped closer and wrapped one of his muscular arms around me, drawing me in close to his chest.

My taste buds tingled, but this time, fear replaced the pleasure. He must have felt me stiffen, and released me. Grasping his arms, I pulled them back into a hug. "Don't let go."

Sam held me warmly in his arms. "You are either very brave, or very foolish, Miss Emily. Which one, is yet to be determined."

Breathing him in, a tickle of smoke in my throat made me cough. "I am not afraid with you by my side."

Sam's hands slipped down my arms until he found mine. "How much bad news can you handle in one day?"

"You mean there's more? What could be worse than going to Hell?"

"I suppose it's all how you look at it, but I don't think you're going to like it."

"What is it?" I asked.

Sam spied something in the grass and kicked it with his boot.

"Stop stalling."

"We shouldn't kiss."

CHAPTER FORTY-FOUR

EXCUSABLE ADMISSION

THE SOUND of my fluttering eyelids filled the otherwise unnatural silence dangling between Sam's lips and my own. Images of Zachary Melcomb, Alex Hibbs, my beautiful white dress, and a prom night spent eating popcorn with my parents flashed before my eyes. The kiss that filled my daytime fantasies and scoured all other waking moments was being denied. Permanently.

I thought of Sam and how perfect he was for me. But no kissing? Ever?

There were many things in life I could deny: after all, I loved denial. But pretending I did not want a beautiful, romantic kiss? This I did not expect. An excruciating desire flared within my flesh.

"It's only a kiss," I lied to myself and then to Sam.

He studied my eyes as I spoke. "I'm sorry, Miss Emily, but I don't see any other way. I reckon that playwright who created *A Prelude to a Kiss* may have been onto something. The people in that production kissed during the day, remember?"

His words came crushing down on my chest, which was no longer pressed against Sam's.

He bent down to recapture my attention. "We'll still have our nights."

I envisioned the white wispy Sam encircling my body. It had been so intense! I looked at his charming face, and found little consolation.

"Last night was incredible, but I'm not ready for that. I want to start with the basics; you know…first base and sneaking into second—"

"I don't need a dating manual. Men are pigs, remember?"

I tightened my fists and questioned why life could be so cruel. "This just doesn't make sense to me. Why are nights safe and daytime kisses outlawed?"

His frame jerked upright. "Work with me, Emily. Remember when we tried to kiss? We sparked. That's just not normal!"

"Sparked! What does that mean anyway? Is it dangerous?"

Sam's head tipped to the side. "You didn't back into a pricker bush, did you."

Now I was embarrassed and angry. He had known all along what had happened. "How do you know *sparking* is normal at night?"

He opened his mouth, but then shut it. His eyes darted from side to side, maybe in search of someone holding up cue cards.

"Tell me right now, or I'm leaving."

His jaw clenched tight. "Fine! Have it your way. Have you ever had a dream that involved groping…you know, making out?"

I nodded. Then blushed.

"That *only* happens when you are being seduced by a ghost."

I'm not sure how much time passed before I finally blinked. "Oh. Oh? Oh my—"

"Hey! You asked. But at least now you know why I think nighttime is safe."

My lips curved in disgust. "Pig! How often do you do that?"

"I *never* said *I* did it. I just said I knew about it," he answered, crossing his arms.

I didn't know what to think, so I just stood there, looking at him. I finally crossed my arms too. There we were, in some sort of stand off. He looked like he belonged in professional wrestling. I probably looked like a bratty teenager.

Contemplating my choices, and staring at his hugeness, my frustration began to melt. And maybe I was being judgmental. My image of angry wrestler transformed into the Grumpy Bunny, and a smile snuck upon my face.

"Do we at least get to hold hands?" I offered him mine.

He remained still.

"I'm sorry." I reached for his hand and unhooked it from his other arm, breaking the lock. Bringing his hand to my lips, I gave it a small kiss and looked into the deep brown eyes that I adored so much. I was quickly reminded that I loved him, and that nothing could change that; time had come to put on my big-girl-panties.

"I suppose that wouldn't be so bad," he said, interlocking his fingers with mine. "In fact, they fit together quite nicely, don't they?" He raised his hand, bringing mine along for a brief visual inspection.

"Perfectly," I said. "All that kissing is probably overrated, anyway."

He returned the affection by planting a smooch on the back of my hand. "Well then, I think it's about time for a little fun, don't you?"

"I couldn't agree more."

"Care to do a little gardening? Or, it'd only take a few seconds for me to fix up the place if you'd like to take a tour."

The house sat quietly, without paint or dignity. It was easy to tell where the barn had been. Daisies topped the mound. For all I knew, Sam's ashes could be under them too. "Not today."

He gave me a quizzical look. "Are you afraid of it?"

"Mmm, not afraid." I couldn't put my finger on it, but somehow my feelings had changed about the house. "How about we pay Lucy a visit."

"Splendid idea," Sam agreed. "She might even have some pups."

Hand in hand, we started off through the open field, heading in the direction of the fox den. The summer sun felt warm against my face; a wild turkey strutted off in the distance. Sam started chatting about the healing properties of a plant, and my insides tickled with happiness because I was the luckiest girl on Earth. And I was in love.

"Hey!" I said, stopping abruptly. "I had a *dream* about you last night. You were about to kiss me!"

Sam laughed and pulled me along. "Well, there always has to be a first time."

A Gift for Emily

BOOK II

Chapter 1

CASUAL CONVERSATION

SAM ONCE TOLD ME that the Grim Reaper was the most frightening thing he'd ever seen. I'd liked to have asked him if that was because the creature was truly scary or because its intent was to take Sam to Hell. I decided against asking, figuring my own morbid curiosity wasn't that important.

There were definite drawbacks to dating someone like Sam. Being seventeen and in love, the "no kissing" rule seemed be the worst part. At least for me. And of course I still wanted my romantic kiss. What girl wouldn't? Determined not to be denied, I was bent on finding some kind of solution.

"What was that word again?" I asked.

"What word?" Sam responded.

"You know, *that* word. Transitori…"

"Transmigration? Why are you asking about that?"

"Would you still look like you?"

My little sister, Kat, was busy feeding the ducks that had made their summer home here at the local pond while I appeared to be a crazy person sitting on a picnic blanket talking to myself. Sam never materialized when

we went into public, even in our little town of Silver
Lake, Kansas.

"I don't think so, Miss Emily." Sam's voice
answered my question.

"I'd prefer it if you would still look like you. Call
me shallow, but at least I'm honest." He didn't give me
a reply and after further thought, I had more questions.

"Do you think you could possess a recently dead body,
or do you have to steal it from somebody?"

"Such creepy words from such a beautiful mouth."
I dropped my head in embarrassment. "Haven't you
ever thought about it?"

"More lately, I reckon. I'd feel less guilty about
taking a dead body, but at the same time, I wouldn't
want to get myself into a worse predicament. I'm not
sure I'd heal up from what the person died from," he
answered.

"I bet it would be a fresh start. Just like new."

A noticeable draft chilled my skin despite the
heated air temperature. It was Sam, moving to the other
side of the blanket. "I wouldn't get my hopes up for a
glorious resurrection if I were you," he said.

"What if you turned into a zombie!"

An exasperated huff filled the air. "You watch too
many movies."

"Hey! Maybe you are forgetting that I am having a
conversation with a *dead person*?" Immediately, I
looked around for anybody who could have heard me.

In all actuality, I wasn't worried. No one from town
seemed to notice the path we cleared in the underbrush
to gain access to the tiny lake. But this was good. It
gave Sam and me another place to be.

"Emmy!" Kat called from knee-deep water. "Look at the babies! Aren't they adorable?" My little sister was obsessed with anything baby. I waved and gave her a spirited thumbs up. Satisfied by my acknowledgement, she resumed her own quacking, taking part in some sort of cross-species dialogue while tearing off another piece of bread and tossing it into the feathery huddle.

Subtle movement beside me brought my attention back to Sam. Pieces of cracked corn began magically arranging themselves on the blanket. A thin row of kernels progressed into an arch, angling down, then sharply going back up, forming a V at the bottom. A smile spread across my face as another arch joined the first one. The heart was now complete.

The taste of smoke settled on my tongue as his breath tickled my ear. "How about if I steal Taylor Lautner's body?"

Swatting the air, I asked, "How do you know about Taylor Lautner?"

Kitty looked up. "Are we going to a movie?"

"No. And mind your own business," I called out. Rubbing my chin in exaggerated thought, I mulled over the offer. "I suppose that wouldn't be so bad. Gorgeous *and* famous."

"You weren't supposed to be that excited." Sam said dryly.

Flopping back on the plaid blanket, I looked up into the cloudless blue sky. "I really just want you." I turned my head to the side, wanting to see him next to me. I heard his voice instead.

"As long as we're on the subject, I also think the donor—"

"Donor?" I echoed. "And you called me creepy."

"I thought it sounded a little less…something…no? At any rate, the deceased should have a good moral background. It would be atrocious get into another body and then be wanted for past crimes."

I sat up on my elbows. "Atrocious. I haven't heard that word for years."

"It means terrible."

"I know that." Ignoring the need to defend my vocabulary, I plunged forward. "There's just so much to think about. We'd probably have to relocate."

"Not if I found the body in a different city." Sam added.

The body?

The body.

I repeated these two words in my head several more times using different tones, yet each time, arriving at the same mental picture: dead body, cadaver, zombie, Frankenstein. "I think you should steal it."

"Stop your fretting, Miss Emily."

Just then, Kat walked up to the edge of the blanket with the empty plastic bread wrapper clutched in her hand, saving me from mental anguish of dating a rotting zombie.

"They ate it all?" Sam's voice asked in sudden up-beat manner.

"Every last crumb." She turned the bag inside out and let the bread-dust scatter.

"I guess this means we're ready to go." I stood and shook the debris from the blanket.

"We'll get back just in time for you to start feeding all the critters at home," Sam added.

"This has been the best summer vacation ever!" Kat cheered as she took off up the path, holding the plastic bag above her head like a miniature kite.

"She wears me out, just watching her," I said, thinking Sam was still nearby. At least until I heard a "Gotcha!" followed by a scream, and a "No fair! That's cheating," and finally cries of mercy because it was impossible to ward off ghost-tickles otherwise.

Without further delays, an invisible Sam rode shotgun while Kitty was forced to sit in the back of my little green and blue VW Love bug. The two exchanged dialog, allowing me to calculate the assumed benefits of stealing a healthy body versus one in need of medical attention, or altogether dead. Then the notion hit me like a flat iron: this entire idea was completely deranged. Twisted. Gross.

But I couldn't let it go. There had to be something we could do.

Before I even had the drive shift pushed into park, Kitty was scrambling into the passenger front seat to get out.

"Look out for Sam!" I scolded.

"Sorry!" she yelled as she slammed the door closed and ran for the garage. It was already past feeding time.

As I watched her run, something else caught my eye in the passenger seat. No doubt, it was Sam assuming human form.

"She's a good kid," he said.

I took a moment to feast upon his good looks before answering. "It was nice of you to collect the animals and bring them home to her."

Since it was my summer job to look after my sister while our parents were at work, Sam was wise to occupy Kat with a brood of her very own. While the living slept, Sam combed the dark forest and grasslands rescuing small abandoned animals that would have surely died without a maternal figure. Now wherever Kat went, she was followed by an entourage of young orphaned woodland creatures: a small black and white skunk, a little furry raccoon wearing her painted black mask, and a brazenly tough white and gray feral kitty who enjoyed pinning the less agile animals in a game of roughhouse. There was also a red-tailed fox, not yet weaned, that still lived in a box inside the garage.

It always made me smile to see the little critters follow their unusual mother in single-file around the confines of the mowed lawn.

"It'll be sad to see them go," I murmured, taking the keys out of the ignition.

"What are you talking about? They ain't leaving," Sam said.

"What do you mean?"

It was a mischievous grin. "They'll never leave. This is their home."

"Seriously?" A nervous laugh snuck out, probably because I knew how my father felt about pets. "You're lucky my dad likes you."

His large frame shook with a chuckle. "Until the raccoon starts chewing holes in the patio screen door to get in."

"In that case, you're lucky you're already dead."

***

Find J.P. Galuska on facebook and keep up with all the currents events with Book II of the Emily Stokes series.

11606854R00236

Made in the USA
Charleston, SC
09 March 2012